# A Candle for San Simón

# A Candle for San Simón

## A Novel

Kelly Daniels

Owl Canyon Press

First Edition, 2019
All Rights Reserved
Library of Congress Cataloging-in-Publication Data

Daniels, Kelly.
A Candle for San Simón—1st ed.
p. cm.
ISBN: 9780998507392
2019956707

**Owl Canyon Press**
Boulder, Colorado

# I.

# Chapter One

An old flat-faced school bus, home-painted turquoise with pale orange fenders and roof, sped east along the Pan American Highway just outside of Quetzaltenango, Guatemala. Dark foliage covered peaks rising to the north and south into a low ceiling of clouds, and garbage lined the road, the old rubbish dissolving into the forest fringe and making way for the freshly-tossed water bottles, bright wrappers, and the occasional plump garbage bag, some split and spilling, others intact. Civilization fell away beyond the outskirts, the highway hugging the mountainside while the highland valley, green and dotted with primitive family farms, rolled off to the passenger side. Norman Caruthers, a white man, middle-aged with a full head of pale hair and a rum-burnt face, drove the bus, bouncing gently on the spring-loaded seat. He let off the accelerator, frowning through the windshield at the line of brake lights clustered ahead. An accident, he figured, a bad one.

Left hand resting on the chipped Stanley thermos in its holder and Hawaiian-print shirt rustling in the breeze, he dropped the transmission into neutral and tapped the brakes. Seba, Caruthers' dark-skinned assistant, a short, squat man marked by a dime-sized pentagram tattooed on his left cheek, clung to the pole behind the driver's seat, squinting at the disturbance ahead, the stopped traffic and flashing emergency lights. Solemn-faced Quiché took up most of the seats, the women in the colorful tipica skirts, belts, and blouses prized by tourists, their men wearing charity castoffs shipped down from the U.S. Among them sat a few ladinos in business dress. Absent were the tourists, scared off by the recent U.S. travel advisory and the violence that had triggered it, violence perhaps linked to the trouble ahead.

No accident, Caruthers saw, downshifting fifty yards from the roadblock, enforced by the machine gun mounted to the bed of a pickup. The boy behind the gun wore a uniform, which did not reassure Caruthers. The categories of good guys and bad guys no longer pertained, if they ever had, replaced by the more useful designations of the armed and unarmed. Six vehicles from the checkpoint, Caruthers had time to appreciate how life had a way of coming at him from the other direction. On his mind lately had been the recent trend of gang murders of bus drivers in and around the capital, the price of refusing to pay the extortion fees demanded by the local thugs, emboldened by the brazen violence from the big gangs up in Mexico. Having fallen behind in his own payments in these lean times, Caruthers had been dreading a visit from his protector and tormentor, Chucho Cruz, but he hadn't expected an encounter with the army. Probably they'd just wave him through.

Stopping beside a boy with a clipboard, Caruthers imagined gunning it through, a flashy version of suicide, but instead he took another gulp from the Stanley and tried to relax. The two soldiers attending him seemed miscast, a dark squat Mayan scribbling down Caruthers' license beside his slim, bespectacled comrade, arms resting on the machinegun hanging from his neck like a pendant. The gunman entered first, followed by the bookkeeper. Neither had been shaving long. The bus had gone silent.

Caruthers wiped his hands on his chinos as the kid looked him over, surprise evident behind the glasses. Who was this gringo, he'd be wondering, and what was he doing driving a local bus? Who did he know; who didn't he know? Caruthers stared at the dashboard while thinking this, and the thinking, the patter of words, distanced him from the action, calming the panic. The gunner moved down the aisle, and the bookkeeper addressed Caruthers. "Papeles," he said, and a stream of sweat trickled down Caruthers' side.

"Papers," he said, smiling like a dog. "One moment!" A case of very bad timing, he thought, fishing through the box he kept under the seat, working around the pistol he'd only fired once at some bottles on the side of the road. It wasn't his fault the tourists had all fled, and with them the economy. How could he be expected to keep up with everything in a bullshit country like this? From the back of the bus, the gunner, shouting, ordered all the men to exit. Caruthers, fingers gone numb, dropped a folded piece of paper to the floor. Unlike the fallen document, the Stanley waited in easy reach, but he didn't dare grab it, not while this dangerous child stood there watching.

Sifting through hand-written receipts from his mechanic, kept all these years for no goddamned reason, he finally found his passport, five years old since his last visit to the consulate, its latest visa expired by a month. While the soldier flipped through the booklet, Caruthers located the title to the bus and route, written by the former owner in black ink and notarized with a blue stamp. Where was Cruz's goddamned letter? Expired or not, it was his most valuable pass in these parts.

Seba left the bus with the other men, offering his jefe no eye contact. The soldier fanned himself with the passport, losing patience, and Caruthers found a gum wrapper bearing a U.S. phone number with no name provided. "Que mas?" the soldier asked. Just in time, Caruthers came upon the letter. He removed it from the envelope and handed it to the soldier. Typed in Spanish on letterhead identifying the office of the Chief of Police, Panajachel, the text offered the bearer, Norman Vincent Caruthers of the United States of America, license to operate a passenger bus for profit for a year following the letter's date, also a month expired.

The gunman reentered the bus and walked down the aisle. Caruthers watched in the rearview mirror as he sized up the women, who stared at their laps or made busy with their children. He nudged open a shoulder bag with his gun's barrel.

"Visa, no good," the bookkeeper said in English.

"Lo siento," Caruthers replied. "A mistake, is all. Everything's okay. Muy bueno. Uno problemo with the date. The fecha. Nada mas." The boy in the back of the bus, excited that something was finally happening, walked forward, jerking the gun barrel from Caruthers to the door. The seat spring squealed as Caruthers stood.

Outside, the male passengers stood shoulder-to-shoulder against the bus, attended by a team of three soldiers, several Indians already selected out for pat downs and field interrogations, while a ladino, after a cursory look at their identification, was allowed to return to the bus. The pubescent gunman and the bookkeeper led Caruthers to the passenger side of the gun-mounted Toyota, where a gray-haired man in an officer's uniform sat reading a newspaper with the door open. Nearby, a female soldier led Seba and a few other dark-skinned men toward an unmarked van. "Hey," Caruthers said, "that's my ayudante." The officer lowered his paper and white light burst through Caruthers' vision. Something slammed into his face and the front of his body, a force he eventually recognized as the ground, loamy and soft. He tried to rise against the pain at the back of his head when an explosion burst between his legs and sent his face back to the spongy dirt. Eyes clamped shut and curled onto his side, he surveyed the damage, deducing that he'd been hit on the back of the head, with the butt of a gun if those movies he'd seen could be trusted, and then kicked in the bony area between his nuts and asshole. The pain in both spots writhed like small animals under his skin, but he thought that nothing had been broken.

"Arriba," someone said. Caruthers touched the back of his head and felt an egg, covered in moisture too cool to be blood, just rain, which had begun to lightly fall. He opened his eyes to a blurry tableau of black boot on dirt. He replaced the glasses hanging from one ear and saw the same sad vision more clearly. Collecting his power, he clutched the tire and struggled to his feet. The pain between his legs continued to pulse, while his entire head now ached. The fall had soiled the knees of his pants, and this seemed a shame.

"Ouch," he explained, rubbing the back of his head. A phalanx of medals decorated the officer's chest. Gilded glasses on the end of his nose, he examined Caruthers' papers, more the manager of a sales team than a death squad leader. Then again, who better to lead a death squad than a sales manager? Regions to assign, bonuses to dole out, pep talks to deliver, a meeting with headquarters once a month. As before, the jive talk in Caruthers' head helped. He encouraged it to continue, to remind him that none of this, this life, this existence, really mattered. "I'm sorry," he told the officer, who frowned down at Cruz's letter.

"Late," the officer decided, and returned the passport and letter to the bookkeeper.

"Please. I'm only a little late. Is there a fine? I'll pay it."

"Fine. Yes." The officer picked the newspaper off his lap, a tabloid whose front page featured a drawing of human organs set out for sale on a bed of ice like fresh fish, each labeled and priced to move. "1000 quetzales," the officer said. According to the headline, the organ stand was located in New York City, the fruits of a diabolical baby-snatching conspiracy. Caruthers considered pointing out that he could buy a new set of lungs for that kind of money.

"Por favor," he said. "I only made 100 today. I have to eat, have to buy gas. Muy caro."

The man turned a page, speaking English through the paper. "You want to see el inspector? Sokay. You can see el inspector." The bespectacled gunner appeared, holding Caruthers' .22 pea shooter.

"There," Caruthers exclaimed. "You can have all my money, plus la pistola."

In the end, Caruthers pleaded and cajoled, and gently dropped Chucho Cruz's name until the officer accepted Caruthers' best offer, which was everything in his pockets plus the gun, no doubt concluding that he'd get nothing else out of the gringo but a headache. Plus, they were both more or less white, the officer and bus driver, and that always counted for something. The paddy wagon had hauled off Seba, along with the poorest and brownest of the passengers, poverty and a tan sure signs of criminal intentions. Besides, they'd driven the van all this way, and it would be a shame to bring it back to the station with empty seats. A few of the remaining passengers had left on foot, but most still sat in the bus. Caruthers started the engine and drove away from the checkpoint, alive but even broker than before. A woman in the back was weeping, but the rain had stopped, and that was something.

# Chapter Two

They dropped her at the border and stood watching until she'd pushed through the twelve-foot, rusty turnstile into TJ. How they finally got her after all these years? Jaywalking, hustling across Pico during a break in traffic. What a joke. The cop only busted her so he could spread her against his car, feel her ass and tits before going through her bag just to make it look official. No drugs or guns in there, only a few bucks, some extra chonies and socks, her makeup, and an old-time shaving kit in a leather case. A gift for my boyfriend, she told the cop, and even though this was true, at least a long time ago, she said it wrong, all nervous like so he knows something's up. "Victoria Aria Valle," he read from her California ID, "sounds like a porn star's name. You sure it's really yours?"

"Yes," she said, not lying but feeling like a liar anyways. The name was the only true part of her ID. Everything else—address, country of origin, birthday—was invented in the street where she met the guy who printed up social security cards, driver's licenses, or whatever else she wanted. Back in the day, nobody checked too hard, and by the time they did, she'd already used fake documents to get a legit ID. After a while, the person on the card starts becoming the person in real life, until a cop calls you out just to grab some ass. No green card was his excuse to lock her in the back seat and drive off, but she figured he was going to take her someplace quiet to rape her, but this chota played by the rules, at least that day. He locked her in a cell, made some calls, and the next day a chick from ICE hauled her off to chill in a cage with a bunch of refugees for a month. Nobody ever connected her to Rico's murder—just another dead gangster leaking out in a driveway. But it didn't matter that they couldn't pin anything on her. After four years living crazy in LA, her man dead and everything they worked for gone, they deport her like a wetback. She wasn't even Mexican.

The whole thing was funny in a way, so she laughed as she walked up to the line of taxis. She couldn't afford bail and didn't want to wait months or years for trial, probably just to lose anyway, so she waived her right to appeal. The judge appreciated that, so he only bans her from the U.S. for ten years, not life. Gee, thanks Mr. Judge. How about I come back with a legal visa after I die and am born again as some rich bitch from Costa Rica? They'd never in a hundred years give her a visa in this lifetime no matter how many rules she followed, a street kid from Salvador, daughter of gangsters both dead by the time she's six. She was born banned, and she'd stay that way to the end, illegal for life. She liked it anyway, every day not knowing if you're going to live or die, kill or get killed. Yeah, she wouldn't a minded a quiet life, safe and clean like the gringas she saw every day floating by on a cloud of money, but that's not the life she got, so she wasn't going to complain.

It's true she got bored with how she and Rico were living, poor and stupid, trading drive-bys with the 13th Street neighbors for nothing but satisfaction, their friends getting killed one by one, the two of them getting high and waiting their turn. So she gets her GED, and then takes some business classes at City College. Rico laughed at her, and everybody started calling her Lisasimpson, but he started to listen to her ideas one day, and after a lot of talking, they got all the neighborhood bangers to call a truce, quit the drive-bys, split up the turf like how companies split up sales regions, and everybody starts making money for once by collecting tolls from the local dealers in exchange for keeping the streets safe and open for business. She and Rico were finally getting somewhere, moved to a nice place with a yard and two bedrooms, bought a 1986

# A Candle for San Simón

Monte Carlo Rico kept saying he'd customize, and that's when they got him, whoever, their enemies, their friends. Same thing. All she knew was she woke in the morning to pop-pop-pop-pop, and in the driveway she finds Rico and the car full of holes. Three days later, after thinking and worrying and hiding out in a shitty hotel until the cash she grabbed on the way out is about gone, she decides to visit the vato she thinks did it, or one of them at least, to either fuck him or kill him or cut a deal with him, but at least do something, and that's when the traffic cop nabs her, for fucking jaywalking. If she wanted to, she could sneak back across the border tomorrow, but no thanks. The deportation, right after Rico's murder, wasn't a coincidence. It was a sign, her guardian angel talking to her through the horny officer, the icebitch migra, and the crusty judge, all telling her to get the fuck out of LA before it's too late. Go home, to where it all started and where it keeps on going on.

The first taxista in line stared as she approached, figuring her out, a chola that just got a ride to the border in a squad car. Nothing special. "Revolucion?" the old guy says.

"Si," she answered, climbing into the back.

The main drag was how she remembered back when she first crossed over, except shinier and taller, big discos standing where the low cantinas used to, but the Indios still begged and sold stupid dolls while their kids ran around pushing chicle, and the American teenagers were still drunk and yelling, already at eleven in the morning. By night, they'd be crawling everywhere, like termites. "Anywhere special?" the driver asked, and Vicki told him to stop in front of a shoe store that appeared ahead. Inside, she bought a pair of platform sandals, shoved them in her bag and walked on to a club saying it was "Lady's Night" even though it was day and even though the sign never changed because every night was lady's night. Beats from giant speakers shook the building almost, and there weren't any customers except three gringas smoking cigarettes and drinking yellow drinks through straws on a table by the dance floor. She didn't know what she was looking for, exactly, but this wasn't it. Too young. Too American. But it was a place to chill for a minute, use the bathroom and think.

The bartender, a kid, was moving bottles of beer from boxes into a metal tub. She whistled for his attention, and then ordered a Pacifico. She paid him two dollars plus one more for a tip, leaving her 21 U.S. The boy thanked her and went back to his job, too young and good looking to pay much attention to Vicki, a small advantage, but small advantages, efficiencies one of her teachers called them, added up and made the difference between winning and losing in the end, success and failure. It had to go one way or another.

She left her beer half-finished on the bar and went to the bathroom, checked herself in the mirror. Her hair was frizzy and dry after a month of commissary shampoo, so she wrapped it in a bandana and tied little ears on top. At the full-length mirror, she pulled her tank top up, showing the band of her Tommy Hilfigers over her low hanging khakis. She took the shaving kit from her bag, placed it unzipped on the edge of the sink. Working fast, she pulled off the shirt, and at the sink, still dry and clean this early in the day, used the straight razor to slice off the bottom. She tried it on, and it looked pretty good, hugging her tits and showing her flat belly. She kicked off her Cons and did the same work on her pants as she'd done to the shirt, turning them into those shorts that show the bottom curve of the nalgas the gringas at college were wearing that year. The cut-off material in the trash, kicks in the bag and the high sandals on her feet, she cinched the belt tight to pull the shorts high. On the streets, they'd call her a puta, but off the street she looked just like the white girls drinking in the club.

Over the month in detention, her eyebrows had grown in, so she painted her face like a white girl or a brown girl who wants to look white, red lips, bronze shadow and black liner that ramped out like a cat's eyes, thick brows. She had practice, making herself up like this in the bathrooms before going to class and then changing back after so Rico wouldn't see her like that. The face was pretty, thin with a narrow, fat mouth, high cheeks, and a straight nose, but her eyes were what men noticed even in a club full of beautiful ladies, large and tilted like a part-Japanese, so light brown they looked yellow, the color of a lion's fur. The beauty was an advantage and a disadvantage. Men watched her, remembered her, gave her things and wanted things from her. It had been that way forever.

She left the bar without finishing her beer. Outside, she walked, acting like she had somewhere to go while hunting for the right place. No swinging doors or accordion music, no dancing. Something else she'd know when she saw, a bar where men with a little money but not too much money drank. A couple of blocks off the strip, she found it, called Sports Bar, in English. Four trucks and a Taurus stood in the gravel parking lot, all facing the building except a red pickup with an extra-large cab, which some fool had backed in, like he was going to have to make a getaway. She entered a bright room with a straight bar in front of four big TVs. The sound of the announcers of a futbol match echoed around the concrete floor and walls, along with the noise of the few customers talking. The place smelled like TJ, like shit and meat and spilled tequila and burning trash and bleach. Two men wearing cowboy hats turned from the bar to check her out. She ignored them, sliding onto her stool on the opposite end from them. The other customers, four men, sat together at a low table in a corner, salesmen in shirts with collars, knocking off early to drink through the afternoon before going home to their families. She ordered a beer from a girl in leggings and a tee shirt that showed her fat belly flopping out from her waistband.

Twenty minutes later, a dark-haired mestizo from the business table came to order beside her, even though there was plenty of room between her and the cowboy hat men. He leaned against the bar, facing her a foot away, his stomach out like a pregnant lady's. Smiling at Vicki, he called out for four shots of Don Julio and four Coronas. "I look at you," he said as the bartender poured, "and I wonder. What brings a beautiful young lady into this place alone?" His thick hair was greased and combed to one side with a straight white part. Low forehead. Buggy eyes. Fat cheeks.

"Are you my angel?" she asked, turning to him with eyes open wide like a child's. They were the first words that came to her, some crazy talk she remembered from a poem she had to read for class because men at bars liked crazy better than clear. Women who said things straight scared them.

"I could be," he answered, and swallowed. He looked over at his friends, like he might need their help.

"Take me away," she whispered. He licked his lips, and then showed his teeth. "Oh, I didn't mean to frighten you, papi."

He laughed like a little dog barking. Ha, ha, ha. "How can a little girl like you scare me?"

"Good," she said. "I like brave men. Come back when your friends leave. Don't tell them, or they might try to take your place—and if they do, I might let them. After you leave, drive around the block. I'll be here waiting. You have a car, don't you?"

He nodded his head all serious, spinning his wedding band with his other hand. "Of course I have a car. What do you think I am?"

"I don't care about that," she said, looking at the ring. "A big boy like you can stay out late, can't he?"

"I come home when I want."

"I know you do, papi. I'll be here, but don't make me wait too long. Someone is going to be a very happy boy tonight. Are you the one?"

He laughed again, ha ha ha, and walked, stiff and quick, back to his friends while the bartender followed, carrying the drinks on a tray. In the mirror, she watched him smile at his friends and shake his head at their questions, following her instructions like the obedient boy she knew he was.

She nursed her beer while other Vicki Valles floated around like ghosts. Was there an easier, safer, less crazy way to get south? No way she'd whore, and even if she did decide to fuck for money, she wasn't going to let some pimp slap her around, treat her like a slave, and take her cash. And a straight job? Like what? Frying burgers at McDonalds? With no place to sleep, less than 20 bucks left, no clothes, and no experience doing anything but breaking the law? The match on TV ended without her noticing or caring which side won. The cowboys at the bar left, and other men walked in. One skinny dude in a mechanic's suit said hello as he waited on his drink. Her businessman watched it happen in the mirror, jealous. She looked his reflection in the eye, puckered her lips, tapped them with her finger. The mechanic got his drink and moved on. Don't worry, papi, she thought, sending the words to his head. Tonight, you are my one and only.

He and his homies finally got up, paid the bill and left. Five minutes later, he appeared in the doorway. She tipped the bartender, left the beer half empty and warm, walked across the room and out the door, ignoring the man in the threshold. He followed and then overtook her. A gentleman, he opened the door of his red pickup, backed into its space. "A real all-night motel," she said as he started the engine, "no hourly love room. American style, where you pull up to the door. I don't want anybody to see me."

"I don't want to be seen either," he said, and pulled out of the parking lot.

She placed her hand on his thigh. "One more thing. I need a bathtub."

"I know a place," he said, steering onto the highway heading south beside the ocean. A few minutes later, they came to a tourist village just off to the right. Instead of turning toward the beach, he pulled into the parking lot of La Auto-Posada Luna Llena, a strip of a dozen rooms painted pink with blue doors right on the highway. "Wait here," he said, and ran into the office. A minute later, he backed into a spot in front of room five, and soon they stood before the sway-back bed, curtains closed, door locked behind them.

Smiling, he looked eager but nervous, not sure what came next. "I'm taking a bath," she told him, "and when I'm ready, I'll call you in. Can you wait?" He nodded his head, and she put her hand on his crotch, felt it grow. "No starting early," she whispered. "Save it all for me."

In the dank bathroom, she ran the water as hot as it would go. She placed a towel on the toilet seat beside the tub, and on the towel, the shaving kit. Through the door, laughter came from the television, the fake kind that told you when the joke was over. She undressed, and folded her clothes into her bag, placed the bag on the toilet tank, and draped another towel over the bag. Steam covered the mirror, and she turned on the shower. Soaped and rinsed, she began to fill the tub. Leaning back and facing the faucet, she took three items from the kit: a pot of shaving soap, a short brush with a wooden handle, and the straight razor. She gave it to Rico for his birthday after she became his lady. An old man for a gangster at 37, they called him Rico Ritz because he liked to wear a suit and a fedora sometimes, and the razor fit his old timey style. She taught him to shave her with it too. Sometimes when he shaved her in the early days, she'd wonder if this was it, the day she'd die, but he never even nicked her. When they got him, she threw the kit into her bag for no real reason she could figure. Just one of those things you do when you don't have time to think.

She folded the edge of the towel over the razor to hide it, and then told the man whose name she didn't know that she was ready for him. The door opened. "Take your clothes off," she said, head resting on the rim of the tub. He frowned down at the shaving supplies, fingers on the top button of his shirt. "I need to shave my pussy," she said, and stood up to show him her body. He nodded his head, unbuttoning his shirt. Nude, his belly almost hid his dick, and she felt sorry for him, a little. But then she thought of the director of the orphanage where she grew up, who first raped her when she was ten, and a familiar numbness took over, a blank feeling that she found useful at times like this, an efficiency. "Come in," she said, lathering the shaving soap with the brush, and then spreading it up and down her legs. He touched himself, moved his hand back and forth slowly, but made no move to enter the tub. "Careful," she said, smiling down at his sex while opening the razor, careful not to look at his face so she wouldn't give too much away. "I want this to last, papi." Ignoring him now, she ran the blade down her calf, rinsed and made another pass.

Her legs smooth, she placed the razor on the towel, soaped the brush, and rubbed the foam onto her nest, grown thick over the time in detention. "Come in, baby," she repeated, holding the blade out to him, handle first. "I need help with this part." He stepped into the water and stood before her, the folded razor held like a wand. "Sit," she said, and he lowered himself into the water. Straddling his outstretched legs, she stepped up to his face.

"I don't want to hurt you," he said, opening the razor.

"You can do it. Slow but firm. Start at the top and go down. Careful." She lifted one leg up on the tub's edge, bracing herself by holding the shower rod. He pressed the blade against her soapy, wet skin, moved it down. A line of red showed just below the edge of her hair, and he gasped. "Keep going," she said, laughing. "It's just some ink, papi. Don't you want to see the rest?" He dipped the razor into the bath and brought it back to her skin, steadied his hand by gripping her thigh with the other, and moved the blade down, revealing a red triangle pointing down. "One inch more, baby." He shaved further, and the triangle tip moved out until the pattern ended and he came to the skin beginning to fold into the cleft of her sex.

She slid her left hand down her belly, slipped her middle finger between her lips while she relieved him of the razor with her right hand.

"This part is delicate," she said, and pulled the lips to one side, angled her leg, and removed the hair in the crease. She did the same with the other side, careful not to miss anything, all the way under and around her butthole. It took precision, and she enjoyed this sort of work, getting every last hair, no matter how light. She squatted, cupped a handful of water, and splashed away the remaining soap. While he stared, his face six inches from her fresh chunch, she checked the clean, bare, puckered skin, the black widow's mark in bright red, her second and last tattoo, a cover-up job. "Do you like it?" she asked, and he nodded without looking up at her, slowly stroking himself in the water, making a soft splashing sound while the fake laugh came from the television. "Look at my face," she said, and pushed his forehead to lift his eyes, and then she slit his throat. Hot blood sprayed against her thighs. His mouth opened, gurgled, and his hands came up to his neck, trying to stop what was happening, to put the blood back in but it was too late for that.

A shock like ice water splashed across her skin in spite of the damp heat of the room, and she pushed his face into the water because she couldn't stand the look of surprise on it, the flap of skin gushing blood. Under, he thrashed, waving his arms, but he couldn't get a grip on anything in the slippery tub, where she, on him, hands on his shoulders and the blade dropped to the floor, both knees pinning his chest down, had leverage. He weakened and eventually stopped fighting. She stood dripping into the tub while the bathwater turned to wine, energy pumping through her veins like she'd just mainlined crank.

She'd killed before, two men and a woman, all gangsters. The men she'd gunned down during a drive by, back in the early days. The woman was caught stealing from Rico and hanging with the 13th Streeters, a betraying puta who Vicki had beaten and then cut with her razor while Rico stood by watching, a test of loyalty and cajónes. For a while Vicki had felt sorry for the girl, and thought maybe she didn't do it, but then she remembered the 13th Street bangers in Salvador, who'd captured her back when she was just a girl, beat her, shaved her bald, tattooed their mark on her, and raped her, all five of them. They made it easy to hurt the girl, to ruin her, at first. Afterward, she puked in the toilet while Rico laughed. Remembering, she grew dizzy, and cold sweat covered her skin. Breathing hard and deep, she turned around to face the back wall, looking up, one hand on the shower rod, the other against the side of the shower. The sick, scared feeling passed, and she settled back into herself. It was easier to kill when nobody was there watching and judging.

Head to the side, she reached under the body and pulled the drain. Blood dripped down her belly and legs, and drops speckled the plastic bath wall and the floor, but her bag was clean. While the corpse stared up from between her feet, with its surprised eyes and plastic skin, she turned on the shower, soaped her body again, shampooed and conditioned her hair, and rinsed. Her hands shook just a little returning the clean items to the leather satchel, but she ignored the feeling rushing through her, and she stepped onto the bath mat, as she'd done a thousand times before, and closed the shower curtain, the water still gurgling down the drain. She dried herself with the last clean towel, and the body in the tub made a noise, a thumping like it was still alive. She froze, her skin cold and tight, but no other sound followed, so she grabbed her purse, left the bathroom, and closed the door. An American comedy played on the TV, a show about high school kids smoking pot and making jokes, how it must have been for white kids to grow up up north in the old days and maybe still today. She didn't know.

Sitting on the damp towel on the bed, she rubbed her body with lotion, especially the shaved parts. She pulled on the clean underwear she'd been carrying in her purse, made up her face, dressed, combed and braided her hair, soft from the conditioner. Mariachi music played in the next room over, and a woman laughed.

The man's wallet held a thick roll of pesos—these Mexicans and their cash—and a Visa card, among identification, snapshots of his wife, two girls and a boy, young in the pictures but probably older by now. She popped open his blinking cell phone and removed the battery. Outside, it had grown dark. Cars and trucks shot by on the highway, and lights twinkled in the little beach town, but nobody was out front of the motel. She took his keys, left the light and television on, and locked the door behind her. In the truck, she looked under the seat, in the glove compartment, and finally behind the seat back, where she found a road atlas of Mexico. She wasn't sure if she'd dare use the Visa or not, though by the time they found him, she'd be a thousand miles away.

# Chapter Three

Caruthers lay under the whirling ceiling fan, dreading the day to come. He climbed out of bed and into the typical morning illness, of stomach, head, joints, and soul. At the kitchen counter, he splashed a finger of rum into his coffee mug and shot it down. Then he filled his kettle from the tap and placed it on the hotplate. The kettle whined as he dried himself, just out of the shower. Naked, he spooned instant coffee into the mug, hit it with water and rum. Today he chose a royal purple Hawaiian shirt reserved for special occasions, which was to say, a shirt almost never worn. He knocked back the coffee in a series of gulps. Hands steadying, he found a screwdriver in a drawer, and he used it, careful not to strip the threads or scratch the paint, to remove two screws that secured the inset medicine cabinet to the interior bathroom drywall. He pulled out the cabinet to get at the space behind, where he kept his money and anything else he didn't want to lose. The checkpoint episode had cost him, though he'd gotten off easy compared to what Cruz might do to him. He counted his cash, a meagre 500 quetzales, half of what he paid last year for the visa stamp and letter. Showing up without the full amount would piss Cruz off, but not showing at all, waiting for Cruz to come knocking, would piss him off much worse.

He screwed the medicine cabinet back into place, a cheap modern fixture retrofit into his old plaster interior, and stood looking at himself, always disappointing. "They can only kill you once," he said to the flabby old man behind the glass.

He ate toast with another cup of coffee, topped off his flask and set out, down the stairs and onto the waking street, Santander, Panajachel's tacky main drag. Cruz worked out of an office above a tipica shop called "Mayan Treasures," across the street from Caruthers' local bar, La Mala Senda, where in more prosperous times Cruz would sometimes pop in to receive a complimentary glass of Johnny Walker contaminated by Coca Cola, chat up any women that happened to be hanging around, and generally set everyone on edge. The one good result of the customers drying up was that Cruz no longer bothered to visit.

Caruthers stepped into the shadow of the store's awning, breathing in the good smell of fresh fabric while offering the old crone working there an apologetic smile. She, recognizing him, didn't bother to rise from her chair. The wooden stairway angled up the side of the building to a landing fronting a steel door painted with block letters: "POLICIA." He opened the door and approached the woman who worked the front desk. Rumor had it she'd been Chucho's favorite whore in another era, and that he'd given her the present job out of affection. The story attested to Cruz's loyalty as a pimp and human trafficker, his sentimental side, and Caruthers didn't believe a word of it. Certainly this woman, Justa was her name, held enough secrets in her head to put Chucho in prison for the rest of his life, if, of course, an uncorrupted prosecutor, judge, and jury could be rounded up, none of which was likely. Even so, if something went down like an outside investigation, a man like Chucho wouldn't hesitate to kill his former favorite hooker.

Doña Justa looked up from one of the little comic books sold in every shop, blinking like an owl at resplendent, purple Caruthers, compressing her thin lips painted a red verging on black. "Estoy aquí para señor Cruz," Caruthers enunciated. Even after all these years, he still had to rehearse his Spanish for such occasions. She lowered the booklet, which featured a blond damsel with unearthly cleavage fleeing a drooling maniac. Her black hair rose from her head in a foggy column drifting slightly to the right; her skin hung slackly from a face as blank as a mask.

"Hay un gringo," she called, though she'd dealt with Caruthers on a dozen occasions and surely knew his name. Chucho Cruz appeared at the doorway behind her, chewing on something.

He cleared his throat and squinted, searching for his English. He swallowed. "My good, good friend. How are you?" he said, waving Caruthers forward. As always, Caruthers felt embarrassed to find himself a head taller than Chucho, who embraced Caruthers around the waist, squeezed hard enough to bruise his kidneys.

"What's the matter," Cruz asked, insulted by Caruthers' tepid hug participation. "You think Chucho Cruz is maricón?" Caruthers began to deny the accusation, but Cruz laughed, squeezing Caruthers once again. "No, señor, I can tell you I am no maricón. You think?"

"No," Caruthers agreed. Cruz was certainly heterosexual, though Caruthers could imagine him sodomizing an enemy just to humiliate him. Today he wore black jeans, tight over his large hips and thighs, a silky shirt tucked in, cowboy boots. A gold watch pinched his fat wrist, as three thick rings did his fingers, a wedding band on his left and two class-style monstrosities on the other. Caruthers followed him into the office. Cruz sat at his desk, which angled off a corner of the room. The window to Cruz's left looked down at La Mala. The back half of the police building, Caruthers knew first hand, was made up of two holding cells. They weren't often used. Chucho's enemies didn't normally live long enough to be arrested.

"I feel sad my good friend is not come to visit," he claimed, indicating that Caruthers should sit in the wooden chair in front of the desk.

"Sadness doesn't adequately describe my emotions over the state of our relationship," Caruthers risked answering. Cruz appeared not to have listened, his way of covering the voids in his English.

"You come to pay, yes?"

"That's the thing," Caruthers said, lifting the expired letter and passport from his front pocket. "I've run into some trouble lately. Business has been very bad, and I'm short." He drew out the 500 in cash, hoping that something was better than nothing. Cruz frowned. "I know this is not good, but I don't know what else to do? The riders just aren't there. I can barely pay for gas. On top of that, my tires are bad, and my clutch is getting loose."

Cruz whistled, shaking his head. He glanced down at the road, where two children chased a dog, laughing and flinging stones. "You have enough money for whiskey, huh? But no money to pay bills."

Caruthers sought for an answer but couldn't find one. *You've been spying on me?* may have worked in a marriage but not for the present situation. "Yesterday I got caught in a checkpoint. Some army guy, a colonel or whatever, shook me down for a week's earnings," Caruthers lied. "Beat the hell out of me and took my ayudante too. I could have come up with the money if not for that. I hate to say it, but the guy basically robbed you and me both."

Cruz nodded, thinking, his hands steepled before his mouth, and Caruthers wondered if he'd overstepped. "Mind if I drink?" he asked, removing the flask from a cargo side pocket. Cruz smiled behind his hands.

"Señor Norman, you have many pockets, many alcohols."

"Verdad," Caruthers said, and filled his mouth. He offered the flask to Cruz, who shooed it away.

"Enjoy," he said, shuffling through the documents before him, the passport, the letter, and the cash. "I am working." He drummed the fingers of one hand on the desk. "One thousand five hundred quetzales total," he said. "Minus five hundred. This comes to…" Cruz pretended to calculate, "…one thousand." He grinned. "A bargain, no? Two-for-one special."

Caruthers felt sick to his stomach, and his face prickled with hot pinpoints. "But," he started, and faltered. Cruz was looking up at him, surprised, concerned.

"Some problem?"

"No," Caruthers said. "It's fine. A short-term loan is fine."

"Ah, excellent," Cruz said, his former good cheer restored. "Twenty-five percent interest, each month."

"But I thought…"

Cruz raised his eyes to Caruthers and offered a look not entirely threatening.

"Last year I paid one grand total," Caruthers concluded. "You're really squeezing me here Chucho." Caruthers concluded.

"Norman, I'm sorry, but we have the inflation." He displayed an expanse of square teeth. Justa entered the room with the new letter. "Okay. No problem. I give the letter," he said, glancing over the print and signing with a flourish, "and you come back for the visa when you have the money." He put away the stamping machine.

"How about I buy the stamp today, and the letter after?" Caruthers asked.

Cruz regarded Caruthers for a moment, then looked up at the ceiling. "Ay, yie, yie," he muttered.

"No," Caruthers quickly put in, uncapping his flask. "You're right. Letter now, visa later. Perfecto."

Cruz rubbed his face, long suffering and patient, like the parent of an exasperating but beloved child. He counted the money and placed it into a drawer. Then he handed the letter to Caruthers. "Thank you," Caruthers said, standing. "Excuse me," he said before leaving, "el pasaporte?"

Cruz looked at the creased, blue booklet, issued from the American Embassy in Guate after the last one expired. "Wait," he said, and snapped a finger. "I have the solution. Yes, perfect."

"Solution? I like solutions, but, you know, I'd prefer to keep my nose out of other people's business, if you know what I mean."

Cruz shook his head, as if dismissing a compliment. "No, no, no. The easiest thing. You give some friends of mine a ride to Salvador. You drive back. Oh, this is the best idea." He plunged the stamper into Caruthers' passport booklet. "Don't worry. I will arrange everything." He tossed the booklet across the table, and Caruthers fumbled it to the floor.

"Uh, thank you," Caruthers said, stooping for the passport, desperately searching for words to reverse what had just happened. Instead, he stood, staring at Cruz, mouth open.

Cruz frowned. "Yes? More problems?"

Caruthers shook his head. "Nope, not a one." He bowed a little, and then crossed over to the door, where he stopped. "One little thing," he said, turning. "I lost my ayudante at a military checkpoint. A good man, and very useful. I'd rather not have to replace him."

Cruz dipped his head in Caruthers' direction, signaling that he would listen.

"They took him away with most of the other men on the bus. No reason that I could see."

"Name?" Cruz asked, all business.

"Sebastiano…" Caruthers had never learned his last name. "Goes by Seba. Has a small star tattooed on his face. Looks kind of funny, but he's fine. Never causes trouble."

"Seba," Cruz said, and nodded to himself. Caruthers, having done what he could, left the office of the Chief of Police and jogged across the street to La Mala, hoping to catch Red prepping for the noon opening hour. The door was unlocked so Caruthers pushed through, only to find young Billy, Red's errand boy, listlessly pushing a mop across the floor tiles.

"Closed," the young man spat.

"I know that," Caruthers said. "I'm here to talk to Red."

"Red not here. You go. Out. Leave."

Caruthers stood for a moment, stuck. He didn't want to let this punk push him around, but he couldn't think of a way to override the pronouncement. Technically, Billy was currently in charge of the business. "Tell him I stopped by," Caruthers said. And then, to save face: "I hope for your sake he doesn't get mad when I mention you kicked me out."

Billy made a farting sound with his mouth, and Caruthers left, embarrassed. Now, on top of everything else, he was a tattle tale. With nowhere else to go, he began walking through humidity that seemed to increase by the step, toward home. The notion occurred to him that Billy was the key to the best of several bad options for the day. Rumor had it the kid had ayudante experience, and Caruthers would be better off making some money while waiting on Seba. Except that now it was too late. He'd insulted the young man, and to go back and apologize… impossible. Sometimes the right thing to do just wasn't worth the trouble. And what was one lost day in an entire life of lost days? What was the point of anything, after all, driving or not driving, earning or not earning? Living or dying. It would all be over soon anyway.

# Chapter Four

Maxwell Caruthers, a rangy, handsome man of thirty-two tucked under a cowboy hat, rode a bus named Esmeralda into the wilderness, where his flock awaited. The village of Zunilito appeared as a dot on his guidebook map, an hour northwest of Quetzaltenago, where Max had started his mission with a week's intensive Spanish lessons. According to Pastor Kent, Zunilito was so primitive they had no phones or computers. The church contact, a village leader named Reina, kept in touch through sporadic Facebook messages, probably sent from a neighboring city. By this time Max should have set up a Facebook profile of his own, to contact Reina as well as post updates on the church page. For some reason, though Kent assured him the process was simple and safe, Max felt uneasy about plugging into a network of people connected only by machines. An out-of-work union carpenter, Max never caught the technology train.

And so, because of his procrastination, accommodations had not yet been arranged in Zunil. He would simply arrive, to press flesh against flesh, to look into the eyes of his charges. The matter of his father would wait. God's work came first.

Rolling over grassy foothills, he leaned back into the undersized school bus bench, drifting into a daydream meeting with his Spanish teacher of the previous week, Karma Muños. What are you doing back? she would ask when they ran into each other on the street, and his answer would lead to a continuation of the long conversation of the previous week, an interrogation that covered politics, religion, family, even the ideal qualities of a romantic partner. At five hours per day for seven days straight, they couldn't help but cover a lot of ground. Max closed his eyes, settling into the rhythm of the bus and the fantasy, which led from chance meeting to impromptu lunch, where he spoke well, expressing his thoughts with charm and ease, unlike the real him.

A tug at his shirtsleeve brought him back to the moment. The little Mayan girl between Max and her mother flirtatiously lifted the fabric covering Max's biceps, exposing a faded tattoo of a jester—a lesser regret. He smiled and shrugged, hoping to convey the message that one should think twice before committing to permanent ink.

"¿Que es?" she asked, touching the jester's face gingerly, even fearfully, as if it might spring to life.

Luckily, the pot leaf originally representing the jester's shoulder mantle had faded into a dull green blur. "Tatuaje," he said, having learned the word from Karma, but the girl didn't seem to understand. Dressed in the colorful Indian gear common to her people, she probably spoke little Spanish.

He frowned, trying to find another way to explain the picture, when the mother at the window seat abruptly pulled the girl away from Max and onto her lap. "Perdoname," Max said, mildly alarmed. The travel advisory still stood, owing to a rash of peasant attacks on tourists, in each case the victim mistaken for one of the rumored baby-snatchers the tabloids kept inventing. Kent and the government both advised to avoid interactions with indigenous children. A dark-eyed man, the girl's father perhaps, watched Max from the next bench up.

"No, no," the woman replied, and then said something too fast for Max to follow, though he guessed it was an attempt to spare his feelings. So hard to understand each other, Max thought, even when everyone spoke the same language. Out here, they didn't stand a chance.

"No problem," he said in Spanish, hoping to have guessed the proper response. She smiled, her teeth edged in silver. She was, Max realized with a shock, younger than he.

Half an hour later, the bus driver's assistant announced the approach of Zunil, and Max waded into the aisle. Built into a hillside, the town surprised him with its size, a walled, medieval-looking cluster of stone boxes bound by winding, cobbled pathways—easily large enough for a thousand residents. A canary yellow church marked the center of the town, pretty but not large. How in God's green earth was he supposed to find his people here? He hadn't even bothered to memorize Reina's Mayan surname.

The bus stopped, and Max exited with a few others. He followed them across a footbridge over a creek and then through an open gateway in the stone wall. Heat radiated from the road and the close concrete buildings on either side. Hat tilted against the glare, he started up the main stem, glancing down the alleys on either side as he climbed, not at all sure what he was looking for. His fellow travelers fell away, through doorways or down side streets, and he felt relieved to walk alone with his private idiocy. Every door stood closed, and all the windows were shuttered for the siesta hour. Halfway up the hillside, he came to the 50-by-50-foot square fronting the church.

With no better plan, he approached the large double doors. Why hadn't he heard anything about a Catholic church in Zunil? He understood the hunger for something else, a more personal relationship with the deity and a less dressed-up approach to God, but shouldn't Reina have at least mentioned the presence of a competing church? Like a trespasser, he entered the cool dark interior, through the antechamber with its fount of holy water and down the center aisle. The place was empty, so he dared to approach the gruesome Jesus on the wall, still suffering. Why keep him nailed to the cross? Max wondered. He'd risen, after all.

Transfixed by the horrible beauty, he sat at a pew in the front row.

# A Candle for San Simón

Powerful stuff, the naked, bloody effigy surrounded by radiating gold and baubles, the glowing stained glass, the sweet, hot smell of candle wax along with some herby incense. All theater, all show, and yet, didn't his hands and feet ache in sympathy for the tortured man before him? He glanced around the chapel, hoping to find someone, a priest perhaps, who might know Reina, but the room was as lifeless as Christ's painted eyes.

He dipped his head to pray, to apologize for judging this church. Only God can judge, he reminded himself, and then went on to ask Jesus to send him to Reina. An intrusive, castigating voice pushed in, marveling sarcastically at Max's gall to think God would entertain such a petty request. If God has a plan for everything, then He already knows whether or not you're going to find Reina. He probably sent you here to fail, to teach you a lesson. "Amen," Max said aloud, and stood, deploying action to silence the critic, striding through the dim, cool room, through the entryway, and out, pulling his hat back on, its band damp.

Attempting to outpace a stalking sense of failure, he walked, looking now only for a store to sell him a Coke, someone to talk to. Lost along yet another desolate side passage, he began to accept the inevitable. He'd have to return to Xela, find some Wi-Fi and finally make the blessed Facebook account and send a blessed note to Reina to set up a blessed meeting with a blessed time and a place like he should have done days ago. Perhaps he should go ahead and tell Kent how badly he'd already screwed up while he was at it. Dry-mouthed and sweating, Max chewed on this new reality when a figure appeared twenty feet before him, a ragged, beggarly man with one cloudy eye, who'd popped out of a side passage barely wide enough for a person to walk. The man, the first resident of Zunil Max had seen since he'd left the others from the bus, nodded his head vigorously while summoning Max forward in the Guatemalan style, a palm-down motion like bouncing an invisible ball.

Max looked behind him to make certain that he was the object of the beggar's signal. The beggar kept nodding his head in encouragement, smiling like a clown. In spite of strong doubts, Max approached, and then followed him into the passageway, away from the sunlight and around a tight corner. Only a thin strip of blue appeared overhead, and a sharp smell had Max breathing through his mouth. Finally, the beggar opened a door no more than four feet high, and smoke poured out while he presented his right palm to Max. With his other hand, he raised his thumb, index, and middle fingers, signifying a request for three quetzales, the price of admission. From inside, a man's voice droned rhythmically. Max gazed into the dark chamber, thick with milling bodies enveloped in a smoky orange light. Could this be Reina's church? He dropped three coins into the waxy, creased palm, if only to satisfy his curiosity.

Stooping low, he stepped through the portal into air so hot and pungent he gagged. The door shut behind him, and sweat sprang from his skin. To the left, candlelight flickered through the spaces between the many figures standing about. Max nearly stepped on a man writhing on his side on the concrete floor, moaning and straining toward a bottle of the local moonshine that lay capped and just out of reach. A woman, middle-aged in business slacks and blazer, squatted to help the downed man sip from the bottle.

Max's eyes adjusted to the dark as he moved deeper into the chamber, long and narrow, like a train car. Someone placed a can in his hand. He passed an obese Indian woman sitting on the floor with her back to the wall and knees up, puffing a thick, hand-rolled cigar of reeking tobacco, dress hiked up to her hips. She spewed smoke and cackled like a B-actor playing a lunatic. Reina? Max imagined asking. The general din absorbed his own laughter.

Moving toward the light, Max came to an island of burning candles in a lake of melted wax, separating him and the rest of the congregation from a barefoot man in an oxford shirt tucked into a striped Mayan kilt. While the man gestured and shouted, a still figure sat beside him in a rocking chair. For an instant, Max thought the chair held a corpse, but then he recognized the thing as a doll, a department store mannequin hidden under the brim of a Houston Astros baseball cap and behind mirrored aviator sunglasses. A scarf covered the mouth, and the idol otherwise wore a wide-lapelled sports coat from the seventies, a dress shirt with a thick tie, and slacks tucked into knee-high, furry boots designed for ski vacations.

Members of the congregation set money, candles, cans of beer, cigarettes, and bottles of spirits on the floor in front of the idol. The shaman attending the mannequin upended a large bottle of the local rotgut called Quetzalteca, pouring the clear stuff into a small glass, showy as an uptown bartender. He spoke in a husky, smoker's voice, then rocked the figure back in its chair, slipped the bandana from the face and fed it the alcohol.

Unthinking and parched, Max popped the can in his hand and drank. Horrified once the warm, sour liquid hit his tongue, he gagged, and, with nowhere to spit, swallowed. He'd been sober for fifteen months. Dizzy, he set the can on the floor with the other offerings. The shaman—demon, conman, or whatever he was—lit a cigarette, and held it to the idol's mouth. A plume of smoke shot through the bandana. Max pictured a Catholic priest pulling the same trick with bloody Jesus on the cross. Outraged by his blasphemous self, he laughed hard and helplessly.

A man and woman escorted a teenaged girl, their daughter presumably, around the candles up to the idol and shaman. All three kneeled side by side on pillows on the opposite side of the mannequin from the shaman, facing the congregation, the girl in the center. The shaman fellow continued to shout, his voice gone hoarse and yet still penetrating. He crossed in front of the idol to stand before the kneeling family at an angle, so the audience could see both him and the girl. He waved the bottle, drank, ducked down low, and jettisoned a mist of liquor onto her left breast. The child, in the early months of puberty, knelt with eyes closed, her face as passive as a carved saint's. The wizard held forth, filled his mouth again, and wetted the girl's other breast. The parents, hands interlocked under their chins, watched with exaggerated bliss in their eyes, somehow both fake and real, theatrical but still felt. The girl's thin dress, now wet, clung to her chest.

The shaman slowed the process down, worked everyone up with his gestures and shouts until finally reaching the climax, kneeling low like a dog and spitting up the dress between the girl's legs. Max felt drunk from that single, accidental sip of beer. Lust and self-disgust slithered in his belly, down into his thighs. This was just a girl, he told himself. But no. Not anymore she wasn't. She had the body of a woman, so she was a woman. That was the story being told here. The conman, for that's what he ultimately was, offered the mannequin another drink before concluding the ritual by spraying the girl full in the face. The girl accepted the blast by squeezing shut her eyes and then resuming her calm expression—a pornographic exchange. Mist from the liquor hung in the air, twinkling in the candlelight.

Horny, nauseated, and dizzy, Max stumbled toward the exit. He tripped in the crowd and many hands caught him by the shoulders and arms, stood him up, helped him on his way, touching his neck, his back, his chest. Someone groped his crotch. The fat woman still cackled on the floor, spewing smoke, folds of fat on her thighs hiding her underwear or bare sex. The drunk at the entrance still twitched toward the still out-of-reach bottle. Max, sopping wet, kneeled to give the man the God-forsaken bottle. He burst through the tiny door and discovered a world outside brighter than the one he'd left, as if a film of dull plastic had been ripped off Max's eyes. The air he gulped, stumbling down the alley toward the road, tasted thick, cold and sweet as nectar.

# Chapter Five

Walking through clouds of car exhaust, Vicki sensed the invisible border from coplandia to mara territory. The big city streets of Salvador looked better all the sudden, the potholes filled by men and boys paid with coins tossed by passing bangers. Her skin tightened, like a breeze had blown across her naked body, even though she was covered in her baggy road clothes, her invisible costume.

She came to the American-style laundromat, across the street from the cantina that served as Mara X headquarters. She entered, ignored by the ladies washing their own dirty stuff, and dropped her new clothes into a machine: loose tan slacks, and a light cotton checkered shirt with long sleeves. She couldn't have them looking just off the rack. She plugged coins into the slot and sat down to wait on a plastic chair by the front window. Across the street, vatos entered the cantina and left a few minutes later. She moved the clothes from washer to dryer, watched them rise and fall, rise and fall. Big metal fans on the floor pushed the hot air around. Vicki went back to the plastic chair, watching for Angel Agular, his famous baby face and short body, but of course he wasn't going to show himself in town like this. The government put a reward of fifty grand U.S. on his ass, so Angel kept to the shadows. He'd been Rico's main contact down south, and the dude was making enough money to hide behind.

Clothes dry, she took them to the bathroom, where she dressed like a gringa college student going to Halloween as a chola. The message, the brand, was that she was from El Lay, vatos. She was going to give these third-world homies what they saw on the internet, a gangster bitch from Hollywood. The pants went on warm, a good fit, not too tight but enough to show her hips. She attached suspenders to the waist and let them hang to her sides for show. Then the black bra, and the checkered shirt open except for the top button, showing all kinds of skin and a peek of lace. She'd already plucked her eyebrows back at her motel room, and so she painted her lips and outlined them in black. Looking almost right, she flashed the X sign for the mirror, grimacing. Her hair was last. Earlier she thought about spraying it into a pompadour, but instead she braided it into two strands that fell down her back like an Indian princess's. Those vatos weren't going to notice her hair anyway. Done, she tossed the old clothes in a trash can full of shit paper and walked out.

She jaywalked across the street. Acting like she belonged, she pushed open the swinging double doors and stood there, shirt open like a cape, the light streaming in behind her, blinding the three homies who stared up at her, frozen around a game of dominos.

"Aye, mama," one of them said. "Come on in." A wagon wheel chandelier hung from the tin ceiling, dark from years of smoke. An old man stood behind the bar on the left side of the room. A boy maybe seventeen sat at the short leg of the bar, an iPad lighting his flat face. The three men hunkered over a table. Banda music turned down low came from hidden speakers. She walked in, letting the doors swing shut, squeaking and knocking as they settled into place.

She leaned against the bar, ordered rum and a Suprema with no glass. She paid, drank the rum in one gulp, hefted the bottle by its neck, and spun toward the seated men. On the table lay scattered dominoes, forgotten now. She climbed onto a stool, legs spread the way men sat, hands resting on her thighs.

"Looking for someone, mama?" said the man she figured led the crew. He wore a white straw cowboy hat, a mustache like a worm over his fat upper lip, and a shirt with fringe across the chest. He was thick and tall compared to the smaller men on each side, one bare-headed, the other in a black ball cap flying the Salvadoran flag edged in gold piping. The hatless one wore a mesh tank over his tee shirt.

"Yes," she said, and stepped off the stool. She walked to the table and squatted so her chin nearly touched the edge. "I come from Los Angeles," she whispered to el jefecito. "I was Enrique Caldomar's lady before they got him." She waited for the name to register. "I have an important message for Angel, from Enrique before he died."

Darkness covered Jefecito's face, a shadow that came from the inside. He shot a look to the hatless man and jerked his head toward Vicki. Moving fast, the two men pulled her to her feet. Hands groped her body, starting at her hair and moving down to her shoes. The man in the cap brushed aside the dominos and emptied her purse onto the table, a few bills and coins, makeup case, and her California ID. She'd almost brought the shaving kit, but no, too risky. "Victoria Valle," Jefecito read from the card. "Sit." The men lowered her into the extra chair at the table. Jefecito replaced the items into her bag. "A message, you say? From Enrique? Give it to me, and if it's important, I'll pass it on to Angel."

"No disrespect," Vicki said, "but Enrique made me promise to not tell anyone but Angel." The darkness remained, bad weather under the brim of the cowboy hat. "It was his dying wish," she said, hearing the bullshit in her voice. She almost flinched.

"You were with him when he died?"

She hesitated, too long. "Not right when he died. They shot him in his car, and I was just inside our place. But he knew before it happened. I don't know how, but he could feel the end was coming. He told me. 'They're going to get me.' That's what he said. I thought he was being crazy, but he was right. 'When I'm gone, you have to promise me one thing. Go to Angel Agular,' and then he told me what to say." She hadn't planned this part; she hadn't planned much at all, except walking in and saying she had a message to deliver. Plans were no good when it came to lying. They came out like lies.

"I'll get the message out of her," the man in the ball cap said, and he yanked open her shirt, popping the button off and onto the table.

"This shirt's from L.A.," Vicki shouted, a lie that felt like the truth. "Rico bought it for me. It was his favorite."

The men looked surprised. The boy with the iPad and the bartender were gone. The music had ended, and the only sounds came from the street, car horns and shouts over the hum of traffic. Jefecito stacked the dominos and placed them back in their little wooden coffin. "As you can see, my men would very much like to ask you some questions." He grinned at them, and they laughed. "Your final chance is to tell me what Enrique has to say. If he said anything. If I like it, well, who knows. If I don't like it, or if you keep pretending you can't talk to us, then it will be time to go to work. So how would you like it to go?"

Vicki, flipping through possible moves, settled on one that would have to do. "I'll tell you," she whispered to Jefecito, "but only you, please."

"Why not?" he said, and sent his men away. "This better be good."

She looked him in the eyes. "Enrique wanted to give me to Angel, to make things right. When he was young, still down here, he took Angel's lady. Many times without Angel knowing. But then Angel discovered them, and that's why he ran north. Nobody else knows, and Angel will go crazy if he thinks somebody found out. You understand? The message is me. Rico wants to be forgiven. He loved me, and he wanted me to be taken care of, and at the same time settle the score."

Jefecito stared at her, the darkness dissipating from his face. "Sorry about your shirt," he said. "Tell me one thing. What happened to Angel's woman? Did she escape with Rico?"

"No. Angel tied her to a ping pong table. He brought men from outside, who didn't know her. They beat her, raped her, while a camera recorded it all. They sawed off her feet and hands while she was still alive.

After she bled out, they butchered her and placed her parts in trash bags. He showed the video to his new wife on their wedding night, so she wouldn't get any ideas."

Jefecito nodded in recognition. The torture and murder of the girl was real. The video was real. Victoria had seen it. So had Jefecito of course. Many stories had circulated over the years about who she was and why she'd been killed this way, but the mystery had never been solved...just another gangster girl going out the hard way. Vicki dipped her head, hiding a cold splash of fear. She'd said too much. How could she have known about Angel showing the video to his bride? She kept quiet and hoped for the best. If Jefecito asked, she'd put it on Enrique, embellishing a true story, like everyone did. But she didn't have to worry. Jefecito believed her story, or pretended to.

"I will tell Angel you're here," he said, and seemed to want to explain more, but then he dropped it. "You will stay with us until then. If Angel wants to see you, it will happen."

"What about my stuff? I can't see him dressed like this."

"If Angel wants you, everything will be taken care of. If not..." he shrugged, and then pinched the loose button from the table. "We'll fix your shirt," he said, rising and extending his hand to her. She took it and stood. Together, they walked deeper into the cantina. For some reason, she felt sad about leaving her crap back at the motel room, another loss along with the rest, Rico, her life in L.A., her parents, the shadow life she never knew as a normal girl, the shaving kit. Everything she'd ever had.

# Chapter Six

Caruthers approached the lake, eager to send packing the juvenile delinquent playing at ayudante, Guillermo. He called himself Billy, part of his worship of everything American, everything American except Norman Caruthers. A week after the checkpoint, with Seba still at large, the new kid just wasn't working out. Caruthers, visa and updated letter in hand, trusted that Cruz's recommendation of the kid was of the light, off-the-cuff variety, and that Caruthers could fire Billy without repercussions.

He crested the rim of the volcanic basin, almost home. 500 feet below, the lake lay gray-blue and flat, like a cataract. The volcano directly across from Pana, the big one whose name he'd forgotten, spewed a jagged line of white smoke into the high, vague clouds. Someday it would blow, or one of them would, and Caruthers half-hoped to be around to see it, to go out like those poor bastards in Pompeii, caught in the act of living to be dug up and studied a thousand years later.

He hugged the cliff cutbacks for fifteen minutes, and then coasted the last stretch to lake level. Finally, he pulled into Panajachel, the gaudy, seedy tourist trap where Caruthers had settled, Disneylandia some locals called it. He passed tipica clothing shops, tour outfitters, restaurants, all as empty as the Stanley thermos rattling in its holder. Weary, hoarse from goading Billy, he parked at his regular spot in the weedy lot behind La Mala Senda, disappointed again not to find Seba waiting.

From the driver's seat, he counted out some bills and handed them to Billy. The youth—skinny, tall, with a haircut like soft-serve chocolate ice cream twirled onto his head—showed his bad manners by tallying the money right there. "That all?" he asked.

"You almost earned some of it," Caruthers said, and shooed the kid out the door.

"I need more if I work tomorrow," Billy complained, standing at the bottom step while Caruthers climbed down. Billy's jeans hung low on his ass, making for slow movement around the bus, and his black tee shirt featured a sparkly design of gothic letters too complicated to read. The kid had been hanging with small-time hoodlums, which accounted both for his connection to Cruz and for the notion that money should be plentiful and easily got.

"Listen you little weasel," Caruthers said, fed up and thirsty, "I wouldn't let you work for me for free, not after this week's ass dragging. I wouldn't take you on if you paid me. Get it? You stunk. You want to know why? Bad attitude, like the world owes you something. Well it doesn't, and I'm here to present you this fact since nobody else has. You can thank me later."

Billy stepped back, mortally offended, though his English was too poor to have understood most of what had been said. Even so, he'd obviously gotten the drift, based on the way his face crumpled up like he was going to cry, but then, after a small tremor of countenance at war with itself, the smirk emerged, like something pushing up through soil. "You die here," he carefully enunciated, pointing at the ground, "and I laugh." He wheeled and strode off, into the darkness that had borne him.

Well, Caruthers thought, not the smoothest human resources transaction in history, but it got the job done. Though it never paid to make an enemy of anyone associated with Cruz, Billy hardly registered as a problem compared to the forthcoming delivery. Caruthers had little trouble evacuating the kid from his mind, pushing through La Mala's back door and finding the place about as busy as it got these days, with three drinkers lined up along the bar.

"Can you believe it?" Red asked as Caruthers mounted a stool, eyes adjusting to the dim light. La Mala was a simple place, dark and smelly, with an L-shaped bar twenty by five feet long, two high tables and four low, and a wrought iron spiral staircase leading to a rooftop bar closed since the first tourist attack several weeks back. Red cracked a Cabro and placed it before Caruthers, then returned his attention to the newspaper spread over the bar mat. "They called her an 'amateur journalist.'" A gangly man with a long ginger ponytail, Red had been in Pana, owning and operating this very bar, since Caruthers first arrived. "What in hell is a amateur journalist anyway?"

"Well, I expect it means she wrote stuff that don't pay, like blogs and whatnot," said a man two stools to the left of Caruthers, a relative newcomer with an unknown source of funding, not that there were many options. A modest trust fund, early pension, disability, or some kind of legal settlement. The shadowy side included pre-Columbian artifact smuggling, gun running, human trafficking, security contracting, and the like, work Caruthers never imagined he'd ever fall into, but life had a way of surprising you, he thought, gulping beer. "Like it's a hobby," the guy went on. Caruthers had never liked his ratty face, the close-set eyes, the pinched features and patchy beard, the five-foot-six stature and the boasts of liaisons with hookers, as if fucking a whore were some kind of accomplishment. "Or was a hobby, I guess. Now that she's brain dead and like that."

Red turned the page, lips pursed with disgust. "Ever notice," he said to the paper, "that it's always the do-gooders that cause all the trouble?" He looked up at Caruthers. "She had it coming."

"Jesus, Red," the rat man said. "That's a little tough on the lady, isn't it?"

Caruthers agreed, but he understood Red's frustration. Red was moderate by nature, slow to anger, and the gringos of Pana depended upon him for this quality. Sleep it off, he often counseled. Drink some water. Take a walk. But everybody with a stake in the economy, legal or otherwise, was on edge lately. Five weeks after the travel advisory, the papers were still writing about the first attack, to say nothing of the two since. The rising gang violence had become so common nobody mentioned it anymore, though it added to the general sense of chaos, along with occasional government-directed disappearances. These days, Caruthers half believed the baby-snatching, organ-selling stories. Why not? No worse or absurd than everything else happening there or abroad. The whole world was going nuts, not that Caruthers spent much time worrying about "the world."

Gone from La Mala were the raucous nights that sent Caruthers hiding in dark corners from hordes of shouting tourists burning through Guatemala's play money, and now it happened that even Caruthers depended upon the trekkers of the gringo trail to balance the books. Until recently, he'd imagined he'd risen above the world's bullshit, or maybe sunk below it. Same thing. His function in life was to drive poor people from one place to another, along a route served by enough other drivers to render him superfluous, redundant, an entity of no account and therefore immune to the good or ill winds of fortune. But no. No escape even for the peons, especially for the peons when an economy sours. Turned out, tourists made up a larger percentage of his ridership than he'd imagined, and no tourists to buy the trinkets in the cities and markets meant no trinket salesmen taking the bus. This go round, he didn't have the money or time to start over. If he managed to survive Chucho's one-off, Caruthers was going to have to dig in and wait, cut expenses and tough it out. Eventually the tourists would return. They always did. The familiar injustice of life in Guatemala would resume. The only question was whether he'd still be above ground when they did. Not that he cared much either way.

He killed his first beer.

"Oh, hell!" Red said, cracking another and replacing the empty on

Caruthers' cardboard coaster. "I almost forgot. The oddest thing I ever saw. You got something in the mail. I never heard of that before." He disappeared behind the bar.

Caruthers figured Red was talking to or about somebody else, but then the envelope appeared before him, written in childish print, his name care of the bar, a local stamp, no return address but posted from Xela. He was afraid to touch it. Could it be from a woman? Certainly not. He'd not so much as held a female hand in years, and besides, a man had scrawled these words. Seba? Unlikely the ayudante was literate even in Spanish.

Caruthers tore open the envelope and unfolded the lined paper inside. "Dear Father," it began. Caruthers sat there sizzling, blinking his eyes. He read the letter, a sappy, wounded missive from Maxwell, his first-born son, informing Caruthers of Max's intention to visit, in person. Caruthers read it once and began again. The style was casual, the outward message reconciliation, the subtext anger, pain, recrimination. Max, a holy roller now, on a Christian mission trip of all things, wanted to confront the man who'd run out on him, sought "closure." Caruthers looked up, breathing now. The others were watching him.

"You okay?" Red asked.

The melodrama his former family had enacted twenty-one years before on that blazing August night flashed through this mind, the event that led to the act that had defined him, his life's single courageous, contemptable gesture. "You're killing yourself," Pam had insisted, a tall male social worker by her side. "You're ruining your children's lives. You're ruining all of our lives." An intervention, the thing had been called, a trend of the time and probably still a trend up in the sanctimonious norte. He'd played his part admirably, crying, apologizing, and worst of all, promising.

By the end of the night, everybody hugged and blew snot into tissues. Caruthers even tearfully embraced the social worker, but by lunchtime the next day he was furious, humiliated, thirsty. Mouth dry, back aching, he walked out of his deceased father's auto parts warehouse, owned now by his father's young widow and managed by Norman Caruthers himself, to the bank, where he emptied the savings of fifteen thousand dollars, half of the recent inheritance they'd been saving for a new, better house. Pam could have everything else, a Chevy paid in full and thirty grand worth of equity in their tract home. Fair deal, he figured, and if she didn't like it, she could go to hell, or hire someone to chase him down and drag him back if she wanted him that bad.

That afternoon, supplied with a suitcase hastily packed before the boys got out of class and Pam returned from her job at the local health food co-op, he sat in the back of a Greyhound heading south, nursing anger and a pint of Beam. He entered Mexico on foot, experiencing an exhilarating sense of possibility. For a moment—the smell of meat and tortillas wafting about, chickens walking along cracked city sidewalks, peasants begging on corners, and a man in a mariachi costume exiting a lowdown bar—he felt justified; he felt right.

Caruthers cleared his throat. "Course I'm okay. Any reason I wouldn't be?"

"Well, probably not. You were just growling like a dog and tearing your napkin to shreds while you were staring at that letter. Aside from that I guess you're tip top."

Caruthers regarded the pile of confetti he'd made of the napkin. "I guess you could say I'm thrown off my game a bit," he admitted. "The issue is that my oldest boy, who I left when he was a kid and who I don't know from Adam, is down here to deliver God's message to the sinners, me chief among them. Not sure exactly where he is or when he's supposed to arrive here. Might walk through that door any minute and bring righteous condemnation down upon me."

"How's his Spanish?" a new customer at the bar asked. "You know that dude ran out on the journalist lady before she got clobbered was a missionary? They'd have killed him too if he didn't know the lingo."

"Well, the Mormons got the missionary thing wired here anyways," another put in. "Your son Christian?"

"I don't know what he is. A zealot of some denomination I assume."

"Jesus freaks are the worst," the rat man offered. "I wouldn't want one of them coming to visit neither."

"Hey there," Caruthers said, moved to anger, aimed mainly at himself for talking in the first place, for allowing his private business to become a topic of discussion. "I been sick of your shit since before you ever arrived. Probably before you were even born. I don't want to hear another word from you about my son. Or anything else for that matter."

The newcomer scooted his stool away from the bar and glared at Caruthers. Dark splotches spread across his face. "Lo siento, hombre," the man said, enunciating like a spaghetti western cowboy.

Caruthers laughed. "Speak American, asshole. We're in an American bar."

"All right," Red said. "Enough. Norman, if you're going to be like that you can take it outside, and if you have to leave then you might as well stay away for a week. I don't need this. Not today or any day."

Everyone, even those who weren't around at the time, knew about that wild Saturday night when Caruthers stabbed Dan Garner, a friend at the time, with a steak knife over dinner at El Patio. Caruthers' recollection of the event jumped from trying to decipher a menu through a roaring tunnel of drunk to waking sick and parched in a cell. It took hours to learn that he'd for some reason attacked his friend, and three days to bribe and wheedle his way out of jail. By that time, Dan was gone, split town even before his stitches came out. Caruthers always wished he could have at least apologized to the guy.

After that, he'd decided that either drinking or friendship had to go. The choice was an easy one to make, and he'd had little trouble limiting his social interactions to occasional barroom chatter with men whose names he didn't bother to remember. The one exception to this social

# A Candle for San Simón

boycott was Chucho Cruz. The Chief of Police liked to practice English, and Caruthers, the white-haired, red-faced, Hawaiian-shirt-wearing drunken gringo bus driver, amused him. Caruthers was unable to turn down Chucho's occasional invitations to dinner, where Caruthers would sit uneasily for two hours at a table with Chucho's homely wife and four homely kids, for whom Cruz showed off his clunky English. Even the incident with Dan tickled Cruz, who sometimes whipped a blade from his pocket and sliced it through the air before Caruthers' face. "You wan play?" he'd ask, laughing. These mock attacks usually led to half-serious invitations to work for him, hints that amounted to a standing job offer as a mule. Caruthers had always laughed them off, until he hadn't.

"Sorry, Red," he said, contrite. He hated to put a bartender on his wrong side. "Bad joke. How about a round of rums on me?"

Red lined up four glasses—he eschewed hard liquor himself, or Caruthers would have bought him one too—and the men drank, wiped their mouths. The rat man slid off his stool to pat Caruthers' back, and Caruthers flinched like a beaten dog. Indulging in the customary self-hatred, he drank hard after that, gulping it back. *Piece of shit, piece of shit*, tolled in his head like a bell. It wasn't like this every night, but often enough for him to know how the rest of the evening would go down.

After two more rums, he pulled the letter from his pocket. He unfolded it, and squinted at the dark blue scribble wobbling across lined yellow pages. Around him blurry shapes moved listless as manatees through the bar, emitting underwater groans. "Dear Father," he managed to decipher, and swallowed some phlegm caught in his throat. The words pissed him off. "Dear father," he snarled sarcastically.

He glanced up and there was Red, wiping a glass and watching. "Sokay," Caruthers assured him. It was imperative to keep hidden what was going on inside. "Jus…" he searched through terrifying emptiness for the rest of what he had to say, the last part of the word. Red turned away. "Justalking," he said quietly. He grinned, found the glass in his hand and slugged back a mouthful. "Just talking to my son," he shouted. "Have a problem with that?" He swiveled his stool toward the rat man, who was looking down at his beer. Red appeared between them, not happy. "Sorry," Caruthers said before Red could send him away. "Sorry," ducking his head as he chanted, "sorry, sorry." Hunched over the bar, he brought the glass to his mouth, hiding a smile because he wasn't sorry at all. Not about anything. He spilled rum down his chin as he chuckled and gulped, crunching ice.

# Chapter Seven

Bored stupid on the porch between the Stupid Brothers, Vicki felt relieved to see Jefecito's double-cab Dodge Ram appear in the distance, dragging a cloud of dust. At least something was finally going to happen. Three nights she'd slept in this desert hideout, guarded by the loser twins and a gray-haired old lady who hated Vicki at first sight. She got her own room at least, and they brought her clothes, a toothbrush, and tampons. She shouldn't of made her move on Angel so close to her period, but she didn't think they'd snatch her the first day she walked into the cantina. Oh well. She'd have to work around it.

The boys guarding her slept in bunk beds like children and weren't allowed to drink alcohol. They'd been grouchy, jittery, and horny, stuck in the middle of nowhere with Vicki always there to remind them of what they weren't getting, even in the loose gym clothes she'd asked for. She knew what they said to each other when she wasn't around. If Angel turned her down, she'd be theirs, after Jefecito got his fill. She didn't think they'd kill her, but who could know? She'd figure it out soon enough. No use dying twice.

Jefecito in his cow herder hat skidded to a stop, dusting his shiny paint job. The window came down, and he gazed through sunglasses at the porch. Vicki stood. "Get dressed," he said, and she went to her room without a word. She stripped nude, tossing the cheap house-clothes onto the bed. Then she pulled on what she'd worn to the cantina—washed and line-dried by the mean old granny—and stocked her purse with what she needed, including some tiny scissors she found in the bathroom. The hall was clear, so she slipped across to the bathroom, where she washed herself and put in a fresh tampon. Her flow had lightened, but she was still bleeding. Some men didn't mind, but most did. She had to figure Angel would be squeamish, even after all the blood he spilled.

"What'd you do, take a dump in there?" Jefecito asked. She ignored his stupid grin and climbed into the back seat with Idiot Number Two. Number One took the passenger seat up front, and Two beside her presented the black sack she'd worn over her head on the way there. She pulled it on and breathed in her own smell, not a good smell or bad, just her, the stuff she ate and the toothpaste she used, the grease and shampoo in her hair, and everything else. Light came through the material of the sack, turning it brown. She tried to relax.

The truck turned left onto a paved road. The men didn't talk. Music clicked on, a narcocorrido she'd been hearing on the radio ever since arriving in Salvador. Too campo for her, these songs. Once again, she missed L.A., the noise, lights, shiny people, all that money, and toilets that flushed the shit paper.

Twelve songs later, all from the same group with no DJ in between, they made a couple of slow turns, and then stopped to wait out an automatic garage door opener. They pulled in, and the door closed behind them, turning the brown of her head sack black. The engine rattled for a few seconds, echoing a little from inside a small space, and then it and the music died. Jefecito did that little chirping whistle of his to signal that it was time to go. Doors opened. Two helped her out, and even though her hands were free, she made no move to remove the hood. Someone else, One probably, took her left arm. Two had her right. They led her forward through the hollow-sounding garage. "Stairs," One said, and she stepped up. At the top, exactly thirteen steps later, she overstepped and stumbled onto the landing. The men held her arms, so she didn't fall, but One cursed Two to be careful.

# A Candle for San Simón

"Shut up, clowns," Jefecito hissed.

A knock at the door. A voice from inside. A lock turning. They led her forward onto another hard surface, tile maybe. The hood came off, and the door closed behind her. She couldn't help whirling around, taking in the place and the company, showing her nerves. She stood alone with a man fully on his back in a reclined fat chair, ignoring her while he watched two women and one man having sex on a big screen television. The room was large, open, and modern-looking, the kind of thing they called a loft in the L.A. rental ads. The walls were brick, the floor shiny concrete. The man in the chair laughed at the sex going on, even though it wasn't anything special, just a couple of hos working some guy's rod. Past the man, Angel, she figured, a sliding glass double door led to a deck with a view of a big brick building with a smokestack. Angel on his chair held a television remote control in one hand, a bottle of beer in the other. The people on the screen kept going with their standard porno thing. Vicki was almost disappointed. She figured the big boss would look scarier.

"Come," he said, and she stepped deeper into the room. The door behind her closed, the men who'd brought her gone. "Let me check you out," Angel said. She stood in front of the television, ran both hands down her hair to smooth it back. She'd been careful to keep the bag off her face. Her stomach hurt and seemed heavy, fat. She felt weak after days under guard, ugly and unconfident. She looked at the floor. Most men liked her this way, submissive, and she figured Angel was the same as most men. He clicked off the television. "I am so bored," he said, and laughed, high-pitched, the way a young girl giggles. Vicki raised her face. He was stocky, dressed in business slacks, shiny cowboy boots, and a pressed western shirt, dark blue with white piping. He wore his hair cut short and spikey, formed into a black fence around the top of his head, guarding the bald patch inside. Probably nobody ever told him how it looked from above. "So you were Ricky's girl, yeah? You're pretty, but lots of girls are pretty, even prettier than you, younger, too. What do you have for me? What makes you special?"

Vicki thought, quickly clicking through a card deck's worth of replies. A blowjob wasn't going to do it. Acting the slut would make her just like the others. Even if he fucked her, he'd tire of her quickly, probably toss her to his stooges a few days later. "Loyalty," she said. "I can keep secrets."

"Everybody says that. And they do usually keep their mouths shut, only because they know what will happen if they don't."

"Fear is not the same as loyalty," she countered, and something changed in his face, a deepening of his brown eyes, like instead of reflecting the world, they now were sucking it in. "I'm not like the others. I think about things. I notice. I see opportunities. If Rico had listened to me, he'd be alive today. I saw what was happening, tried to warn him, but he didn't believe me."

The eyes grew troubled, and the body shifted, as if he were trying to escape the big chair. Vicki thought she'd taken the wrong path, from loyalty to competence, to ambition. Fear sizzled through her, but she showed nothing, not on her face or her body. She was awake, standing straight up, hands still at her sides, chest moving with her breath. Angel brought his seat up by pulling a level at his side. He placed his feet on the floor, and rested his elbows on his knees, stuck between rising and staying put.

"I have something to show you," she said, faking the courage she didn't feel. "Which way to the bathroom?" Angel touched his thin, gringo lips with the tip of his index finger, and then used that finger to point at a door opposite the one she'd come in from. "Give me fifteen minutes."

In the bathroom—large, with a long granite sink and gold-colored faucet—she pulled the shower curtain aside and found what she wanted. A metal rack hung from the shower pipe, holding shampoo, body wash, shaving foam, and a chunky steel safety shaver. She unbuttoned the shirt

# A Candle for San Simón

and shrugged it from her shoulders. She removed her bandana and bra, and then, kneeling beside the tub, turned on the bath water. Careful not to smear her painted face, she wet her hair. After a couple of seconds, she cut the water and twisted the hair into a large strand, squeezing out the extra moisture. At the mirror, she rummaged through drawers and got lucky, finding a pair of scissors, small but much better than the nail cutters she'd brought. Her twist of hair in one hand, she cut through it with the other, as close to her head as she could. Afterward, she threw the damp trunk into the trash, ignoring the feeling of sobs in her throat and continuing to clip away at the loose clumps remaining on her head. Working fast, she got rid of everything she could, leaving her head an ugly, lumpy brown gourd. The feeling of sobbing had moved from inside her throat out to her skin, and now it burned like a cunt, more painful than the cramping low in her stomach. She dealt with it, the pain inside and out, by moving from her body, like stepping out of clothes so that she watched herself both in the mirror and in the flesh, a trick she learned when she was a child. She shook the canister of shaving cream, filled her palm and spread it over her head, smoothing it into a helmet. She rinsed her hands, brushed the loose bits of hair from her shoulders and breasts, and then cleaned the cream from her hairline with the hand towel. Finally, she folded a towel and placed the razor on it, thinking of a doctor show she used to watch, where the nurse would prepare a tray of knives before surgery. She filled the cup at the sink with water, and after some thought, took off her shoes, socks, and pants, and then clipped the bra back on. Water in one hand, the razor and towel in the other, she walked out, toward Angel and whatever was going to happen to her.

He stared as she approached, mouth open, on the verge of laughing. She'd surprised him at least. The porno played again on the television, though he'd spun the chair around toward her. The plan was to kneel in front of him, presenting the razor, head down like a sacrifice, but she changed course, set the things on the small table by the leather couch across from him. Ignoring him, she lay on the couch with her head draped over the puffy arm, neck stretched wide to the ceiling. "Come," she said without looking at him. She heard the chair squeak as he struggled out of it. "Wait." She turned her head to see him. "Take off your clothes. I don't want you to get them dirty."

He chuckled, paused, and unbuttoned the fancy shirt, top to bottom, exposing a white undershirt. He unclipped gold cuff links, shaped like small horseshoes. Shrugged out of the shirt. Pulled off the tee. Kicked his boots off. Unbuckled his belt. "Enough," she said when he'd gotten down to boxer briefs. His legs were as skinny as a boy's, and dark rings of hair circled his nipples. The gold chain around his neck was as thick as her middle finger. "Now shave me," she said.

"Yes," he replied, his voice thin, like his throat was as narrow as a straw. She looked up at the rough bare beams of the ceiling. She heard the razor dip into the water, and felt the blades touch high on the center of her forehead, slide back over her skull. The sensation of wet, cold metal on her newly exposed skin, touched by the air in the room and sharpened by the minty smell of the cream, was nice. She closed her eyes as he worked. "Don't miss anything," she said.

"I won't," he replied. She knew that women who played this game of bossing around big men demanded to be called "mistress," or some kind of name like that, but Vicki hadn't ever done it before, and she didn't want to say the wrong thing, break the spell of seriousness and make it seem like a joke. Angel sucked in a sudden breath, and she knew he'd uncovered the tattoo. Rico had shaved her head a few years back, with the straight razor. It was her idea to cover the old tattoo, like a brand on a cow, he said, laughing as the artist worked. She hadn't seen it in years, except in her mind. The thick, gothic X behind a floating banner reading "Siempre." In the background loomed the Madonna of Death, her grinning skeletal jaw clenching a blood-red rose, her dress fine and lacy over white bones.

"This is going to be our secret," she said. "Isn't it?"

"Yes."

The groove of their talk was off. She needed a name, and he needed a name, and they both had to mean it. "You'll be my little Angel, won't you?" she asked, as a mother to a baby.

"Yes." His voice quavered, like he was about to cry, and Vicki knew she'd found something worth more than pure coke.

"And I am your love. Say it."

"You are my love."

His warm belly touched the top of her head. "Say, 'yes, my love.'"

"Yes, my love."

"That's good." She eased up on the couch arm so he could shave her neck. "When you're finished, wet a new towel from the bathroom and clean me off, good."

"Yes, my love."

"If you do a good job, maybe I'll let you rub my shoulders."

"Yes, my love," he said, and went over her head once more, scraping away every last hair from the puckered scalp.

# Chapter Eight

After three hours clicking through screens in a dark and hot Internet café, Max was happy to open his tangible bible, a worn King James in a leather cover, out in the air of Xela's Parque Central. At the computer, he'd soon found his mistake in the village of Zunilito, too small to appear on most maps, miles from and unrelated to the city of Zunil, whose underground religious ceremonies he now knew better than he'd ever wished. Creating a Facebook profile and sending a note to Reina was even easier than discovering the location of her hidden village, but then the internet trapped him, half-reading articles and scrolling through images until his eyes burned.

He'd learned about the eerie idol, Maximón, also called San Simón, one of the many pagan gods incorporated into the Catholic pantheon as saints, a result of the church of old ransacking primitive cultures, torturing and enslaving their people, outlawing their religions. This particular saint, naturally, stood for fornication, alcohol, cigarettes, and cash.

His browsing led to an ethnographic study of the Quiché Maya around Lake Atítlan, conducted in the 1950s and posted on the internet for posterity. He learned about courtship and marriage, which generally took place during a girl's daily trips to the lakeshore for water, where her hopeful lover would wait, flirting as she passed. Her job was to ignore him, and his job was to persist. Sometimes her indifference was put on, part of the game of hide and seek; other times she just didn't like him.

# A Candle for San Simón

The boy wouldn't know which until he put the time in.

Max learned that the Mayan did not strike in their children, and this surprised him, given the otherworldly obedience and maturity he'd seen in all Mayan children since arriving in the country. They were sweet, serious, industrious little versions of their parents. He'd never seen one cry, shout, or whine, in spite of obvious and extreme poverty. For the first two years of a Quiche's life, the ethnography read, he or she was the center of the world, doted upon by mother, father, grandparents, and the entire village. Children accompanied their parents to whatever work was done, be it weaving, collecting firewood, building huts, or agriculture. While the parents worked, the child played with dolls and toys carved from pieces of wood, perfectly content with primitive amusements. When the next baby came, however, the child lost paradise, a fall both sudden and devastating. This was a difficult period in every Mayan's life, but after a couple of months, the toddler adjusted to the new reality, put aside the toys of infancy, and helped Mom and Dad at work.

The ethnography chose to focus on everyday life, and so ignored religion, which seemed to exist apart from family and labor. Max clicked around and found plenty on the Mayan's ancient beliefs, beheadings and rivers of blood, journeys into the underworld, betrayals, sacrifices. This was entertaining, bracing stuff, but Max couldn't see how it would affect his approach to the village; he couldn't imagine they'd actually believe any of that outlandish stuff at this point in time.

Before signing off, he studied road maps to plan a course of action. Common buses followed no published route, but they tended to cluster in larger cities, and spread out from there. The closest urban area to Zunilito was Panajachel, the major city on Lake Atítlan, where his father apparently lived. Was it a coincidence, or a message? Was his stumbling into the Maximón service a coincidence, or a message? Was the similarity of names, Max and Maximón, a coincidence or a message? And if any of these coincidences were actually messages, then from whom? In

Guatemala, he'd read, rebels dressed as military, military dressed as rebels, and gangsters could impersonate either, or each other. The devil lived here, and so did God.

Lounging in the sun, on a steel park bench in the garden-like park, Max flicked through the pages of his Bible until the spirit moved him, and he stopped, eyes closed, his finger on a random passage, a habit he'd adopted since joining Kent at The Fortress. While his prayers to Jesus tended toward the casual, a little sibling asking his wiser brother for advice, Max's interaction with God, the Father, came directly from the book. Today, his finger rested on Hosea 11.1-11, an unfamiliar passage. "God's Compassion Despite Israel's Ingratitude."

*When Israel was a child, I loved him, and out of Egypt I called my son.*

*The more I called them, the more they went from me; they kept sacrificing to the Baals, and offering incense to idols.*

Max looked up, through the shifting leaves of a pepper tree above, letting the words sink into him. Hadn't he just witnessed, even participated in an offering of "incense" to an idol? What did that make him? Israel? Not the country, but a person, he thought. Who was "my son"? Who were "they"? And where did Max fit into any of this? Was he the son? he wondered, and read on.

*They shall go after the Lord, who roars like a lion; when he roars, his children shall come trembling from the west.*

*They shall come trembling like birds from Egypt,*

*and like doves from the land of Assyria; and I will return them to their homes, says the Lord.*

Max closed his eyes. Home. A bird sang nearby, a sweet little melody. When God roars like a lion, Max thought, he will return all of his children to their homes. Even the sinners. Even Norman Caruthers. He closed the book and opened his eyes. The birdsong stopped, and Max surveyed the world he'd done nothing to earn, a gift the sunlit gazebo, a gift the tall homeless man sweating in a trench coat, a gift the cars honking and smoking around the three-lanes of one-way traffic circling the park. A breeze cooled his face and died, another gift.

He decided to find Karma, to ask her to lunch, to ask her for more than lunch, if God saw fit to lend him the courage. He left the park, and four blocks later passed through the metal gate outside the Instituto Xelaju de Idiomas. Karma sat across from a blonde gringo, tall and slim, wearing round wireless glasses. Plants in big clay pots stood around the 30-by_30 foot tile square, surrounded by plaster walls topped in broken glass shards. A dozen tables stood about, half of them occupied by student and teacher pairs. Karma's gringo wore a long-sleeved office shirt, pinstriped and rolled up to his elbows, his haircut fresh, his skin like milk. Max felt inferior to this adult, foolish and jealous; he felt ragged and dingy, an out-of-work carpenter playing at missionary. Before he could slip out, Karma spied him, smiled, and waved.

Trapped, Max approached her table, assembling an introductory speech in Spanish. "Perdoname," he began. "No quiero inturuptarles, pero me gustaria hablar con te cuando estan terminado para almurzar." Max was pretty sure "inturuptar" wasn't a word, but Karma got the gist, and by her smile appeared to appreciate the effort, a simple, honest smile.

"Claro," she said. "Max, this is Doug. He's a doctor from Canada. Before starting work in a hospital up there, he's spending his vacation vaccinating the poor. Isn't that amazing?"

"Sure is," Max said, and shook Doug's hand.

"Glad to meet you," Doug responded, a friendly man, conscientious, clean, and appropriate. Max hated him.

"Igualmente."

"If you two want to talk, I'm happy to take a break," Doug said. "Wouldn't mind stretching my legs a bit."

"No. Not at all," Max insisted. "Nothing important or that can't wait. I can come back once lunch starts. Twelve thirty, right?"

"I'll meet you in the park," Karma said. "At the gazebo. ¿Si?" She was chubby, with creamy brown skin, soft-looking cheeks, reddish-black hair, and dramatic dark eyes. "Soy mestiza," she'd said about herself when they'd first met, indicating through gestures the Spanish eyes, Mayan nose, and plump body. "What kind of women do you like?" she'd once asked during a lesson. He'd sputtered, aiming for something spiritual and intellectual, an honest, trustworthy woman or whatnot, but she'd cut him off. "No. I mean fat, skinny, light, dark." She smiled, turned her face and side-eyed him. "Nalgota?" She mimicked wide buttocks. "Chichona?" she asked, cupping invisible breasts in front of her own generous bosom.

"All types," he'd finally said, and she'd snorted, dismissing this lie with a shake of her head. The truth was, he'd always been drawn to tiny, girl-like women, short and petite, but he wouldn't tell Karma this, because he found her sexy, smart, funny, occasionally intense. Often she'd turned their training conversations toward vaguely Marxist political ideas. Max— a non-voter whose sympathies vaguely ran toward Republicans, the only party that seemed to believe in God, and also the party endorsed by Kent—pretended to agree with her convictions, easily crossing to her ideological side since this wasn't his country, so why should he care how they governed themselves? He hated politics anyway.

"I'll be there!" he said. "Again, sorry for interrupting your lesson," he added to Doug.

"Not a problem," Doug said, and Max escaped back to the park, his dignity more or less intact.

The gazebo rose from the center of the rectangular park on a concrete pedestal twenty feet high. A bum, not the one in the trench coat but another, slept under the black iron dome, so Max sat on the steps leading up. The air was cool, and the sunshine felt good along with the warmth radiating from the concrete. He stretched his legs out and tipped his hat over his face, gunslinger style.

He woke an instant later, nudged by Karma beside him. "The shoeshine kids will steal the money from your pockets if you sleep here," she told him, smiling. He sat up, cleared his throat and rubbed his face. His back ached from where it had pressed against the edge of a step.

"Just resting," he claimed. "I'd have woken if someone tried to pick my pockets."

"¿De vero?" Karma asked, and unsheathed the silver blade from the Swiss Army knife in her hand. He felt his pockets, a few local bills, his driver's license, and the church debit card in his left front pocket. "What does this do?" she asked about the short, thick spike in the knife's arsenal.

"I've never been able to figure that out," he said. "I keep thinking that one day I'll need it, and there it'll be."

"My favorite is the cork screw," she said, folding the doohickey back into the knife and then handing it to him. "Not to open wine necessarily. I like the way it looks." She made a corkscrew motion with her finger in the air. "It was on the step beside you. I don't want you to think I'd put my hand in your pocket. I don't know you well enough for that, at least without asking."

He laughed, his face hot. "Can I take you to lunch?" he asked.

"I know the perfect place," she said. "This way."

They walked uphill, past the city's sole fancy hotel, along a cobbled passage too narrow for cars. At the top of the hill, his collar and hatband wet from the exertion, they entered a small place featuring Don Quixote on his old horse on a sign out front, under the name, Taverna Don Rodrigo, a crowded and dim cafeteria.

They found the last free table, just under the raised television in the corner. A soccer match was on, and it seemed that everyone in the place was watching the two of them with intense focus. Karma ordered, and Max, winded from the climb and trying to keep up, ordered the same. "I like it here," he said, looking around, taking in the funky smell of yeast and fried meat, the urgent shouts from the television.

Karma took a lime wedge from a bowl in the center of the table, dipped it in salt, and ate it whole, including the rind. "It's the only place in town that makes its own, how do you say, cerversa de barril."

"Barrel beer?"

"That's how you say?"

"You must mean draft beer." He mimicked pouring a pint from a tap.

"Yes. Draft beer. Draft beer." She wrote in a notebook from her leather briefcase.

Max prepared to ask for what he wanted as a great groan came from everyone in the room. Almost. They'd almost scored a goal. Costa Rica, an extreme underdog, faced Germany in the World Cup. The score was zero-zero. Max wished Karma to accompany him to Panajachel for the weekend, to get to know one another and maybe even to play interference while he met his father. *Crazy*, he told himself. *Are you crazy? She's your teacher. You barely know her.* How could he expect her to drop her life, spend an entire weekend with some gringo stranger? Could he be any more forward? While he fought with himself, two of the famous draft beers arrived in short, fat mugs, the beer black as tar. Karma hoisted her mug, smiling. "Cheers," she said, and Max, trapped within his carelessness, lifted his own mug. He'd pretend to drink, he thought, touching the glass to Karma's, on the verge of panic. Why not just tell her the truth? he finally asked himself, and then tipped the glass, filling his mouth with the smoky, wild liquid. He swallowed. "Good?" Karma asked. She wore her straight hair down today, side parted and covering both ears, mahogany against the black lapels of the business coat that matched her skirt.

"Yes," he said, trying to keep the desperate sadness from his face and voice. "Delicious." He wasn't lying.

"Have a lime," she said, and plucked one from the bowl. She salted it, and trucked it through the air between them toward his mouth. On the verge of opening his mouth like an infant, or a Catholic, he intercepted it with his hand. The acid scoured his mouth, but he'd finish his beer, he reasoned. The fact was, he hadn't been such a bad drinker, just a few beers after work, the occasional blowout with friends. The quitting had more to do with an overall change of self, focused on joining the church. After more than a year, he could handle a beer over lunch. What was the big deal?

"Listen," he said, placing the rind on the scarred table, "I need to ask you something."

"This doesn't sound good." Her deep maroon lipstick glistened moistly, and a faint trace of dark, dewy fur ran in the shadow of her hair, down from the front of her ears to her rounded jawline. A plain silver cross lay against her throat, a few inches above the crease of her breasts disappearing into the folds of her white shirt.

"It's good, I think. Well, good or bad, it's about my father."

"You finally met him?" They had naturally covered this subject over their 35 hours of talking.

"Not yet, but I sent a letter to where I think he is. I need to go through Panajachel anyway, and so I figured this weekend would be as good a time as any to look him up. My guidebook says there's a small village across the lake with a beach that's supposed to be really nice. I thought maybe I'd invite him to have lunch there, outside on the water. Sort of a picnic. You know what that is?"

"¡Como no! It's the same in Spanish."

Max looked at her directly. He could find no way to present his request in any way but clearly. "I'd like you to go with me."

"Me?" she asked. The waitress came with their sandwiches, long, narrow missiles smashed flat in Cuban toaster presses. Everyone in the room groaned in unison. Germany had scored.

"I mean, if you're not busy. I could really use your...support." Max cringed inside at the note of begging in his voice. Just tell her, he exhorted himself. Be honest.

"It's a long bus ride for lunch," she said, lifting the sandwich, stuffed with fried baloney and melted cheese.

He considered offering to pay her, the worst idea possible. He breathed in, and out, smiling. "I like you. I want you to meet my father if it works out that way, and for him to meet you. I'm not sure why exactly, and I know it's a long trip. I'm not making any assumptions, like, at all, but I figured we could get a hotel for a night or two, separate rooms of course, my treat. They say the lake is beautiful and the town is lively." He sat back, satisfied that he'd taken his shot for better or worse. She set the sandwich down, and he tasted defeat on his tongue, bitter as lime rind. "I'm an idiot, aren't I?" he asked, reaching for the mug.

"Shh," she said. "You were doing good, until now. Yes, I'll come with you. Friday after my class finishes, okay? We'll meet at the gazebo. Now eat your sandwich. And finish your beer. You can use it."

# Chapter Nine

The bus pulled into the border checkpoint, new tires droning over the first smooth road in a hundred miles. A kid in a green ball cap waved Caruthers through, uninterested in the gringo driver and the twelve girls in the back. Caruthers never aimed to get into the human trafficking industry, but here he was. Throughout the morning, he'd tried not to think too much about it, though driving a crew of whores for six hours had proved too long a stretch to keep the brain offline.

In the end, Caruthers figured the morality of the situation wasn't so clear as the holy rollers up north would have it—moral certainty being a luxury reserved for the pampered. The options for these girls came down to an impoverished, brutish life humping firewood on their backs in the campo, or a dangerous, degrading life as a traveling American hooker. In their place, Caruthers probably would have chosen the same path as these girls.

"Yeah, fuck you, buddy," Billy the pretend ayudante muttered, directing his pent-up machismo at the somnambulant border guard waving them through the corridor of orange pylons. Southbound crossings rarely merited scrutiny. Contraband almost invariably went the opposite direction, part of what Chucho saw as the genius of his plan. How the girls would travel from there, Caruthers neither knew nor cared. He just hated being forced to hire Billy, but with Seba still missing in action, Chucho had insisted.

Two hours later and approaching the capital city, Billy pulled out his portable doodad and tried to program it to direct them to the rendezvous. "Hold on," he said.

"Hold on to what?" Caruthers asked, slowing into a smoky dystopia of imported mega boxes surrounded by generalized rubble. In spite of the stench and the racket, or maybe because of it, a feeling of happiness filled him. He liked it, the teeming life of the urban poor. From the cab of a bus, they looked quaint.

"I got it," Billy said, staring at the thing they called a phone.

"Turn left on 9th Street in one and a half miles," said the female, robot voice, a nice voice, just bossy enough to trust.

The street narrowed as the asphalt ground to dust under the tires, the box stores behind them, increasing poverty ahead. The lady in the phone guided them to the spot, the empty lot of a long-fallen edifice. Caruthers pulled off the road, avoiding head-sized hunks of concrete strewn about. The torched frame of a sedan rusted in a back corner of the lot. Men, women, kids, and dogs hung around, up and down the street, not particularly interested in the bus. It fit into this scene just fine. The acrid smoke of trash burning somewhere out of sight stuck in the back of Caruthers' throat, and the good feeling of a few minutes before had gone. He killed the engine, glancing back at the girls, huddled in the back several rows, silent and watchful. Caruthers hit the Stanley, glad he'd thought ahead to bring a refill. Today was going to be a long one.

Nothing happened. Billy left the bus to wander about, followed by the whores-to-be. Caruthers eventually stepped out after them and stood leaning against the side of the bus, wishing he still smoked. That's when the SUV pulled sideways behind the bus, a black-on-black Chevy Tahoe, brand new. Caruthers wondered if gangsters leased or owned. The doors flew open, and Caruthers' soul contracted like a sea anemone that's been poked, as simple, ball-shriveling fear silenced the smartassery running through his mind. From behind the wheel a tall, thick man stepped out first, his face, neck, and bare shoulders covered in tattoos like the graffiti scrawled over a public bathroom stall. The other three emerged after: a short, preppie man in a mustache; a woman with head buzzed nearly bald, showing a lot of lean flesh on arms and belly; and a Chinese-looking man dressed in a blazer and slacks. A white, kidnapper-special van pulled up behind the SUV.

Billy approached the gangsters, ludicrously young and skinny among these criminals, while the girls half-hid in front of the bus. In Spanish, Billy asked after "Oscar," and the newcomers grinned, sharing an inside joke among themselves that Caruthers didn't like. He couldn't follow after that, didn't want to follow, though he could see by the anxiety in Billy's face and body that things weren't going as planned. The preppie laughed at one of Billy's questions, and the Asian pulled a baggie from his jacket, tossed it to Billy, who caught it then dropped it, shrieking and jumping away like a school girl from a bug. The laughter turned to knee-slapping hilarity all around. Billy sprinted back and into the bus. Before Caruthers could follow the kid inside, the crew advanced, so Caruthers, still leaning back against the bus, stared off into the distance, working up the words in Spanish, *I'm just the driver. No speak Spanish.*

Led by the buzz-cut lady, they passed Caruthers, paying him no mind. While they inspected the girls, a mixed lot heavy on Mayan features, curiosity got the better of Caruthers, and he ambled over to where the baggie sat on the dirt. He didn't need to stoop to ascertain the contents, several bloody stumps of fingers, hairy little sausages with dirty fingernails. Caruthers hustled back into the bus, where he waited behind the wheel. Billy caught his eye in the rearview mirror, but Caruthers shook his head, no, don't talk, and the kid for once obeyed. Caruthers wondered what Chucho would do if he returned without the girls or the money. Jesus Christ. One measly smuggling run and he was already going to get killed. Served him right for not keeping his shit together, for letting himself get sucked into Chucho's orbit.

The gangsters deposited the girls into the white van, and Caruthers wished these poor souls luck. They'd been playing some kind of jacks game on the ride up, just kids. Not for long. The bald woman entered the bus, toting a carry-on suitcase, the hard plastic kind. A shoulder holster held a thick pistol at her ribs, and she pulled a camo-print light jacket on over her sports bra. "Is that the, um, thing I'm supposed to deliver to my boss?" Caruthers asked, stupidly in English, and she sat in the front seat, behind him. Who knew what the suitcase contained? Could be the minced remains of the former owner of those finger sausages back there in the dirt.

"I need a ride to wherever you're going," she said in English. "You're a bus driver. So drive."

The van and SUV pulled away, and Caruthers, disturbed by this development, backed out into a three-point turn, and began the reverse of the long trip in. Excuse me, he was too scared to say out loud, but who are you and what are you doing on my bus? "Tell me about this boss," she said.

"Boss? I wouldn't actually call him my boss. I'm the owner operator of this vehicle, and he just sort of hired me for a one-time gig."

"Chucho Cruz. Tell me about Chucho Cruz."

Caruthers steered into the heart of the city, tense as piano wire with that lady practically breathing on the back of his neck. He looked for Billy's gaze in the mirror, but the kid had suddenly grown absorbed in the street scene out the window. Was he about to deliver an assassin to Chucho's doorstep? Jesus Christ. "He's the Chief of Police," he said, hoping to dissuade her from violent plans. "A scary guy, to tell you the truth."

He flinched as she stood behind him, and then she moved over to the front of the bus to lean back against the dashboard, a long, lean woman, beautiful even with the stubbly head, her eyes like little flames in her face. He wondered if she'd gone through chemo or something, though she sure didn't look sick. Caruthers wanted to know whose fingers they'd left in the dirt back there. In what ways the plan had gone awry, how and why. Mainly, he wanted to know if he was going to get shot in the head by the trip's end, or if he'd have to wait for Chucho to kill him later. "You're an American, down here while everyone down here wants to be up in America. ¡Que raro, cabron! What are you? A joker?"

"Not on purpose." Caruthers imagined guiding the bus into a telephone pole, sending her out the windshield—while mashing his own face into the steering wheel. He hadn't buckled his safety belt in years.

She grinned. "An accidental comedian. So, you try to be serious, but everyone laughs. I met people like that before."

Caruthers braked gently into a traffic jam, careful not to unduly jostle the lady. "I never quite thought about it that way, but yes, I guess you could say I'm like that. Someone people laugh at."

"Don't be sad baby," she said, poofing her lips in matronly sympathy. "Everybody likes to laugh."

"Say," he said, impatience overriding the fear, "I'll tell you what I can. I have no secrets. But do you mind letting me know what's going on? I mean, I'm just the driver, and probably it's not my business, but I'd like to know what to expect over the next few hours. It'll help me concentrate on the road if I have a pretty good idea that I'm not about to get killed at any moment, if you get my drift."

"No problem, señor," she said, parodying the white guy accent in that nasally voice black and brown people always use. "The organization your boss made a deal with has been acquired by the organization I represent. You know, like a hostile takeover. I'm going to personally meet with Mr. Cruz to apologize for any inconvenience this might of caused him, and to direct him to contact us for any future transactions. We're legit, and plan to pay him the same rate he'd previously negotiated for the goods delivered. Does this answer your question?"

"Yes ma'am. I now understand this isn't any of my business, and the less I know the better."

"Sure it's your business, Sly. That's your new nickname, like when you call a tall guy tiny."

Caruthers watched her in his peripheral vision, a woman who'd obviously spent many years in the States. He wondered what had motivated the haircut, and guessed it was a beautiful woman's way to look scary—more fuck you and less fuck me. "Sly it is," he mumbled. "I've never had a nickname before."

She laughed, moving back into the bus toward Billy. Caruthers was grateful for the break, though in a strange way, he already missed the attention she'd given him. No matter. He looked forward to never seeing her again.

# Chapter Ten

Caruthers hailed a tuk-tuk with flames etched onto its miniature mud flaps. "Embarcadero para San Pedro," he told the young driver, and they whined down the strip toward the lake, to rendezvous with Caruthers' firstborn son, Maxwell. A yellow mongrel ran beside the go-cart a few paces, barked and veered off. Caruthers never thought he'd see the day, but here it was. Max had appeared like a ghost at La Mala the night before, and Caruthers felt as if he'd been doused in ice water. Red and company stood chuckling behind their hands or outright gaping while Caruthers stammered. Max refused his father's offer to buy him a beer, and the ensuing conversation stumbled along, brief and painful. Caruthers had felt so desperate to end it, he'd immediately, gratefully, agreed to spend the next day, today, with the kid, anywhere, any plan, which is how he'd come to the present moment, puttering along in a tuk-tuk for God's sake. The driver turned onto a side street, hooked back toward the lake and pulled up a few yards before the dock, on which Max, a tall slim man in a cowboy hat, waited with several others for the boat to launch.

Climbing out of the three-wheeler, Caruthers waved, moved to happiness by his son's strong, healthy frame and good looks. Beside him stood a woman, short, dressed in navy slacks and a coat, like a bank employee. The idea hit him that Max had hired a lawyer for the occasion. Take it all, kid, he thought, the bus and all the troubles attached to it. Behind Max and the woman, an indigenous family, man, woman and three kids, waited beside the green, fiberglass lancha rocking softly against the old tires screwed to the side of the dock. This would be his last duty to his son, he assumed, hobbling forward. Soon the young man would be too busy saving the poor to spend more energy on disappointing old Dad. Even so, he'd try to give the kid something useful to take home with him, a story of a happy, harmless drunk playing hooky with his life. Toting a plastic grocery bag full of soda pop, he split the gauntlet of underemployed tour guides hassling him about volcano hikes and stood before his son, scratching a mosquito bite on the back of his hand. "It's been a while, not counting last night."

"Twelve years," Max said, and moved in for a hug. Caruthers complied, barely, patting Max's back in a way that felt wholly wrong. "Dad," Max said, stepping back, "meet Karma, my friend and Spanish teacher. Karma, my dad Norman."

"Nice to meet you, sir," she said with that winsome accent of the fluent second-language speaker.

"Igualmente," he replied. And then, "That's about all the Spanish I know, so don't get your hopes up."

She smiled, and they walked along the dock to join the family where the captain squatted, holding the end of a rope attached to the boat lightly in one hand. The lancha was a narrow, V-hulled vessel with four rows of benches and a steering wheel on a podium in the back, the cabin enclosed by a canopy of the same homemade-looking fiberglass. The captain, a large-headed ladino, stared up at the gray sky. Just after Max had left the bar the previous night, the first rain of the season pounded the land, but the black clouds had backed off since daybreak. Sometimes the rain appeared in increments, other years it came on like a barbarian horde. Today the air was thick, still. A swampy smell rose from the lake, which lapped the shore with a soft sound.

Another tuk-tuk sped up to the dock, drawing everyone's attention. A woman in a pink and gray camouflage ballcap stepped out, and Caruthers' stomach twisted into a knot. "Sly!" she called, waving. "Wait up." Dressed in tight jean shorts, a tee shirt, and combat boots, she jogged over to the trio. "I saw you on the street a few minutes ago, and just as I'm going to say hi, you get into one of these golf cars. So I think, where is he going? And here I am."

"A friend of yours?" Max asked.

"I'm Vicki," she said, extending her hand. "Sly and I know each other from work. I'm visiting from out of town."

"Max," he said, taking her hand.

"And you are?"

"I'm, well, I'm his son."

Vicki's mouth opened, and she turned to Caruthers. "You didn't say you had a son!"

Caruthers shrugged. "We haven't seen each other in a long time."

"And so handsome!"

"We're about to head off across the lake," Caruthers added, for no good reason at all. "For a picnic."

"This must be your girlfriend," Vicki said, smiling at Karma.

"No. We're just friends."

"Oh, friends." She winked. "Okay, sure."

"She was my teacher," Max said.

"Oui la la!"

The kid frowned, more confused than insulted, or so it seemed to Caruthers. "So you work with my father? I don't understand."

"A little side job. Right Sly?"

"Yeah. A one-time thing."

"Well," Vicki said, "that's why I hunted you down like this. I wanted to tell you about my meeting with your boss. What a guy! Oh, he's funny.

We're going to be working together a lot, and that means you and me will be seeing each other around. I knew you'd want to know." Caruthers, scratching the bleeding bite on his hand, couldn't find any words, except *no, no we won't be seeing each other*, but he didn't dare utter them. For one thing, he knew they weren't true. "I didn't meet you yet," Vicki said to Max's friend. "I'm so rude sometimes."

"Karma," she said, warily taking Vicki's hand.

"Like, that thing where if you do something bad to someone, something bad will happen to you?"

"Short for 'Carmelita,' actually," she clarified, "but also what you say. I believe that what comes around goes around."

The captain stood from his spot on the dock and helped the woman in traje into the boat. "Listen, Vicki," Caruthers said, "this is sort of a family thing here. You understand. We haven't seen each other in years, and we're going to sort of catch up."

"Oh my goodness," she said, hand covering her mouth. "Am I intruding? Go, go. The boat will leave without you. We can talk later." She addressed Max. "You see, I'm stupid about these things because my moms and pops died when I was small. I don't have no family."

"I'm sorry to hear that."

"It was a long time ago. I'll see you again. And you too," she said to Karma. "Watch out for the rain."

The captain escorted Karma into the boat, and Max hopped into the seat beside her. Caruthers had the front bench to himself. Vicki, playing a game Caruthers couldn't figure, stood on the dock to see them off. He hoped she was just messing around.

The engine started, and they backed away. Once they left contact with the dock, a wild, ecstatic, frightening sense took hold, the feeling of freedom. Caruthers relaxed when the nose swung around, putting Vicki out of sight. It could have been worse. She could have insisted on coming along, and then what? The engine wailed, and the front of the boat rose

A Candle for San Simón

over the leaden, riffled surface of the water. Caruthers, reflecting that freedom wasn't free as the jingoists never tired of saying, held his ass over the unpadded seat. He twisted in his seat to regard Max, frowning at the misty volcano with a crescent-shaped wrinkle deep between his eyes, his hat held on his lap. He'd always been a scowler, an intense kid, and Caruthers felt sorry for him. Karma watched the scenery pass, occasionally glancing down at the foamy wake. Whatever impression Vicki made was already fading, except perhaps those bare thighs over big boots. Caruthers wondered if Max was a hound like Caruthers had been in his youth. He figured that probably yes, somewhere deep inside the dog howled.

Up ahead, a distant fisherman paused with his net in his hands to watch the lancha approach. He flung the net and clutched the rails of his hand-carved kayak to absorb the wake. The man watched the gringos pass, his eyes flat and impassive.

Twenty minutes later they thumped lightly against the dock at San Pedro. The village lay up the steep hillside, hidden behind trees. A squat cinderblock cube painted white, a cervesaria, stood beside the rutted dirt path. A narrow side trail led to a small stretch of sandy beach. Apart from a circle of hippie kids kicking a leather nugget, they had the place to themselves. "I swear these are the same guys that were here when I showed up back in the time of the dinosaurs," Caruthers told Karma. "And damned if they haven't aged a minute."

Karma offered a neutral smile as she pulled a folded blanket from her backpack and unfurled it onto the sand. In spite of the disturbing appearance of Vicki the gangster girl, Caruthers felt cheerful, talkative, even perhaps capable of some of the old charm. Why not make the most of a good, early-day beer buzz, enjoy himself for once?

"Nice spot," Max said, surveying the volcano visible across the small bay.

"Beautiful," Karma added.

Max opened a sack filled with rolls, a couple of avocados, tomatoes, a hunk of cheese wrapped in paper, and a plastic baggie full of sliced ham. Caruthers produced his own offering, an overpriced six-pack of Fanta orange soda cans. Bottles would have been cheaper, but then he'd have had to return them for the deposit, not to mention carrying the weight. "Should I make the sandwiches now, or wait until we're hungry," Max said. The sun wasn't visible, but the time was around ten a.m.

"Wait, I guess," Caruthers said, for some reason irritated by the question. "Unless you feel like making them. Then by all means."

Karma stepped out of her platform sandals and sat on the blanket.

"What you're looking at," Caruthers pointed out, "just to the left of the volcano, is called The Sleeping Indian. Can you see it? The big nose pointing up, the chin. His forehead kind of slopes back too much, but the rest is pretty conceivable."

"I see it," Karma said.

"And now you'll never be able to unsee it."

"A giant sleeping Indian," Karma said, smiling to herself. "I wonder if he'll ever wake." She turned and caught Caruthers with his hand in his back pocket, touching the flask. "Or she. It might be a lady Indian."

Caruthers glanced again at the mountain ridge. "Not too well endowed if it's a woman."

Karma laughed, and Caruthers, relieved that she hadn't taken offense, nipped at his flask. Returning the booze to his pocket, he regarded his son, sawing through the rolls with his red pocketknife. The boy wasn't smart enough for this woman, which was probably for the best. He wouldn't see what was happening until it was too late. If Caruthers had to do it over again, he might have done what so many other gringos had, gone native with a Guatemalan maiden. Even an ugly, poor American could score a beauty, if he was nice to her and provided their children with dual citizenship. Another reason for the local men to resent the invaders.

"Sandwiches are ready, whenever you're hungry. I'll just put them back in this paper bag. We've also got bananas and mangos. Let me know and I'll slice up the mangos."

Cheers from the hippie camp diverted attention from the feast and Max's pocket knife. Apparently one of them really kicked the hell out of the thingy. Caruthers felt the hatred deep in his heart. They'd never harmed him, but there it was, burning like coal.

"So," Karma said, glancing over at Max, who had walked off toward the shore, "are you a religious man, like your son?"

"Religion? You get right to it, don't you, sweetheart?" He laughed. "I don't believe in invisible men in the sky. Or giant sleeping Indians for that matter."

"Do you believe in justice?"

"Ha," Caruthers barked, involuntarily.

"Is that funny to you?"

"It's not that," he claimed. "You just caught me off guard. I don't believe in it, in justice, not as a force in the universe. I definitely don't believe humans are capable of making it happen. But I'll drink to it." He raised the flask and belted a large one back, liking this young woman his son brought to play interference. Over the mountains to the west, lightning flickered, not visible bolts but plenty of light illuminating the clouds. Seconds later, waves of thunder rolled over them. "Wow!" Caruthers said. "Maybe I do believe in invisible men in the sky."

Everyone stared up at the dark sky, the black cloud gathering over the western ridge. "We're gonna get soaked," Max decided, returning to the picnic. One of the hippies pocketed the little kick ball, and they took off up the trail toward town. "Isn't it time to go?" Max asked. A spittle of rain fell. He grabbed the sack of sandwiches. Caruthers helped Karma fold the blanket and slip it into her pack.

"The Fanta'll be fine," Caruthers pointed out, but nobody laughed. The light rain turned to a few heavy, stinging drops.

The clouds broke open, dropping thick curtains of water that pelted them by the bucketful as they ran across the beach toward the path. The ground turned to puddles and streams. Their lancha was gone, back across the lake. "There used to be a little restaurant up in town," Caruthers said. "Follow the trail. I'll meet you there."

As they ran ahead up the slithering path, he paused at the whitewashed stronghold where they sold beer. It was closed and locked. No awning or roof overhang protected him. He knocked on the door, then pounded on the door while the rain pounded his body. Nobody answered. His feet squished in his shoes. This could be bad, he thought, but no. Not bad. He had half a flask of rum in his pocket, and the restaurant sold beer, probably rum too. A hippie from the kicking party materialized from the gloom, ambling forward holding a banana leaf over his head. He was a white kid with a loose brown afro that sagged under the leaf.

"Nothing left," he said, pointing with a sparsely bearded chin at the cervesaria.

"How's that?"

"No alcohol." He smiled. "We killed it last night, man."

Caruthers thought about this. Surely, surely they'd have restocked at some point today. For God's sake, they only had to travel to Pana, thirty minutes away. Yet he couldn't find another reason for the place to be closed.

"You okay, brother?"

Caruthers took a long look at the young man. Most likely, he hailed from some posh suburb like the rest, his ragged clothes a costume, dressing like a pirate for a Halloween that never had to end. He'd buy a Harley when he hit thirty-five. "You're not old enough to be my brother."

The kid straightened his back, lifted the banana leaf higher over his curls, turned and walked on. "Whatever," he called into the rain. "It's all good."

# A Candle for San Simón

Caruthers reached into his back pocket and pulled out the rum. He was a half-empty kind of perceiver. He looked up at the sky, too wet to get any wetter. The rain would let up. The boats would take him home before things got rough. The café would sell beer. It was all good.

He found the others in the hut-like restaurant, a place that hadn't bothered with a name. The hippies had set up camp there as well, at home enough to have pushed half the tables to a corner so they could continue kicking their doodad. The waitress, a lanky woman standing with arms folded across her chest, glared at Max and Karma, who sat munching sandwiches and drinking Fanta. "Glad you made it," Max said. "Thought maybe you'd been washed away."

Caruthers didn't laugh. Trembling inside but trying to act casual, he asked the waitress what kind of beer they had. She executed a horizontal slicing motion with her arm, decapitating the request. "Rum?" Caruthers continued. "Whiskey? Quetzalteca?"

"Nada," the woman said. Her teeth were long and gray. "Coka. Fanta. Agua."

She left Caruthers to consider his options. Agua, he thought, gazing out the window. He looked around the room, took in its crumbling plaster walls, twisted wooden furniture, cracked tile floor, the dirt road outside gurgling with brown water while a cascade fell from the palm frond awning over the bank of windows and open front door. The rain on the roof sounded like a stampeding herd of bison. The situation, in short, unacceptable. The hippies' leather ball escaped them and bounced off of the back of Max's chair.

"Sorry, bro," someone said. Caruthers retrieved the ball and handed it to the girl chasing after.

"Here you go," he said, placing it in her hand, formulating a plan of sorts. She wore a gypsy wrap around her head, and smelled of sage smoke and body odor. Mud caked her bare feet halfway to her knees. Caruthers followed her to the circle. She dropped the ball and kicked it with the inside of her foot. A boy juggled it expertly with his feet and knees. Caruthers clapped his hands. "Good, stuff. Very nice." Some of the kids glanced suspiciously his way. He played it cool by strolling to the window, where he hit the woefully light bottle. Brown rivulets had taken over the mud road, pitted with hard drops. The waitress lit candles. The bison charged in a burst. The girl with the gypsy head wrap ignited a joint and passed it. Caruthers, drenched to his shorts, drank again from the flask. Why hadn't he brought beer? Would it have been so hard, to carry an extra few cans? He was an idiot, again and always.

"Sandwich?" Max called out. Caruthers, shaking his head no, returned glumly to the table.

An hour and a half later, the rivulets outside had grown to a single river, spanning the road. Caruthers dripped the last drops from his flask into his mouth. The girl with the head wrap had a guitar and everyone, including Max and Karma, sang along with the songs she played. "When will it stop?" one of the hippies asked herself.

"Never," Caruthers answered, but was ignored.

"Join us," Karma implored him. "'Come in,' she sang in a pretty voice, 'I'll give you, shelter from the storm.'" The guitar player didn't know many songs and they'd played this one three times already.

Caruthers raked his fingernails over the mosquito bite on his hand, making it bleed fresh. The song ended, and Caruthers approached the hippies, sitting in a cluster on chairs or the floor. "Hey, kids, hate to interrupt the jam. Great songs, by the way. I was just wondering if any of you happens to have a stash of booze of any sort. Here, maybe back at your room?"

They stared at him, as if trying to decide what language he spoke.

"Sorry, bro," the turbaned girl said, and strummed a chord. "We crushed it last night. You should have seen us hassle the store people after they ran out. The whole thing was out of control."

"Come on," Caruthers said. "I know one of you has a bottle

somewhere." He looked from face to face, and they avoided his gaze. "A bottle of wine? Beer? Anything. Something stashed away in your backpack. I'll pay good money. Name the price."

"We got ganja," one of them said.

"No," Caruthers replied. "I don't want ganja."

"I thought you weren't my brother," the curly-haired boy said. He sat Indian style on a table, a level higher than everyone else. "Now that you want something from us—" He faltered as the moment turned intense. Everyone was looking at him. "We had a negative connection earlier," he explained.

"Dad," Max said. "Please. Let it be. You can go without a drink for one night of your life."

Caruthers turned, walked up to his son. "No, Max," he said softly. "I can't." Tears welled up in Karma's eyes but didn't fall to her cheeks. "I'm already starting to shake, and pretty soon I'll get real sick. It's no party, nothing you want to see."

Caruthers barged into the kitchen, where he found the waitress staring at a small radio warbling trumpet and snare drum music. "Lancha?" he asked, scanning the shelves for alcohol. She made the same slicing motion with her hand. No. "I pay," Caruthers said. "Money. Mucho dinero." She scowled, caressing her front teeth with her tongue. He reached into his pocket and retrieved a stack of bills Chucho had forwarded him after the delivery, too lazy to deposit them behind the medicine cabinet. He counted off two hundred, three hundred, money that should have gone for gas and to tide him over until he got back into the swing of his route, money he owed Chucho. The woman motioned for him to follow, back into the dining room.

"Where are you going?" Max asked. The kids were playing a Grateful Dead song. Only a couple of them knew the words.

"Home," Caruthers said, walking out.

"And you're leaving us here?" Max called from the doorway.

Caruthers thought to explain that it was dangerous, that the possibility of being struck by lightning or swamping and drowning was high, and that he wouldn't dream of putting Max and his girl in such peril, but that would have taken too long, and who cared if the kid understood or not? Caruthers deserved no sympathy, no understanding, so why bother asking for it? The waitress led him ankle deep along the edge of the flowing road to a wooden shack three buildings down. Here she negotiated with the man inside. A couple of minutes later, Caruthers parted with his money, some of which went to the waitress and the rest to the boatman, whom Caruthers followed half sliding down a winding footpath to a tiny private dock. Soon he would either be home or dead, and the tight pain in his chest loosened. His breathing steadied. One way or the other.

The man flipped upright his six-foot open boat, fastened on the small outboard he'd carried down the hill, and after some tugging managed to start the engine. Blind, they traveled into a pocked gray infinity. Under slashes of lightning, shaken to their centers by thunder, they bumped and swayed through a strange other-element of air and water, white froth boiling around them, darkness punctuated by white flashes. Caruthers bailed nonstop with an old coffee can, hands trembling, pummeled by hard cold drops, one step from hail. A surreal, timeless period later, a dark shape appeared dimly in the murk, the shore. From there they hugged the coast until Panajachel's drenched lights twinkled weakly ahead. At the dock, Caruthers pulled his body from the boat and lay for a spell in three inches of water on the concrete, face resting on his folded arms. He climbed to his feet and ran through the rain, covered in mud, saturated, shaking from cold and sickness, but saved.

# Chapter Eleven

Every leaf and cobblestone glistened, but Max couldn't shake the image of his father, groveling for a drink and running out on him, again. Walking beside Karma, he almost laughed, but instead he maintained a silent fury, chewing his thoughts, swallowing them down. "Your sandwiches were very good," she ventured, grinning, but he wouldn't take the bait. For the first time since he'd met her, she annoyed him.

Now that the rain had stopped, they'd soon be back in Panajachel, where he'd already moved from the previous night's garret to a lakefront room with two double beds, basic but pleasant, meant to impress Karma, on Kent's dime. Oh, if he could take any message from this reunion it was to set aside his petty affairs and focus on the real prize, nothing less than God's work. He regretted luring Karma out here, and he considered leveling with her, apologizing and sending her home on the first bus out of Pana, cutting both of them free.

Walking downhill through what passed for a town, piecing together the necessary words for Karma, he drifted deeper into shame and self-recrimination, the sort that used to attend the worst hangovers back in the drinking days. He'd been a mopey baby since his father ran off. Hell, since he'd asked Karma out. Why couldn't he be better, for her sake if not his own? She'd come all this way for him, and she'd gotten nothing for it but rain, drama, a sulking toddler for a partner, a sandwich, and a pop.

"Thanks," he said, trying to smile. "Personally, I thought they sucked."

She looked at him, frowning.

"My sandwiches."

"Oh! I thought…something else." She laughed, and he managed to join her with a brief chuckle. Forced or not, it felt better than scowling.

Gravity pulled them forward, and Max had to stop himself from breaking into a jog down the steep hill. Steam rose from the jungle all around. The damp heat clung to the air, pressing in on him, and his wet clothes chafed his sweating body. He longed for a cold shower, dry clothes. "Are you sure you want to do this?" he asked.

"Do what?"

"Stick around for the night? I mean, if you've had enough, I totally understand."

She snorted like a horse. "After today, you better take me out somewhere nice. You know I had to get up at 5:30 to catch the bus?"

"Hey," he said, smiling for real, "that was your choice. I invited you to come with me yesterday."

She fanned herself with a hand. "I know, I know. Just get me out of these wet clothes, okay?"

He curbed his reply, something suggestive. On either side of the path, narrow trails snaked into the jungle, leading to tiny homemade houses with small, neat gardens, chicken coops, clothes hanging out to dry in the new sunlight. They passed a table covered in fruit for sale, attended by a little girl. "I know what you mean," Max said. "I could use a long shower."

"Mmm," Karma moaned, and looked over at him with a half-smile. He waited for her to continue, his gaze sliding from her face to her body, imagining the skin under the fabric, covered in dewy hair, puckered in the breeze of a hotel fan. She looked forward and so did he, at the last stretch of path to the dock below. The lake sparkled under the sun, so blue it looked dyed.

They sat on the end of the dock, bare feet dangling over the water.

"What if nobody comes?" Karma asked. The boat service normally ran once an hour, but who knew after the storm.

"I guess we'll be stuck here." He looked out over the smooth water, the blue-green, smoky image of the sleeping Indian. "That'd be nice," he muttered, and then chuckled, embarrassed by the vocalized thought.

"Yes," she said. "I was thinking the same thing. Staying in this tiny village forever, away from all the troubles of the world. Sometimes I dream of escaping like that."

Max lay back, smiling at the sky. A sense of wellbeing seemed to rise from him like steam from the jungle, but no matter how much left his body, the feeling did not diminish. He was producing it, too much to keep in himself.

"Here comes the lancha," Karma said. "I guess we won't get to escape after all. It was a nice illusion, though."

Max sat up. The boat zipped toward them, tiny in the wide lake. "Too bad," he said.

Five passengers sat in the boat, a well-dressed couple—Europeans or South Americans by their clothes—and their toddler; plus two local men, probably coming home from work. Cardboard boxes took up the rest of the space in the boat. The family climbed out first, and then the men began to unload the boxes. "Que es?" Max asked one of the men.

"Cervesa," the man replied.

Karma snorted, and then began to laugh. "I'm sorry," she said, gasping between fits. Max watched her. Everybody did, and the more they looked, the harder she laughed. Finally, she covered her face in her hands and looked down at the dock. When she lifted her face, she shook her head, wiping her eyes. "I'm sorry. I know it's not funny, what happened today."

"Oh, it's a little bit funny," Max said, smiling.

They had the boat to themselves for the return trip, their elbows and shoulders touching as the lancha slid over the glassy water. From the dock, he led her to the room in the cheap waterfront hotel, a bit shabby, with plaster walls and concrete floor, but fronted by large sliding glass doors looking out over the lake.

The beds took up most of the space, and Karma plopped onto the farthest from the bathroom. "Feels good to lie down," she said, eyes closed.

"It'll feel even better with dry clothes."

"Ah," she said, sitting up and grabbing her backpack. She unzipped it and pulled out the blanket, and then a stack of clothes, all quite damp. "I forgot."

"No problem," Max said.

They marched into town, to a small department store, more like a Walgreen's than Macy's, where Max, tired of wearing jeans in this weather, grabbed a pair of Adidas athletic shorts, a soccer jersey modeled after the Guatemalan national team, and for good measure a packet of white socks, and a packet of boxers. He found Karma in the lady's section, clothes draped over her left arm. She examined Max's selections, plucked the boxers from his hand, returned to the men's aisle, and replaced them with boxer briefs.

At the hotel, she showered first, and emerged in black tights under a large tee shirt embossed with the Puma logo, her hair wet and combed back. When Max finished with his shower, he found her with two thick braids, one over each shoulder. She looked beautiful. Max, on the other hand, looked a dork, with his brilliant white socks and dirty work boots. The underwear Karma had selected for him clung in an unfamiliar way, not unpleasant, but, combined with the silky shorts, keeping him always in mind of his genitals. "I'm starving," she said.

They ate at a rooftop restaurant on Santander that served an elevated version of Guatemalan food and featured a view of Pana's rusted tin roofs, most weighed down by stones, cinderblocks, and old tires. Karma ordered fish from the lake, Max a knob of roasted beef, tough as jerky.

He hardly hesitated before ordering a bottle of wine from Chile. After the plates were cleared, Karma asked for coffee. Max, not normally a p.m. coffee drinker, followed her lead.

Candles stuck in wine bottles lit the patio, shared with a young Guatemalan couple constantly snapping pictures of themselves with their phones. The pictures, instantly posted on the Internet no doubt, reminded Max how slowly his project was progressing, how much of the church's money he was spending without results, and how little time he'd put into his job. In the silence of his musings, Karma dug her own phone from her bag, tapped off a text. The humid air had cooled enough to be pleasant, especially when a vagrant breeze traveled by, riffling his bare head. Loud music started up from somewhere in town, trumpets and snare drum and wistful crooning.

"I have an idea," Karma said. "How about I take you dancing?" She laughed at the expression of terror on Max's face. "Don't be scared. We'll start slow."

"Well," Max said, unable to find a suitable excuse to refuse, "I'm not really a dancer."

"Come on, follow the music. If we don't like where it leads, we go home. Yes?"

They declined dessert, and Max paid, promising he'd secretly reimburse Kent and the church once he got home and back to work, by dropping anonymous cash into the collection basket above his normal tithe. The thought relieved him, and he stood from the table. Looking out toward the lake, Karma stretched her arms over her head, raising the shirt above the crotch of her leggings while making a squeaking sound of satisfaction. "Oh, I need to wake up," she said. "You?"

"I'm a little sleepy myself," Max said, caffeine burning through his veins like fire.

Up Santander, they approached Norman's bar, La Mala Senda. Talk about truth in advertising, Max thought, crossing to the far side of the road to avoid an accidental encounter. Let the old man drink in peace, he thought, and put him out of his mind. Down a side road, they found the source of the music, an adobe storefront featuring a wooden sign with burned-on letters, reading, "Xibalba." Electronic dance music had replaced the banda, and the place surprised Max, how chic it felt, like a hip spot down some back alley in the warehouse district in some big American city. He looked down at himself, ready for a day at the gym, his naked head exposed. One look at Karma's smile and flashing eyes dispelled the hope that she'd pass.

"Okay, let's do this," Max said, and Karma took his arm. Inside, the place was candlelit and misty, full of milling bodies, very much like the Maximón service at first impression, except the smell. A hidden fog machine rather than cigarette smoke clouded the air, filling the room with an odd but not unpleasant chemical aroma, mixed with various perfumes, colognes, and the usual boozy smell of barrooms. Light came from dramatic thick candles flickering from high on the walls all around. The average age in the club was a good decade younger than the Mayan church's. The music was too loud for comfortable talk, so Max let Karma direct him to the bar. She ordered a cocktail, something clear in a class, and he asked for a beer. A clap on his shoulder brought him suddenly around, to find himself in kissing distance to an attractive woman with the cropped haircut of a runway model and yellow eyes that seemed to glow in the soft light. Max tilted his head, trying to place her, and then he did, the woman they'd met that morning at the dock, grinning between he and Karma, a hand on each of their shoulders.

"What are you two doing here?" she shouted, and Max noticed a man standing behind her, a boy really, frowning the way teenage boys always do in public. "Come," said the woman—Vicki was her name, and she pulled them gently away from the bar, through the room and to a back corner where an arched passageway, dimly glowing, stood three-feet high in the wall, a little hobbit hole. Vicki spoke into Max's ear: "Crawl through to the other side. We can talk in there." Max glanced past Vicki at Karma, who looked dazed by the sudden takeover of their date, and beyond her the boy, unhappy to occupy the outskirts of the cluster.

Max nodded, smiling, and took Karma's arm, dragging her into the center of things. Vicki got down on hands and knees, and Max had to glance away. She wore a tiny party dress that hiked up over her butt, showing two smooth mounds split by a red swath of underwear, not a thong exactly, but the thicker kind of bottom the young women wore on the beach that season. She still wore the black combat boots though. Max motioned Karma to follow, and he crawled through next, a tunnel only a couple of feet long that opened into an intimate cave-like room occupied by a dozen drinkers standing around a bar or at tall tables. Medieval torches burning along stone walls lit the place more brightly than the candles of the main room. "Isn't this place wild?" Vicki asked.

"It's like a torture chamber," Karma said, looking around.

Vicki laughed. "It's a mezcal bar. They have like a hundred kinds. Come on. I'll buy."

"I don't know," Max said, holding up his beer. "I think I'm good."

"Think you're good." Vicki laughed. "What are you talking about?" She slid between a couple on one side and a small group of young men on the other, and leaned against the bar. Max took one of Karma's hands.

"Looks like she's buying a round," he said. "We can go after if you like."

"I'm fine. It's just that she's a lightning bolt." Karma zigzagged her hand through the air, making the sound of thunder.

While the bartender set up three small glasses in front of Vicki, she and the boy were talking, maybe arguing. Smiling, she flicked her hand toward the passageway, and his face took on a pout. Sure enough, he shambled off, scowling off into space. Max glanced back in time to see his sneakers disappear into the tunnel.

The couple left the bar, and Karma and Max took their place, Max between the two women. The bartender, a thin young man with a mustache and long sideburns, welcomed them in accented English, and delivered a short speech on the pale gold liquor before them. Apparently, a small company in Mexico put a lot of care into their product. Following Vicki's lead, Max and Karma stuck their noses into the miniature wine glass and sniffed. The smell was funky and smoky, not exactly good, but Max had never found beer good tasting either, and that had never stopped him.

I shouldn't do this, he thought, lifting the glass to his mouth. A pint with Karma for lunch was one thing, a shared bottle of wine was one thing, same with a bottle of beer at a nightclub, but this was really drinking. He filled his mouth with the stuff, swished it around, and swallowed, his face heating up while a feeling of calm moved from his head down to his neck, his shoulders, his arms and chest. "Very smooth, isn't it?" the bartender asked.

"Delicious," Max said.

"Ei, yi, yi," Karma said, fanning her mouth with her hand and blowing bursts of air. Max, Vicki, and the bartender laughed. The trio stood with their backs to the bar after that, contemplating the room, each in their own space. Max stole a glance at Vicki, the sort of woman who back in the States would wrinkle her nose at him, a tradesman with dirty fingernails standing in line at the bank to cash his check after work, stinking up the joint. He lifted the tiny glass of liquor and sipped again, feeling the warmth in his head, an old friend, well met. He'd never been a bad drunk, had never called in sick from hangover, hit a woman, puked at a party, or crashed a car. He'd been a six pack after work kind of guy, always a little buzzed at night, a little thirsty in the morning, with an occasional Saturday night blow out and Sunday spent on the couch watching footfall with a bag of fast food and the hair of the dog. Quitting had coincided with joining the church, not because alcohol was forbidden, but as an overall change of self, a starting over.

# A Candle for San Simón

First his live-in girlfriend Lisa left him, for a variety of reasons, the drinking and pointlessness of his life among them, and after a period of heavy boozing which amounted to a whirling dream of sadness, anger, self-pity, and finally nightmare visions that swung from suicide to murder and back, he accepted a co-worker's invitation to Sunday at The Fortress. The cleanliness of it all—the people, the place—helped, eased some of his hurt, and soon after he remade himself in the congregation's image, trading in the old, damaged Max for a shiny new model that ran perfectly and didn't have a scratch. But now, apparently, he was drinking again. And not only that, but drinking between two beautiful women, both of whom seemed to like him, seemed, maybe, to be fighting over him.

"What are you so happy about?" Karma asked.

"Happy?"

"He's possessed," Vicki said. "Poseído by the spirit of mezcal."

"Why shouldn't I be happy?" he asked and raised his glass for a toast.

They finished their drinks, and Karma excused herself to the bathroom. Max watched her go, her thick backside shifting through the long tee shirt. He remembered that they were both underdressed for this establishment. "Another drink?" Vicki asked, and Max shook his head, claiming to have had enough, even as his thirst raged.

"One more," she said, "a quick one while your girlfriend is peeing." Before he could respond, she called over to the bartender and ordered. The drinks were expensive, at least locally, and Max realized Vicki had paid a lot for the first round. He jumped in with cash, and after a short skirmish over the bill, Vicki allowed him the honor. "Before we drink," she said, holding the new glass, "I want you to close your eyes." He'd been calculating the amount he'd need to repay the church as her words took shape.

"What?" He didn't understand, though his heart raced, and Vicki's body seemed to give off heat and the smell of smoke, like a campfire on a chilly night. He'd never seen eyes that color before, and he found himself moving closer to the fire.

"Close your eyes," she repeated. He did so, picturing powder dropped into his drink, the sort of thing he'd seen in movies and which happened to girls in night clubs. Something touched his lips and he jerked his head back in alarm, opening his eyes. "It's okay," Vicki said, her index finger moving along his upper lip, wiping some sort of balm around his mouth, sticky, faintly sweet and familiar.

"What is this?"

"The juice of the forbidden fruit," she said, smiling, "to go with the mezcal." Confused, he licked his lips with his tongue. "Is it good?" she whispered, and he turned from her, lifting the glass to his mouth. He downed the liquor, tasting nothing but the memory of the stuff she'd rubbed on his lips.

"Welcome back," he called as Karma approached. She looked at the glass in his hand. "Would you like another?" he asked. "I didn't know if I should order one for you or not."

"No thanks," she said. "If I have any more, you'll have to carry me home."

He laughed, too loudly. "Well, I guess we'd better be off," he said to the room in general, only glancing at Vicki. "Great to meet you," he said. "Thanks for showing us this place."

"My pleasure," she said.

Karma and Vicki said their goodbyes, and Max followed Karma through the tunnel, feeling Vicki's eyes until he stood in the front room, and finally they exited to the dark, quiet street. "Wow," he said, shaking his head. "That stuff was strong."

Karma agreed. A block later, he took her hand, and she leaned into him for a moment. Again they approached Norman's bar, and Max imagined the old man stumbling out, identifying them, breaking the mood. "That woman," Karma said, "she's something."

"Yes," Max said, licking his lips. "She's…intense."

"I've known girls like her before. They are trouble."

"Good thing we got out when we did."

They entered the hotel in silence, passed the unoccupied front counter, and went into the room. The ceiling lamp, a bulb covered by a grayish plate full of dead insects, made shadows of their eye sockets. "I guess we forgot pajamas," Max said, and they embraced. For a long time, dreamtime where he lost himself in the warmth and wetness of her mouth, the softness and firmness of her back, her ribs, and then her ass, they kissed and caressed and rubbed their bodies together, standing at the foot of Max's bed.

"Thank you," he said when they broke, still holding her tight, the pleasure so strong it hurt. "I've been waiting forever for this." He laughed, not at himself or the world or anyone in it, but just to let out some of the happiness. Karma laughed with him, her boozy breath sweet in his face. He inhaled it through his mouth and nose, all that he could catch, though he still tasted the crazy lady from the bar on his lips.

# Chapter Twelve

A figure appeared on the side of the road, a ghost in the rain. Two figures, Max saw as the bus pulled over to let them on, an Indian woman with a toddler. Karma sat on the bench behind Max, stretching out in the half-full bus. He and Karma hadn't slept the night before, but didn't have sex until dawn. For hours they'd alternated, talking and making out. They'd had no condoms, for one thing, but beyond that, Max tread gingerly through this age of changing sex rules. As light edged the curtain, they kissed and grinded, his shorts pushed down to his thighs, she in the tee shirt and nothing else, when he simply entered her. "Be careful," she'd whispered, and he decided this meant to pull out before coming.

Over the course of the night, Karma had confided that she'd been asked to take a week off work, and maybe more depending upon future enrollments. In other words, she was currently laid off, so Max asked if she would travel with him, help him find the elusive Zunilito, help him communicate with his mission if they could ever find it. Maybe he could talk Kent into hiring her as a translator. She had agreed, and here she was. Max could hardly believe it.

The ayudante leaped out to help the woman with a box covered in a plastic garbage bag. The little girl led the way, dressed identically to her mother in a striped wool costume, except for a straw hat on the girl and a red sling across the mother's chest. Max had somewhere seen it all before, the drenched, scowling woman, her hair pulled severely back, the girl under a grown-man's hat, both moving up the aisle, the gothic lettering backward on the top of the bus's windshield reading "Corazón," cartoon hearts on either side. Once he put a name to the feeling, déjà vu, the magic vanished, but the woman and girl did not. Max knew they'd sit beside him, so close he would smell the wet clothes, feel the cold of their bodies—and he was right.

The girl sat on her mother's lap, snuggled into her belly and closed her eyes. She coughed, a grave-sounding rattle. The sling, bulging like a pea pod, held an infant Max hadn't noticed before. He shrank away instinctively, afraid of catching whatever they had, a virulent despair.

He glanced back at Karma, who stared through the dripping window at the soggy land passing outside. The rain didn't so much come down from above as exist in the air around them. Max sensed the Mayan woman's gaze. The road was gray, and so was the rain, the land and the sky, the trees. There was no difference among anything. Beside him, the woman—just a child really—paid the fare from a wet fold of bills.

"Buenas tardes," she addressed Max, after the ayudante had gone. Max smiled, and she said something he didn't understand. Her dark eyes sucked everything into them. She repeated herself, and Max understood two words: "cien dolares."

"No," Max said, not sure what she was selling though certain he didn't want it. Karma gripped Max's shoulder.

"It's okay," the woman said in English. "No me importa. Cien dolares, no mas." A black wisp of hair showed through a crease in the sling.

Max pulled in a deep breath. "I'm sorry," he said.

"No me importa," the mother repeated. Max stared forward, squirming inside. The bus was climbing, switching back up the face of a mountain. Out the window, the mountain fell away, a steep drop into a gray void. The woman spoke again, but Max refused to understand. Even so, he knew that she was lowering her price, and that the product was her baby. The bus braked hard, dodging a pile of pine branches blocking the lane. Up ahead, a flatbed had stalled against the oozing side of the mountain. They passed and kept climbing into the clouds. Max could hardly see ten feet outside the window. Two dull orbs appeared and grew larger. Another bus flew by, wailing like a demon.

The road leveled out. They drove for a while without speaking, and Max thought he'd outlasted the woman. The bus began to coast downhill, the sound of the engine all but disappearing. They fell through the bottom of the clouds, and now sailed under a solid white ceiling.

"¿A donde va usted?" Karma asked the woman, and Max thought, no, please don't. "¿Que va a hacer?"

"No se," the woman answered. The girl coughed. She wiped her face with a piece of the baby's sling. The woman continued, too fast and too accented for Max to follow.

"She wants me to tell you what she's saying," Karma said. "I told her you—we, she thinks we're married or something—can't take her baby. She just wants to talk." Max sat still, staring at the backward letters on the windshield, unable to refuse and unable to accept the situation. He felt betrayed by Karma, who seemed to be conspiring with the woman against him.

"I received the letter from my husband," Karma translated. "He's been gone a year and ten days. They have him."

Max reminded himself that these words were not Karma's, but still they disturbed him, coming from her mouth.

"He dreams only of death. I pray to God he's already gone." The woman continued, lifting the infant in the sling, holding it in both upturned palms. "It isn't his. One of the men that took him made this baby. There were two of them. I don't know which is the father." The woman showed no emotion, save the blunt resentment in her voice. "No se," she concluded, words that Karma didn't bother to translate.

The ayudante whistled, and the bus pulled over. "Zunilito," the young man cried, though he stood only two feet away. Max, energized by a sense of relief, escape, rose from his seat, and the tiny family cleared the way for him. As Max hoisted his backpack onto his shoulders, the ayudante pointed to the left of the paved street, where a muddy road rose into pines. It was only two o'clock in the afternoon but dark as night. Max hopped out, into a deep puddle. He helped Karma avoid it. The door closed, and the bus pulled forward, only to stop ten feet away. The door opened, and the woman, with her sick daughter, her unwanted infant, and cardboard box full of possessions, stepped off.

"No," Max said out loud, and the bus drove away, leaving him in the rain, backpack on his shoulders and girlfriend beside him. Maybe she lives here, he thought, he hoped, he wished. He set out, across the street and into the glop. The woman, he saw, glancing back, followed ten feet behind, like a stray dog. Wasn't there some rule against this? In the States it would be called stalking, maybe. But here there were no rules about anything, and even if there were, nobody followed them, nobody enforced them. A local would either show pity and take her in, or throw rocks at her until she went away, but he was not local, and she knew it.

He trudged up the sloppy road, through mud that rose over his boot tops. From up ahead, a mongrel came running to investigate. It stopped short, a skinny, skittish animal, covered in scars. Max looked up into the rain, saw individual drops plummeting down around him. The dog ran off, back where it had come from.

A half a mile later the rain let up to a drizzle. The path led to a red clay clearing where half a dozen structures the size of yard sheds lay about randomly, like tossed dice. Smoke slithered from dark windows, the only sign of human occupancy. Max turned to Karma, and the family huddled behind her. Out of better ideas, he decided to ignore them, to pretend they didn't exist. He walked into the middle of the clearing, spooked, half expecting an arrow through the ribs, a blow dart to the neck. No missiles or people came out to greet him, so he approached the nearest hut, its door of thin sticks fastened horizontally by wire and string. Max thought of the second little piggy, a little bit better off than the first, but still a goner. He tried to knock, but the door wasn't solid enough to generate a sound. "Hello!" he called. "¡Hola!"

The door cracked open, revealing an old creased face. "I'm here," Max announced in Spanish, "from The Fortress."

"Si, si," the old woman said, opening the door to let herself out, not him in. She seemed neither welcoming nor hostile, neither enthusiastic nor put out as she led them across the muddy clearing. Faces appeared in windows, and a small group of children materialized from the fog, everyone eager for a look at the visitors.

"You're taking us to Reina, correct?" Max asked.

"Si, si. Reina. Si." She brought them to another hut, more or less identical to hers, built of scraps of plywood and corrugated iron, filled in by sticks and mud and plastic sheeting all held together with baling wire. "Aqui," the old woman said, and turned to leave.

"Reina?" Max called, and the door opened, revealing a girl, skinny as a straw and perhaps twelve years old. She wore jeans and a tee shirt embossed with a Japanese animation creature, a rabbit maybe. Her thick black hair was cut in the shape of a motorcycle helmet. She invited them in. Max wanted to explain that the young Indian mother wasn't with him, but he couldn't find the words or the cruelty. Besides, he was still processing Reina's age. Somehow, everyone had assumed she'd be an adult, but here she was, a girl, apparently a fan of Japanese cartoons.

"Max, yes?"

"Yes. And you're Reina?"

"It's nice to meet you."

"But you're just a girl," he couldn't help blurting out.

"I am young," she said. "But I'm the only one here who reads or uses the computer or does maths. I am the only one who goes to school. Welcome to my home. My mother is dead. My father left for the north. I live alone."

The hut, one room twelve-by-twelve foot, smelled like smoke, and no

# A Candle for San Simón

wonder. A fire smoldered in a stone pit in a corner. No chimney—an innovation that hadn't yet made its way to Zunilito, though Facebook apparently had. A coarse Mayan rug covered the center of the dirt floor, and a cot, a table, and two chairs completed the furnishings. Madonna, the singer not the mother of God, posed on the wall at the foot of the bed, the paper yellow and curling, ripped along the edges. Opposite hung a wooden cross made of lengths of two-by-four notched and glued together. A facsimile of a wristwatch decorated a third wall, face the size of a dinner plate with two-foot-long bands. The battery must have died because the hands were frozen at six o'clock sharp. "Sit," Reina said, pulling out a chair for Karma. Max sat beside her. Reina glanced at the tagalong family in the corner. When no one offered an introduction or explanation, Reina sat on the edge of her bed.

They struggled into a conversation in which Reina tried to impress upon Max her devotion to the Lord. She didn't know much about the Bible, but she believed. Max felt like an impostor, his abilities, even his faith dwarfed by Karma's skepticism and the worldly troubles of the family in the corner. Pushing on, he asked how Reina had come to find, and reach out to, The Fortress, out of all the other churches in the world. "I was online," she said, "searching, and The Fortress showed up on Google when I put in 'California, Church, English.' I sent a message, in English." She shrugged. "Pastor Kent wrote to me, and then we wrote every day. Sometimes I didn't understand, but I like to practice English on the computer."

While the talk sputtered on, the young mother lay back against the wall on the floor and closed her eyes, the toddler on her lap, the infant quietly nursing while light rain pattered the roof. Reina, aside from glancing quizzically their way now and then, went along with the trend to ignore them. Her English was almost as awkward as Max's Spanish, and the communication barely functioned. Max wondered why Karma hadn't jumped in, and he supposed she was still teaching him, forcing him to do the work. Or maybe she was, wisely, keeping her distance from an obviously bad situation. For Max, physical discomfort soon overtook the strain of conversing in the hierarchy of displeasure. His feet were wet, hands swollen, knuckles aching. He'd forgotten what cold felt like.

Reina yawned. Her wide mouth gave her the aspect of a jack o' lantern. Her nose was a nub, her eyes in the shadow of her bangs. "I'm sleepy," she said. "English makes me sleepy."

"I know the feeling," Max said.

"We have a house for you," she said, standing. They followed her out, into the rain that had returned. "This one." She pointed to a shack across the clearing, dim evergreens behind it forming a jagged horizon. Max, grateful for Karma's presence and guilty over dragging her into this place—took her cold hand in his, pretending to comfort her while actually seeking comfort himself. He glanced back, and there they were, of course, his strays. Go home! Max wanted to shout, but they had no home. Weren't there official places for people like them, shelters and the like? He'd ask Karma later. The thought comforted him, a potential solution that would neither inconvenience him overmuch nor burden his conscience. He could post about saving the family on Facebook. Max looked back and saw them as a picture, sopping, sad, desperate. Kent would love it.

As they approached the hut, Reina explained, half in Spanish, half in English, that it stood unoccupied because the previous resident, whose wife had died years before and whose two sons left soon after for Xela, or maybe Guatemala City, or maybe farther still, up into Mexico or even the U.S., had himself died. No one knew how to contact the boys, and so they probably didn't know their father was dead. The nearest mail was a half hour bus ride away, where Reina attended school, and nobody in the village had a phone. The boys couldn't read or write.

In school, her ninth and final grade, she'd learned that what killed the man, his wife, and many others in the village, were problems with their lungs. Emphysema, cancer, and other diseases caused by the smoke from their fires. "No one believes me," she said, sloshing through the slick clay, children watching from a safe distance. "They send me to school but then won't listen to what I learn." She looked up at Max, smiling like an adult, which is to say, without pleasure. "Usually it's a boy who goes, but there's no boys left except Eduardo, and he's too dumb."

They entered the dead man's hut, cold and bare except for a stack of blankets folded on the floor. "I am sorry," Reina said, gesturing toward the empty space. She seemed to want to say more, but instead left them to their lodgings.

The young mother promptly found a corner to lie in, covering herself and her children in a blanket from her cardboard box. "Well," Max said to Karma, shrugging, "here we are." He smiled, without pleasure. "I won't blame you if you take the first bus home."

"How about a nap?" she said, stepping out of her muddy sandals. The time couldn't have been much past three, but it felt like night.

The door opened without warning, and the old woman they'd first met stood there, holding a platter, an old hubcap actually, filled with apples not much bigger than walnuts. Max accepted the gift, and the old woman left without word or gesture. The apples were sour, starchy, but Max ate two because he was hungry. Karma ate one, and Max looked over at the woman in the corner, hidden under the blanket, perhaps feeding the infant. Max placed the hubcap on the floor near her and set about changing his wet clothes, too weary for modesty.

A few minutes later, he lay beside Karma, blankets under them, his unzipped sleeping bag over. He was tired but so wound up he was certain he'd not sleep, but he did, immediately and deeply.

He opened his eyes, disoriented in a strange darkness. He blinked, looking left and right, and the past few hours returned, the bus ride, the family, Reina, the dead man's hut. He sat up and made out Karma beside him, sleeping on her side, barely visible in the gray light seeping in through the single glassless window. In the corner lay a lump of blankets, emitting the thin squeak of a baby whining. He stared at the blankets while a leaden sadness spread through the room. He got up to verify what he already knew. The baby, a foot long, shriveled, red skinned and black haired, lay on its back in a nest of tipica blankets, naked except for a cloth diaper. Both its arms rose toward Max, slowly, with a strange reptilian motion. Its cries were barely audible. He didn't want to touch it, as if physical contact would implicate him in some irrevocable way. "Karma?" he whispered, but she was out, faintly snoring. Standing, he sighed, looked up at the low, metal ceiling. I hear you, he thought, and kneeled before the baby.

He didn't know its sex, and the mother never called it by name. Its eyes were open wide, and it ducked its chin at Max, waving its arms helplessly. Max presented his index finger and the child grasped it, a solid grip that surprised him, the grasp of a creature clawing up through the muck and into the world. He felt enormous weariness at the thought of dealing with this pitiful infant, weariness and something else. Love. Not love of this particular baby, whom he did not know, but a wider, less discriminating force. He had no idea what the laws were concerning such matters, what facilities and services, if any, were available in a country as poor as this. What would the baby eat? The nearest store selling formula must be hours away, Xela probably. Perhaps someone in the village was nursing. Now that he understood his role here, the reason God had sent him, the task ahead no longer troubled him—it was a problem, and problems had solutions, sometimes.

At least the infant didn't appear sick. How it had avoided its sister's illness, Max couldn't guess. Temerity? Luck? Genes? God's will? "What's your name, little guy?" Max asked, and he understood that the child didn't have a name, and wouldn't until Max gave it one.

# Chapter Thirteen

The infant, a boy, squirmed in Max's lap as the bus leaned over the abyss. He passed him to Karma, who'd dubbed him Jesus pronounced the American way, her idea of a joke. Since Max hadn't come up with anything better, they'd been referring to him as Jesús. On Karma's advice, they were heading to a Catholic orphanage in Xela, where the poor kid might stand a chance. Little Jesús calmed down in Karma's arms. He preferred her to Max, the softer body, the confidence of touch, or perhaps her smell. Max handled the child too delicately, and the kid sensed his fear.

Black haired and black eyed, he'd drunk greedily from the breast of the young mother in Zunilito, who'd agree to nurse him without hesitation. Max had hoped she'd offer to adopt the boy, but she hadn't. One of these days the kid would wonder about his parents. What would the nuns tell him? That his father was a rapist and that his mother abandoned him? More likely, he'd be treated to a convenient lie, or silence. One way or the other, the kid would eventually be devastated by his origin—or would he? Maybe that was an American idea, this obsession with who you were. "That's one thing you've got going for you," Max said, presenting his finger to the strong grip. "You'll be too busy surviving to worry about all that stuff, huh?"

The baby fell asleep with his face on Karma's shoulder. He wore that same cloth diaper, laundered by the pack of women who ventured down to the stream every day, and wrapped in the blanket he'd been left in—

his inheritance. Karma wasn't much more prepared than Max was to care for an abandoned baby, though she had lived with two nephews and a niece. During their long night of talk, she'd confided a near hatred of her older sister, the one with the kids, a bossy, superior woman who'd always picked on Karma. They hardly spoke to each other, and Max formed the theory that she'd run off to Zunilito more to escape her family than to be with him. And yet, she looked sweet with the infant, the tiny black head leaving a slobber stain on her smart jacket.

"What?" she asked, and he realized he'd been staring at her.

He shook his head, smiling. "Looks like we're about here. Should we get a cab?"

"We can take a minibus."

"No. We'll ride a taxi. It's not every day…" He let the rest of the sentence die. They were doing the right thing, of course. He couldn't be expected to adopt the poor child, after all, but still he felt guilty, betraying this tyke already let down in so many ways and by so many people. The least he could do was hire a taxi.

"What?" Karma asked.

"What what?"

"You were laughing."

"Was I? I didn't know."

They exited the bus and hopped into a cab. Along the outskirts of town, they passed a fenced lot, a medical clinic, a private school, several small shops, a first-class bus office. Large, built-in flower pots lined the center of the median, full of trash. Dogs wandered everywhere. Max had never seen a cat in this country, not one.

Without realizing he'd done so, Max had expected a grim factory of an orphanage, standing alone on a hill outside of town, so it surprised him when they pulled over beside a gray stone building indistinguishable from the rest of the buildings along the street. Two stories high and shapeless, it stood across a narrow alley from a modest Catholic church (if there was such a thing). Outside, the air was cool and the sky the same gray as the orphanage and church.

They approached the cluster of indigenous people, mostly women of middle age and older, standing outside a heavy wood door. Jesús yawned and lifted an arm, stretching much like an adult stretches upon waking. He'd be hungry, and they had no food. The idea—never stated—was to get rid of him between feedings.

Max held open the door and followed Karma into a lobby full of more indigenous people. Many of them sat along the walls on orange plastic chairs with metal legs, and the rest formed a line snaking out from a sliding glass window, the DMV of orphanages. Karma spoke to a woman in line. She pointed back toward a hallway leading into the building.

"This is a free clinic," Karma explained, leading Max into the hallway. "The orphanage is this way." Rain began to tap the corrugated fiberglass sheets that formed a roof over the internal, atrium-like courtyard, where convalescing patients stood, sat in wheelchairs, or ambled about. The rain crashed down harder, making a great drum of the roof. The baby, whining before, began to cry.

"Want me to try?" Max asked.

"Can't hurt." Karma passed the bundle, which predictably made matters worse. Max held tight and felt it pumping, this hot little machine, squirming with power, like something that could explode. A shriveled old man parked in a wheelchair along the wall watched them pass, his eyes vacant. It occurred to Max he'd never seen a Mayan over the age of ten smile, though he felt certain they did smile in private. They'd learned to hide their joy from gringos.

They climbed a flight of stairs, pressed through a doorway, and entered a hall lined by doors on either side—the building much larger than it appeared from outside. The sense of the place changed. A faint smell of bleach, sour milk, and soiled diapers, the muffled sounds of children playing and babies crying, walls painted yellow. Karma stopped in the middle of the hall, looking around. Max bounced Jesús on his shoulder, to no effect. The crying made the moment feel desperate, as if time were running out. "What now?" he asked.

"I don't know who to talk to. Should we knock?"

"Of course," Max said, and impatiently rapped on the nearest door. A woman in a gray nun's habit answered. She was plain and young, with a long chin extending past her neck wrap. Karma explained their business. The nun led them farther down the hall, knocked at a door and opened it to a small office, where an older nun looked up from a heavy wooden desk. Max somehow expected this woman to bound up like a grandmother and soothe the baby, ease him from Max's arms, take over and send Max away, but this old lady barely seemed to notice the screaming infant.

Karma introduced herself and explained the situation. The nun stared. She didn't invite them to sit. The younger one had gone, leaving the door open to the hall. Max put the tip of his pinky in the baby's mouth. Jesús clamped on it, sucked, and began to cry even louder. Max tried to settle into a peaceful state, a state of infinite patience. This was where he was. It would end when it ended. The nun's window looked out on a gray wall. Max didn't bother trying to follow the discussion. A chill entered his body. By the tenor of the voices, Karma's and the nun's, he could tell that things weren't going as planned. The old woman was turning them down, rejecting this baby as his mother had rejected him, as Max was trying to reject him. The crying physically hurt, entered him like a blade, and Max felt something like hatred toward the baby on his shoulder.

Karma fell silent, and the nun sat there, waiting. Karma turned to Max. The baby had inexplicably grown silent. Karma sighed. She bent to the desk and wrote something on a piece of paper proffered by the nun. This gave Max hope, until Karma straightened up and said, "Let's go." They left the office, walking quickly the way they'd come. Max asked for clarification, and Karma told him to wait. They left the building and headed along the sidewalk in very light rain, more like mist, walking without apparent destination. The nun, Karma explained, wouldn't take the baby. She didn't have a free cradle, the food, or the staff to care for him. They could barely feed the ones they had. Karma had put him on a waiting list, but it could take months for a space to open up.

"What about all the Americans dying to adopt?" Max asked. "It's all over the news. They pay thousands of dollars."

"How do I know? Something's in the way. Papers to sign. People to bribe? There are too many orphans, not enough time. They grow up and nobody wants them."

"Could you hold him for a while?" Max asked. "My arms are killing me." Karma stopped walking, accepted the baby, and while the transfer happened, the panic returned to Max, now from outside rather than in, like the air had gone solid, pressing on him, impossible to breathe, like drowning. Karma resumed walking.

"There's a grocery store up here. We'll get some formula and diapers. Then we'll go to my parents' house and try to think of something else."

Max lagged behind. He didn't want to buy formula and diapers. He didn't want to go to Karma's parents' house and sit there figuring out what to do with the abandoned baby while Karma's mean sister scowled. He just got to this country, and already they were forcing their problems on him. It wasn't fair, and it wasn't right. He'd done nothing to deserve this. He had too much going on already without this mess. "I'm sorry," he blurted, and stopped on the sidewalk. "I've got to go." A truck started up beside him, spewing black smoke. The red light had turned green.

"Excuse me?" Karma asked, facing him fifteen feet ahead.

"I can't handle this right now. I need some time to think." He was backing up, slowly at first, but picking up speed.

"Wait. Where are you going?"

"I'll talk to you later," he called, and turned, away from her questions and demands, her shock and outrage, her utter disillusionment. He didn't look back. Instead, he concentrated on walking, fast. It was easy without the baby in his arms, and the farther he went the easier it got. Far behind Karma shouted, but Max couldn't make out her words. He took the first corner he came to, and the moment he was out of sight, he began to run, as fast as he could go.

# Chapter Fourteen

Caruthers had driven the road from Xela to Caminos too many times for the details to register anymore, until he saw something that cut through the video loop, his very own son climbing aboard among the undifferentiated masses. There were no open seats in the front, and Max lifted his palm toward his father while passing. Caruthers watched him in the mirror, lanky and careless with his body, flopping it onto a vacant bench four rows from the back.

Seba, who had appeared beside Chucho Cruz that morning, a happy reunion marred by the reality that Caruthers had once again found himself in Cruz's debt, collected Max's fare as if he were just another passenger, which Max was for all intents and purposes. Caruthers drove his route back to the lake distracted, trying to avoid looking at the cowboy in the back but unable to help himself. The kid looked different somehow, agitated and unfocused; certainly Caruthers saw no sign of the other day's self-righteousness. Cresting the volcanic rim, he popped the shifter out of gear and coasted toward Pana. Most of the late-afternoon passengers had gotten off at Solola, but Max still kept his seat, staring out the window at the lake below. Once in Pana, Seba announced the final stop, and Max made his way to the front behind the other stragglers. He stood there while the bus idled at the three-way intersection, door open. "Were you looking for me," Caruthers asked, "or was this a random event?"

"Both," Max said.

Caruthers glanced back at Seba. "Hold on," he said, closing the door. "We can talk after I park this thing." In the lot behind La Mala, Caruthers killed the engine. "Welcome home, Seba," he said, while the ayudante gave him a stack of bills and a handful of change. Caruthers placed the money in the nylon pouch he kept clipped to the side panel, and then he counted thirty quetzales into Seba's hand. The ayudante cast a critical glance at Max before pocketing the cash and walking out. Caruthers climbed to his feet, the empty Stanley in one hand, the pouch of cash in the other. "After you," he told his son, and then followed him out the door.

"I could use a drink about now," Max said.

Caruthers turned in surprise. A light beard covered the boy's jaw, blond and already speckled with gray. His eyes were small and red. "You sure about that?" he said. Max nodded, and they entered the bar.

Inside, they bellied up. "Max, meet Red, the best bartender in all of Panajachel."

Red either didn't get the joke or chose not to acknowledge it. "We've met," he said, wiping his hands on a towel. "The prodigal son."

Max smiled. "I wouldn't say that, exactly."

Caruthers ordered two Cabros, and Red plopped them onto the bar. "What the hell's a prodigal son anyway?" he asked, popping the caps.

"I'm not sure what it means exactly, but I do know the story. The younger son of a rich man asks for his inheritance early, so he can go partying and traveling."

"Partying?" Red asked, looking through a shelf of old fashioned LPs. "What kind of partying did they do in those days?"

"Pretty much the same as now, wine and women."

"Hookers, you mean, or amateurs?"

"Prostitutes, I think. At least that's what the older brother tells their father, but, maybe he's jealous. Hard to say. But what happens is that the prodigal son spends all his money, and then, broke and hungry and all that, decides it's time to come home."

"That takes balls."

"One way to put it. He figures his dad is going to tear him a new one—"

"I know I would—"

"—but for some reason, he doesn't. Instead, he throws the kid a big party."

Red took a record from its sleeve, placed it on the turntable. Caruthers, who'd been watching and listening, stunned by the transformation of his son, the casual bar personality in place of Mr. Upright. Stunned, and though the change was for the better, a little worried.

"All's well that ends well," Red said, and placed the needle on the disc. Warren Zevon filled the room.

"I don't like it," Caruthers said. "I mean, what kind of message is this?"

"Redemption," Max said, tapping his fingers on the bar. "We should cut people slack if they come back to us and say they're sorry."

"The question is," Caruthers said, "why does the kid return? Because he missed old Dad? Because he suddenly saw the light? Hell no. He needs a hot meal and a place to stay. The real story is there's no reason to do the right thing, like that poor sap of an older brother who works in the fields while little brother has a good time, because you can always just say sorry at the last minute, and everybody will love you even more than the kid who never did anything wrong to start with."

"Take this song," Red said, pointing at a speaker. The tune was called "Excitable Boy," a narrative about a kid who rapes and kills a girl he knew, but it's not his fault because he's got mental problems.

"It's tough stuff," Max said. "Forgiveness only counts as forgiveness when the person being forgiven isn't worthy. Otherwise, we're talking about an even exchange, not grace."

"An even exchange," Caruthers said. "In other words, right and wrong."

"Listen," Red said, smiling with glee. "This is my favorite part."

"So he dug her up, and made a cage of her bones," Zevon sang, "excitable boy, they all said." Red laughed.

"I still don't buy it, no offense," Caruthers said, enjoying himself, an actual bar debate of substance, the way he used to pass his time when drinking was new. "The real lesson is that everyone loves the asshole and dumps on the nice guy. Oldest story in the book."

Max drank his beer, awfully comfortable on the barstool. "Sad, but true," he said.

A couple of young women, each laden with a full-sized backpack, walked in and sat at the bar. Big girls in two shades of blond, they ordered beer in Australian or English accents. Caruthers could never tell them apart.

"First round's on me, ladies," Red said, plopping down a couple of bottles. "Don't get many lookers like you these days."

The girls laughed. "Lookers," one of them repeated, "that's what we are, eh?"

In Red's heyday, he'd spent as much plying ladies with free drinks as he would just paying outright—with considerably less consistent results. But Caruthers understood. He remembered the desire to take home women from bars. It hadn't been about sex really. He was chasing the illusion that someone out there, a stranger, wanted him for him and him alone, whatever him was. Never mind the woman in question would have gone home with any of twenty different men on any particular night, given slightly altered circumstances, such as who happened to be there at closing. For whatever reason, it had been crucial in those days to imagine himself special, different, unique, a need growing from the fact that in the end we're interchangeable. Especially after midnight.

"Your friend still around town?" Max asked, glancing over at Red and the women.

"Friend?"

"The short-haired Latina lady. Co-worker I guess."

"Her? Jeez. No, haven't seen her since it rained on our picnic. Thank God."

"What's the matter? You don't like her?"

Caruthers squinted into the dim bar light. He wished to tell the kid everything, confess the smuggling, the yet unpaid debt to Chucho Cruz, the real job of the short-haired beauty, but he clamped down on the urge. It could only get the kid in trouble. "It's not that. I just don't really know her. She's barely more than a passenger, but I get the feeling she's, well…"

"I know," Max said. "She's dangerous. I ran into her after the rain storm. She was coming onto me hard, right in front of Karma. I was sweating bullets."

"So where is your former teacher? None of my business, but I thought you two made a nice couple."

Max exhaled, shaking his head. He upended his beer and gulped it down. He glanced at Caruthers, and then signaled to Red for two more. "The less said about her the better."

"Got it," Caruthers said. Red dropped off the beer, and then slid back up the bar toward the big Aussies. "So, how's your mother, and Danny?"

Max stared up at the small television playing a music program without the sound, where long-haired men in mariachi outfits jumped around behind rock and roll instruments. "They're fine, I guess," he said, absently twirling the bottle on the bar. "Mom's out east, having a good time of it. I call her now and then. Danny went the other direction from me. Seems he was born the other direction. Went into 'business,' whatever that means. We basically never talk. He travels a lot."

"That's a shame," Caruthers said.

Max shrugged, shifting on his stool.

"So, one more question. What happened to you not drinking? No judgement, of course, just curious."

"Things change," Max said, still fixed on the television. "You just find yourself doing the wrong thing and you do it anyway."

"I don't want to help you do the wrong thing. If you need to be somewhere else, or do something else, I say go. Beer's on me. Get out of here. I'm serious."

"Forget it," Max said, and dragged his attention from the tube. "I'm already here. I made my decision." After a pause, Max continued. "I've been wondering how you got into the bus driver business. Strange occupation for a gringo down here."

"It was all an accident," Caruthers said, "like most of my life."

Max examined his beer, reading the label. "Accident, okay, but how, exactly?"

"I was here in this very bar when I first arrived in town, spending through my savings, drinking hard. Figured at first I'd die before the money ran out, but for some reason, my body was holding up better than it should have, strong drinking genes I guess, and I knew I was heading for trouble. Dropping dead was one thing. Going broke in Guatemala was another. I needed some income. Simple as that."

"So?" Max said, lifting his empty bottle for Red to see.

"Well, I got worse and worse. Passing out in the street, getting myself beat up, mugged. Surprised nobody killed me."

Red appeared with fresh beers.

"For whatever reason, I never thought about necking myself." Caruthers kinked his head to the side and mimed a noose.

The Australians walked out, laughing and toting with them the happy atmosphere. "And I'm all strung out on heroin," came Zevon's sweet singing, "on the outskirts of town."

"So you're a mess," Max said. "How'd you end up with the bus?"

"I bought my way into it. Pure chance. Couple of brothers were selling a bus and route they inherited when their pop died, but they had jobs in Guate. They wanted to liquidate; I had some money left. That's it. I met them here at the bar along with a $20 lawyer, and we did the transaction." Caruthers turned, surprised to see another customer at one of the high tables, a red-faced regular. "Signed the papers on that table there."

"Jimmy Buffet bought a fishing boat with his first million," the newcomer added. "So he could, you know, fish if the music thing ever dried up."

Red flipped the record, and Max laughed.

"What?" Caruthers asked.

"I was just thinking that of all the possible jobs for someone who drinks all the time, driving a bus has to be about the worst."

"Cheers," Caruthers said, and they touched glasses.

"Red," cried the new customer. "How about you put on something more cheerful? 'Margaritaville' or 'Cheeseburger in Paradise,' something we can sing along to?"

Max glanced around the place, at the iron spiral stairs, the filthy ceiling fans, the bric-a-brac and wall curios. "What do you say we switch to something harder," he suggested, swirling the dregs of his beer. "The beer's starting to weigh me down. How about Quetzalteca?"

"No thanks. That's pure poison."

"It's cheap."

"So is radiator fluid, but I don't want to drink it either."

"It's traditional."

Caruthers laughed. "Tradition. You mean the great tradition of debased natives getting turned on to alcohol by invading hordes of white folks?"

"Firewater. Yes. That's what we need about now."

"Couple of rums, Red, on me."

"What do you take it with?" Max asked.

"Neat. Or rocks. Don't let me catch you polluting this fine beverage

*Kelly Daniels*


with Coca Cola."

"No?"

"They make good rum here. Cheap too, relatively."

Red poured the golden stuff into two rocks glasses, dropped two ice cubes into each, and served them up. The stuff smelled sweet and slightly burnt, like caramel, and went down hot and smooth. "That was so good, I'm ready for another," Max said, and ordered before Caruthers could slow him down.

Later, either a long time later or just a few moments later—Caruthers couldn't tell—his kid changed again. The serious, thoughtful young man now couldn't shut up, hands moving around his head as the mouth ran, hat tilted back like young Ronald Reagan, hat tilted forward like Henry Fonda, unaware and uncaring that no one was listening, no one gave a damn. Caruthers tried to focus on the words, tried to hear them, understand them, but he couldn't. Instead, he saw the kid's lips, a sort of cocky twist to them he didn't like. Angry, he lunged at the kid, tried to pinch those lips together. The kid leaned back, the stupid smile fading. Max's fuzzy eyes narrowed to slits as the crescent in his forehead darkened. Fuck this, Caruthers thought, sliding off his stool. With no words but a backward sweep of his hand that caught Max on the arm, he stumbled through the bar and out the door, surprised to find that night had fallen.

# Chapter Fifteen

She stepped out of the SUV into a wet cool night. A few drops of rain tapped the ground and the shoulders of her leather jacket. Five men stood grinning or serious, lazy or attentive, but all fronting and wondering what the hell they were doing working for one of Angelito's whores. The big man himself came around from the other side of the vehicle and stood by her. The boys' backs grew stiffer.

Arturo, the bodyguard and driver, stepped out to show himself while Angel looked over the men, boys really, even the old one. Angel had chosen them, while Vicki had scouted and prepared the site of their new Guatemala headquarters, a former bus yard encircled by a high wall, containing two buildings—a workshop and a two-story office—all renovated to Vicki's specs. She hoped the boys were as tight as the grounds, but she doubted it. Buildings, machines, locks and walls you could trust, more or less, but never people.

"Listen culeros," Angel started, "this is Vicki Valle, Double V, your new boss. Any questions?" She folded her arms over her chest, the new leather creaking. "She's from Los Angeles California, homies," he enunciated in bad English, stepping to the side and waved his hand at her like a gameshow lady showing off the prize. "That's where the women's liberation is," he laughed, reverting to Spanish and giving the boys permission to laugh too. "I know what you are thinking. Angelito likes the pussy so much, he gives her a crew." The men kept laughing, playing it safe. She identified the leader of the bunch, about thirty, marked by faded Xs tattooed on each cheek, someone to watch. "But no," Angel continued, "for reals. She's solid. And it don't matter anyway, because what she says is what I say. You understand? When you look at her, don't be looking at her tits. You see Angelito standing there. When you hear her, you are hearing Angelito." The boys quit laughing because this was the serious part. Vicki felt like slashing Angel's throat, but she kept still like a mannequin. She wasn't going to forget though. She never did. "Except this Angelito has a beautiful little ass," he went on. "Yes?" He glanced over at her, and she thought he might command her to turn around. Either the look in her eyes or a second thought changed his mind. Instead, he played like a ladyman, cupping his breasts and turning around to show them his back. The boys loved it, or pretended to. Angel was always like this around men, a real joker, even when he was torturing and killing people.

The boys stopped laughing, and Vicki took over. "There's another reason..." She was going to say "to follow me," but instead went with "...to listen to me." The boys waited. "Money." They nodded to each other, checking Angel for cues. "You're here to make money, true?" No response. "No?" She turned to Angel. "Are you sure these are the right men?"

"Yes," the youngest of them said, while Angel chuckled. The kid had a sweet face for a gangster, with a thick wave of black hair over his forehead. He wasn't against her like the others, and she felt he wanted her to do okay. She would remember.

"Right now, this territory is held by punk ass bitches, taking pennies from bus drivers and store owners, selling their garbage dope with nobody there to regulate them. First, we disinfect, clear these pests out. Then we, *politely*, introduce ourselves to the community as the new players in town. We form *partner*ships with the police, the mayors and shit. This is the start. Our goals are international. You follow me?" They were following her with great interest. "No more dicking around, homies.

Are you ready to join the big game? The major leagues?" They nodded. "We'll see how ready you are, because those vatos down south and up north don't play."

"We don't play either," Double X said.

"Are you ready to die?"

Every one of them said yes, no hesitation.

"So serious," Angel cut in, and the men chuckled. "See? I told you. This lady is scary. You do what she says and everything will be good. If not…" He mimed scissors snipping his nuts, to another burst of laughter. "Baby," he said to her, "show the men their quarters, and I'll meet you in the room." He slapped her ass, sending her on her way. She smiled like she liked it, and maybe she did like it, the dull sting and the sound of flesh hitting leather. Sometimes she lost the line between pretending and real. Maybe they were the same thing.

"This way, gentlemen," she said, sauntering, very much the rich bitch, the rich slut. She led them into the main building, boots crunching over the gravel with a good sound and a feeling of protection. The rocks couldn't hurt her, though she'd been walking on a blade since the day she met Angel. He'd told her right off, after his first orgasm, that the games they played ended in her apartment. To get where she was now took patience, gradually steering their after-sex talk toward what she'd learned in L.A., not just what she and Rico were up to, but ideas and examples from life all around in the city, the world of money. Her broad plan was to expand influence and territory without starting a war with the Mexicans, by performing a service for them, cooperating rather than wasting money and lives on revenge and fronting. After weeks setting the table, she served dinner: a presentation with slides on her laptop plugged into the widescreen TV, like her final assignment in Business Admin 100, the same kind of thing the money people did in their glass towers downtown. When she finished, Angel sat there thinking, surprised maybe, not sure whether to get pissed or laugh. He nodded his head, lower lip pushed out in that way he had when thinking. She wasn't asking for much, but the fact she was asking at all broke all kinds of rules. On the other hand, what if it worked? Money, territory, getting in on the big time. And if it didn't work? She'd get herself killed, but none of it would rub off on Angel. Sure. If you want to do it, let's do it, he decided, like he was humoring her.

The gamble was that he needed her more than he'd admit, in the bedroom. She wouldn't be easy to replace there, and he couldn't use threats to keep her in place without ruining the game, the dream that she was in charge, not him. Sure, he could hire a whore who specialized in this kind of play, but Angel didn't like to pay outright like a John. He liked girlfriends, not hookers, and he installed them in nests about the country, to visit when he wanted. The difference between these girls and Vicki was that no matter how they acted, they were afraid of him. Even a professional dominatrix would tip her hand, hold back on the punishments Angel needed. Vicki feared him too, but so far, she hadn't blinked, and that's what kept her alive. Maybe one day she'd grow big enough to relax, protected by a wall so high nobody could climb it, but for now, she was in it deep.

She showed the men the chillin area, a large basement room set up like a bar, with a pool table, foosball, and TV with a Play Station. Doña Antonia, who would be cooking and cleaning for them, came out with a platter of tostadas and a bucket of beer in ice. The boys smiled, slapping each other in appreciation. Maybe it wasn't going to be so bad working for Angelito's bitch. She brought them to the bedrooms, three of them, lined with bunkbeds and metal lockers, enough space for twelve men, in anticipation of the enterprise growing. The bathroom was large, industrial, with three showerheads, two shitters, a piss trough, and a wide concrete sink, all with hot water. The conditions of working for this crew had been spelled out beforehand. Four days on, three days off in the compound, on a rotating schedule, subject to emergencies or special projects. All crew members were welcome to live fulltime on the premises, but no women, buddies, or families were allowed inside the walls. Everyone received a weekly salary, depending upon rank, experience, and skills, plus bonuses representing a cut of profits. Aside from all the technical stuff, what she'd mostly learned at the college was how to use words, not guns, to beat down the competition, take advantage of the weak, control employees, all to gather more money because money was power and power kept you safe even when the shit went down, because eventually the shit was going to come down. That's why all those CEOs sailed away in luxury yachts when the companies they ran sunk like the fucking Titanic. Bangers, the ones in prison or stuck in their stupid blood feuds, mistook power for the posture of power. The real gangsters didn't carry nine millimeters, didn't fly colors. Those vatos wore suits and ties, drove Mercedes Benzes, hired scrubs like Angel to clean up their messes, because this is what Vicki had learned during her time with Angel: he was small. No way Vicki would ever get to the top, or even near enough to see it, but at least she knew where she was, unlike the rest of this sad crew. Knowing was a tool, and words were tools. She was learning how to use the tools in her toolbox.

"That's enough for tonight," she said. "Meet here at 8:00 a.m. tomorrow, and I'll assign you each a region." They stared at her, waiting to be dismissed. "Goodnight," she said, and walked out.

The driver stood against the wall outside the bedroom upstairs. She smiled, and he nodded in response, always serious, always Angel's and nobody else's, even his own. She closed the door behind her and found Angel on the bed, dressed but with shoes off, feet crossed at the ankles. She slung her jacket over the back of the desk chair and sat to unlace her boots. Long day, she thought to say, a good night to relax. She wanted to shower, dress in soft pajamas, slip into bed and sleep, maybe even fuck if it went down that way, but as long as Angel was there, she was on the job. That he hadn't left yet meant he wished to play, never simple or direct with him. Working herself into the role, she spun around on the chair to face him, her legs spread the way a man sits, though not exactly the way a man sits. "I bet you're scared I'm going to fuck these boys while you're gone, aren't you?"

He grinned.

"Wipe that smile off your face."

"Yes, my love."

"Oh, I know what you're afraid of. That I'll fuck them right here, in front of you, while you sit there watching, crying like a bitch."

"Yes, my love."

"Come here, take off these boots"

# Chapter Sixteen

Max craved meat and a Coke. Two Cokes. Bleary-eyed and raw, he took an outdoor seat at a restaurant on the strip called El Patio. Two tables over sat a white man with a large bandage on his bald head, drinking coffee with the red-haired bartender from Max's father's bar. Flesh-colored prosthetic arms extended from the man's shoulders, ending in rubber-coated pinchers, which he used gracefully to raise a mug to his mouth without spilling. Max tried not to stare.

The tiled patio was pleasant but would have been better if the fountain in the center were functioning. Max had seen a dozen fountains in Guatemala so far, and not one of them had worked. The waitress, a pretty Indian lady with a wide bottom and narrow top, strode up to the table, pulling a note pad from her apron and a pencil from the bun over her head. Max ordered a plate of stewed pork and a Coke. The girl kept writing, too many words for a meal and a drink. When satisfied with her account of the situation, she stalked off to the kitchen.

"With a rock," came a voice from the other table. The armless man, flushed and wide-eyed, leaned toward the bartender. "That pissant Billy and his puto friends hit me with a rock. I know it's him, and I know you know where he is, Red. Don't fuck with me."

The bartender, reclining so that his head nearly touched the chair back, lifted his coffee mug from the table, brought it to his mouth. "If I see him I'll tell him you're looking for him," he replied, replacing the mug on the wrought iron tabletop.

"You don't need to tell him jack shit, because that particular dude is a dead man. Fifty U.S. dollars. That's how much it'll take to wipe him off the face of the planet. And you know how much I've got in my pocket right now?" He leaned in again.

Red folded his hands over his chest. "You carrying cash after just getting rolled?"

"That's not all I'm carrying. I'm sick of the abuse, Red, the blatant lack of respect. I'm going to do something about it."

Red nodded slowly, thinking it over. "You sure you just didn't pass out and hit your head last night? And some bum went through your pockets, or maybe you just spent all your money and don't remember? Maybe at the titty bar up the hill? It's been known to happen."

"No Red. I know what I know." But he didn't seem quite so sure anymore, and he settled back into his seat.

"I'm on your side, Frank, but wouldn't it be a shame to spend all that money knocking off a kid who might not have done anything? Not to mention maybe getting tagged for it. The cops get lucky once in a while, and after spending all your check, you won't have anything left to get yourself out. Chucho Cruz is hanging around these days too. I seen him yesterday. You don't want that guy up your ass. And me, why, I'd have to find a new cleaning boy. I've got Guillermo trained and all. That's a major pain that I don't currently have to deal with. A lot of hassles, is what I'm saying."

Frank clipped his mug and gulped. "*No*," he said, and belched impressively. "That's what *I'm* saying. No to your bullshit. I'm not listening."

The two drifted into silence, Red nearly horizontal, coffee at his chest, Frank spooning sugar into his mug, lips moving. "I got to go set up," Red said.

"Yeah, yeah. I'll see you later."

The waitress delivered a thick glass bottle of Coke, and Max sucked on the straw protruding from the mouth. While he drank, a parade of salesmen from the street harangued him across the low, metal fence. Belts? Reggae berets? Towels? Blankets? Beaded necklaces? Volcano tour? No thanks, no thank you, maybe next time. It was sad, and the Coke failed to quench his thirst. He wished he'd chosen a different seat, one set back from the fence, but the effort to move seemed too great.

A resident gringa in her late thirties rode up on a beach cruiser, and he smiled at the unexpected companionship. "Hi," she said, holding herself up on the bike by gripping the fence. "I noticed your aura from down the street."

Max continued to smile, unsure whether or not to outright laugh. Two braids hung behind her outwardly cupped ears and lay on her breasts. She wore loose cutoff jeans and a flannel style shirt tied at the waist and rolled up to her elbows. Her unpainted face was ordinary, pretty, her body lithe. Max thought of Karma, how he'd treated her, and his interest in the hippie lady disappeared. He needed to get up now, catch a bus to Xela, beg Karma's forgiveness, help her with the kid, take care of his responsibilities, and return to Zunilito. But of course, he couldn't, not now. He'd already ordered, and here was this woman, requiring his attention. *You're fucking up*, his inner voice told him, as if he didn't know.

"My aura?" he asked.

"It looks like a bruise. Or a sunset. There's an ending quality to you. A wound healing. A day closing."

The statement, the opening line of a con, irritated him. "Something I've always wondered. Can you see your own aura?"

"No." She regarded the basket on the handlebars. "But I can guess at it, depending upon my mood. I think it's greenish-blue right now. I feel calm."

"That must be nice." Drinking alcohol, Max reflected, even a single night of it, had already changed him, back to the way he used to be, easier, lighter, removed, the words there at the ready without his having to think about them. The world appeared as a joke when he drank, most of the time at least, and he realized that he preferred this mode of being to the other, the serious weight of sobriety. Who cared, really? Did it matter that he'd run out on Karma and that poor bastard child? He'd liked her, but so what? He liked a lot of women, this one here, for example. He imagined her inviting him to her smoky lair, to twist like snakes on pillows and rugs. Before sex, though, he needed food. He needed drink. Life really wasn't so complicated after all.

"It *is* nice to be calm," she said, "but hey. I was wondering if you'd be interested in a loaf of bread."

Max looked at her face, trying to decipher her codes. Bread? She folded back a tipica cloth in the bike's basket, uncovering a dark, coarse loaf. It was fine-looking bread, though Max didn't currently crave that sustenance.

"For sale?" he asked.

She rang a small bell on her handlebars. "Fifteen quetzales," she said, the nightly rate for his hotel room.

He laughed, not to mock but because he'd thought she was kidding. Bread at the market cost a couple of quetzales.

"I grew the wheat myself," she added, offended.

"Wow," was all he could come up with, but they might have been tapping telegrams across an ocean by this time, and she turned her eyes from him, scanning the road for better prospects.

"See ya around," she said, and rode away.

"Don't worry about her," Frank interjected from his table. "She's sensitive about her bread, is all." Max turned to him, for some reason embarrassed. "You okay?" Frank asked.

"Sure," Max said, as two boys in army fatigues with M16s slung over their shoulders sauntered by on the road, openly staring at Frank.

"What are you lookin' at?" he muttered, but not loud enough for the soldiers to have to react.

The waitress appeared with Max's food. He ordered a second Coke. "I ask," Frank said, "because you look a little spaced out, if you don't mind me saying."

"Spaced out," Max repeated, stabbing a hunk of pork. "That's a good description."

"What I mean is, a little shaky, a little under the weather, if you get my drift."

"I'm fine," Max claimed, and put the meat in his mouth. He chewed it into a paste and swallowed, tasting salt and grease, experiencing a moment's pleasure followed by nausea.

"What do you say we head on out, after you eat, and get a beer or two. I got some money. I seen you with Norman the other day, so I know you're okay. At least, kind of okay."

No, Max thought. Absolutely no drinking. He had a bus to catch, the thought of which nearly caused him to retch, the curves and dips, ripe peasants pressing against him. He closed his eyes and breathed deeply until the wave passed. A beer didn't sound so bad, actually, to fortify him for the journey. And the poor guy, disabled as he was, could probably use some company. "Why not?" he answered.

"That's the spirit!" The man stood and came to Max's table. "The name's Frank," he said, and offered one of his pinchers. "Don't worry. I won't hurt ya."

Max accepted the mechanical hand. It was made of metal tubing, covered in rubber. Frank grinned. "Weird, ain't it?"

"A little bit," Max admitted.

Frank laughed hard. "How you think I feel?" He sat down, still laughing. "Hurry up with that. You can eat any time. We got more important matters to attend to."

# Chapter Seventeen

Caruthers walked in at quarter to three, and there hunched Max, drinking with armless Frank. Caruthers didn't like it, this thing he'd facilitated. He mounted a stool at the opposite end of the bar, wondering how this unholy combination had come about and how to undo it. One silent regular and three vacant seats buffered him from them, though hiding wasn't a solution.

"What'll it be, Norman?" Red asked.

"You know what it'll be," Caruthers said.

"Well, last night you and that young gentleman over there were drinking shots and whatnot, concoctions the boy learned about in disco clubs all the way up in the United States of America. Thought you might want a fuzzy snatch or somesuch."

"I wasn't myself."

Red pinned a napkin to the bar with a bottle. "I thought maybe you finally were precisely your exact self," he said, and walked off the way bartenders do when they've managed a zinger.

Halfway through Caruthers' beer, Max appeared at his elbow, plenty drunk already. "Hey there, Pop," he said. "Care to join us on the dark side?"

"I've been there before," Caruthers said, "and I'll pass. I'd like to cool off with a solo beer if you don't mind, unwind after a day on the road." He didn't want to hurt the kid's feelings, but he didn't want to encourage him either. The fact was, Caruthers, after many years dormant, craved the company. When he'd first settled in Pana, he'd made friends, drinking buddies, but they'd dropped off over time. Some died, others turned enemy, most left town, and a few even quit drinking. As they disappeared, Caruthers hadn't replaced them. Friends had a way of usurping, forcing compromises over when to drink, where to drink, whether or not to talk, what subjects to cover. Somebody was always wanting to go somewhere else and take you with.

"That's sad, Dad," Max said. "Drinking alone."

"Not sad to me," he replied. "I'm as happy as a Mexican in a beanery."

Max snorted. "That's what we call 'offensive' these days, at least back home."

"Mexicans to Guatemalans are like Americans to Mexicans. They're richer, so you can say whatever you want about them."

"Sure, if you're Guatemalan. Last I checked, you're still a gringo."

"True. You can't help who you are."

"So hey. We going to drink or not? I stayed an extra day just to keep the party going a little longer."

Caruthers shrugged and cocked his head toward the vacant stool to his left. "Can't stop you from sitting where you want. And if you're tired of old pinchers, feel free to use me as an escape hatch."

"Listen to him," Max said, sliding onto the stool. "He hasn't even noticed that I walked away. He ever tell you how he lost his arms?"

"Many times," Caruthers said. "Many versions. Which one did you get?"

"Everybody who goes to Afghanistan is automatically a hero these days, and here's Frank, both arms blown off in Nam, throwing a live grenade away from his men."

"Yeah, that's a good one. Implausible, but who cares? What are you having? On me."

"Be flattered," Red said, flinging a napkin like a Vegas card dealer. "He doesn't usually treat until he's out of money."

"Rum, splash of soda, squeeze of lime."

"Now you're talking," Caruthers said, and ordered a rum on rocks.

"What do you mean, implausible?" Max asked. "Frank's lying?"

"How do you blow both arms off to the shoulder without taking the head along with them?"

Max shrugged. "I believe him," he concluded, and the drinks arrived.

"Here's to youth," Caruthers said, clunking the glass against Max's. He felt great, downing the first sip. Who'd have thought it could be so easy. The kid could say whatever stupid thing he wanted, but Caruthers didn't need to argue. It was a revelation. "And speaking of youth, how old you guess Frank is?"

Max glanced over at the pasty, flushed man down the bar. "A rough mid-fifties, I guess."

"And he served in the Vietnam War? At what, the age of ten?"

Max grinned. "I choose not to doubt," he said, and sipped his drink.

Sometime later, tears filled Caruthers's eyes, and he didn't hide them. They were on at high table now, though he couldn't remember having moved from the bar. "The truth is, I dumped you guys. Took off and left. And you know why?" He considered his fresh drink, paused in his confession to try to count the rums. Hadn't he just arrived? Time didn't seem to be working right. He drank a mouthful, looked across the table at his handsome son, the white hat tipped way back to show his face. "I'll tell you why. You, your mother, poor little Danny, you guys were getting in the way of this," he held up the beverage, glowing golden in the barroom light, "this damned alcohol." He chuckled, set the drink down, wiped his running eyes. It was that simple, that sad, the tragedy of his life. A fucking country song.

Max swayed, frowning. He blinked hard, seemed to come back into himself. "No biggie," he said. "I forgive you."

Caruthers looked away, cringing inside at the memory of the time he'd been forgiven for, just before marriage, just after marriage, ten years into marriage. He'd fancied himself a neo-beatnik in college, too young for Vietnam, too old for whatever came after. He'd protested in his own way though, studying the Yippies and the Black Panthers, sharing the Truth with any who'd listen—the story of FBI as Secret Police, the United States Government as overgrown Banana Republic. His friends at college listened, agreed that it was a shame, that something should have been done, and that's where it all ended. The stories became shtick, and the shtick became him. Skipping class, he hung around the kiosk with the marginally enrolled, dressed in surplus military rags and a Che Guevara beret. He talked the talk, wore the costume, loitered in coffee joints and bars, affected to write poetry for God's sake. His father, the great capitalist, had dismissed him early as a loser, and though Caruthers hated the old man and everything he stood for, he later accepted Dad's offer to run one of his businesses, a specialty auto parts shop for collectors, more hobby than investment, even though it turned a profit. Caruthers was the nominal boss, but he hated the dull, pointless work and hated even more the retro grease monkey jumpsuit accented with a bow tie—specifically designed by Dad, who described the getup as "working man with class." He hated the shop, and the shop hated him. Caruthers did a bad job, especially as the drinking began to really kick in—lost parts, unhappy customers, jumbled books. By the time he understood what he'd gotten himself into, he was married, with two kids, a mortgage and two car loans.

Caruthers lifted his head and regarded Max, looking off into a private distance, one finger in his drink as if testing the temperature. "Well," Caruthers said. He clapped the kid's back. "Thanks for trying to understand. That's more than I deserve."

Max brought his finger from the glass to his mouth. His bleary eyes focused on Caruthers. "Mom always told us you changed after Grandma died. Is that true?"

Caruthers shifted on his seat. He'd had no idea this was the story Pam had been spinning. He took the idea seriously. Thought it through. The timing was about right, yes, but no. He and his mom had allied against the tyranny of his father, who'd openly enjoyed long-term love affairs throughout his life but kept his wife, no longer pretty or a social asset, hidden away in the big house, to dose herself silly with pills from morning to night. "Mom's death was a great relief and kindness," he said, "and she had nothing to do with how I turned out." Red was playing his Best of Van Morrison record, and fucking "Brown Eyed Girl" came on. For some reason, though, the song came out fresh, beautiful, the way it must have sounded the first time. A kind of miracle.

"You two ready for another round?" Red called. Caruthers and Max were the only customers left.

"Yes we are," Caruthers said, and turned to Max. "You see much of your mother before coming down this way?" Max shook his head, no, and then spit a sliver of ice back into the glass. Red served the fresh drinks, carted away the empty glasses.

"She moved east with Bill, the guy she married after you left, so they could take care of his parents. One of the Carolinas. I forget which. I talk to her on the phone every couple of months. She sends a card for my birthday and Christmas. That's about it. On the phone, all she does is tell me about people I've never met."

"So you're all alone up there, huh? I'm sorry to hear that."

Max shrugged his shoulders, and the chorus of "Brown Eyed Girl" resumed its customary tediousness. Caruthers thought about his own father, mean and vital to the day he died of a stroke at 84. Caruthers recalled the funeral with military honors, the fifty grand willed to him, while the rest went to his uptight, ass-kissing sister and her smarmy gold-digger of a husband. Caruthers looked at Max, excited to share the sudden revelation, that it wasn't the alcohol intervention, or the pressures of family life that had driven him to Guatemala; he'd run off as the ultimate slap in the face of his daddy, a good decade too late for the message to land. Max gazed back, and Caruthers knew he couldn't explain any of this, and didn't want to. What was there to explain anyway? That his entire life had hinged upon a miscalculation, a hopeless, useless gesture of vengeance? "Let's get out of here," he said, standing.

They caught a cab out of town, up a switchback road to the ridge overlooking the lake, the opposite side of Caruthers' usual route. "Where are you taking me?" Max asked, staring out the window at the black lake, like a hole in the earth.

"You'll see."

They drove through a village, over rolling pastures, and finally pulled into a dirt lot filled with a hundred jalopies. Behind a wall of pines stood a warehouse, lit by a single bulb hanging over the front door. A couple dozen men loitered around the entrance, many of them smoking, most wearing cowboy hats. Caruthers paid the driver with money he couldn't afford to spend, but who cared? The world might end tomorrow. It probably would. "I hope you're not taking me dancing," Max said. He seemed refreshed by the cool air. Hard rock music came from the building.

"Dancing. Yes. It's kind of like dancing."

"I don't dance. I told Karma that."

"That why she's not around anymore? Women love to dance."

Near the entrance a white sheet stretched between two posts, spray painted with: "¡Hoy Lucha! El Gringo vrs Julio de la Rosa."

"El Gringo?" Max asked.

Caruthers paid their covers to a large, bearded man who wore sunglasses in the dark.

The music blasted through the door, and they entered a vast cavern full of metal folding chairs and bodies milling about. Floodlights lit a sagging fight ring, on which several masked wrestlers paced about. An announcer kept up an incomprehensible patter, competing with nerve-torture guitars, drums, and shrieking. In all his years in Pana, Caruthers had never attended a lucha, until now. He and Max drifted toward a kid selling canned beer from behind a table.

"Look," Max said, pointing out Frank, standing among several men exchanging bills, his bald head glistening, pink as his mechanical arms. He held a stack of bills clipped between his pinchers.

"Is he doing what I think he's doing?" Caruthers asked.

"Gambling."

"On the outcome of fake wrestling? Incredible."

Max begged to sit up close, so they took seats in the second row. The wrestlers wandered around the ring, decked out in ill-fitting homemade costumes. One guy wore a simple red mask emblazoned with a face-sized swastika across the front. Continuing this theme was the wrestler in the Ku Klux Klan robe, marked with three Ks across the forehead of the pointy hood to drive the message home. Caruthers hoped this wasn't El Gringo.

Four other wrestlers wandered about, two with plain masks, one barefaced, and the final sporting six-inch devil's horns flopping from his forehead like half-hard dicks. They paced like zoo animals, hopped, stretched their arms and legs, waiting for some signal to start clobbering each other. No referee had yet arrived, but a girl in a short dress climbed into the ring. The Nazi promptly put her in a choke hold.

"That's not right," Max pointed out.

"I'm just glad he's not the hero. You never know around here."

The man without a mask pretended to punch the Nazi on the back, sending him to the mat. Valiantly, he carried the ring girl to the ropes, where she climbed to safety. Meanwhile, the rest of the wrestlers stood about slapping each other in the face, taking turns in a most orderly fashion, every swing attended by a foot stomp to the mat. Everyone participated in this exercise except the devil, who had somehow managed to smuggle an eight-foot ladder into the ring, which he smashed over the bare-faced man's head while he stood at the ropes distractedly and stupidly watching over the ring girl.

The fight continued on like this, somehow escalating. Everyone kept getting hold of the ladder, using it as a giant saber, until the KKK guy and a generic wrestler with a black mask climbed each side of it and stood at the top, slapping each other across the face like a couple of gentlemen robots stuck challenging each other to a duel. Caruthers finished his beer, and Max slipped a small bottle from his pocket. He hit it, winced, and passed to Caruthers. Quetzalteca. Caruthers took a large gulp. It tasted fine, like pure alcohol. Caruthers immediately felt it in his head, even as the burn continued down his throat and into his belly.

The black mask had knocked KKK off the ladder, and now he balanced precariously on the top rung, wobbling with arms out. His two comrades were both outside the ring by this time, defeated by evil, and now the three ghouls, Nazi, Klansman, and the Devil himself, stood below the ladder, pretending to menace but really just waiting to get trounced. Black mask leaped, landed on the three, pinned them all for a spectacular victory. A ref must have crept into the ring at some point, because he was there to count the bad guys out. The forces of good prevail again! The crowd stood, shouting themselves hoarse and knocking the folding chairs aside to get closer to the ring. Caruthers lost sight of Max in the melee, and he took the opportunity to withdraw to the sidelines. He had to use the bathroom anyway.

When he returned to the main room, the crowd—a mob really—was chanting, "De-la-Ro-sa, De-la-Ro-sa…," everyone pressed up against the ring. Their hero was a young man, barrel chested with a humble manner, a thick mane of black hair, and Mayan features. Caruthers, looking around the crowd for Max and not seeing him, went to the beer table for a can. El Gringo entered the ring, a beautiful woman on each arm, one blonde, one dark headed. His costume was sewn together, perhaps by his mother, from a cut-up U.S. flag, all red-white-and-blue, stars-and-stripes but so fragmented the eye couldn't take it in as a single unit. He appeared to move strangely, shifting as if his borders weren't solid, amorphous.

Rudely, he pushed the girls away and grabbed the microphone from the announcer. Looking around the room contemptuously, he addressed the crowd in perfect Spanish. More than perfect, his Spanish was highfalutin, how a gringo would talk if gringos could talk. His tone, his message, his bearing all conspired to insult every last Guatemalan. He listed the great northern cities where he normally wrestled: Los Angeles, New York, Chicago, Miami...places beyond even the dreams of the dirty denizens of this Guatemalan backwater. Boo! Boo! went the crowd. The guy was good, probably Mexican. He had that Mexican exuberance and flair for overstatement, so distinctive in taciturn Guatemala.

The local hero pushed El Gringo aside, and the crowd howled as the cowardly Gringo hid behind his girlfriends. Soon De la Rosa was chasing him around the outside of the ring. All in good fun until an audience member, attempting to brain El Gringo with a folded chair, accidentally knocked out De la Rosa, which allowed the wily and craven Gringo to pounce on the hero.

As El Gringo dragged the dazed De la Rosa back into the ring, a disruption broke out in the crowd. Chairs and cans flew around as if caught in a small tornado. The general cheers and boos turned into shouts of fury. The wrestlers stopped the show and stood there, watching. The brawl grew as those outside its whirling edge rushed in, either to fight or break it up. Caruthers backed away until he was at the wall. He could only assume Max was somewhere in there.

Wouldn't that be something, he thought, if the kid ended up dead, trampled, brained? Another great move by Norman Caruthers, leading his first born to a laughable death. He guzzled the last of the beer in his hand and bought another while he still could. Five minutes later, cops came storming in. One of them, insanely, fired a shot. They began pulling men from the brawl, peeling it like an onion. Those who'd been plucked out slunk off into the background, but the vortex still blazed.

Caruthers shouldn't have been surprised to see Max dragged from the center by two cops; he shouldn't have been surprised to see none other than the King of Bad Vibes, Chucho Cruz, emerge from the shadows to take charge of this unusual prize, a real life gringo tourist, caught fighting—but surprised Caruthers was. Max's face looked a little puffy, but otherwise he didn't show any obvious damage. In fact, he was smiling and laughing until Cruz took over. Caruthers really, really didn't need this. He was out of favors with Cruz, but what could he do? Let the gangster take Max downtown? Max might never see the sky again if Cruz decided to take things in that direction. He poked his index finger into Max's chest. Four cops stood around to witness, while elsewhere the night was ending, the wrestlers gathering their props and walking away, the audience meeting up, hustling for rides home.

Caruthers downed his beer and approached. "My good friend Norman," Cruz said in English. Max held a couple of quetzales unfolded in his hand, an insult of an attempted bribe.

"Señor Cruz," Caruthers said, grasping a thick paw, surprised by the gentle grip, the dry, silky texture of his palm. "¿Que pasa?"

Cruz frowned, as if unfortunate news had just been brought into the conversation. "This boy. He has caused disturbance in this place."

"This boy?" Caruthers asked. "This boy is my son. I was hoping you'd get to meet him, under better circumstances."

"*This* boy?" Cruz glanced around, as if another boy might be hidden nearby. He settled a stony glare on Max. "This boy is lying to me," he concluded. "He has no passport. Why? He won't tell."

"No, this boy's okay. He's a tourist. Spending some money. Helping the economy, you know. Visiting his old man. We've been drinking at La Mala. He just got caught up in the whole thing. No fault of his own."

"What's his name?" asked Cruz, the cop, the criminal. Caruthers, insanely, blanked for a moment.

Cruz's face began to brighten with victory, and Caruthers said, "Max.

Short for Maxwell."

Cruz looked the kid up and down, scowling. Max wore a humble face, playing possum. Cruz let the moment stretch. Caruthers felt five years old, a neighborhood kid asking if his friend can come out and play.

Cruz smiled, straight teeth under the severe mustache. He clapped a hand onto the back of Caruthers' neck, and, just as happened when his father used to do the same thing forty years before, Caruthers flinched. Chucho Cruz had a light touch though, massaging Caruthers' tight neck like an expert. "Don't worry, my friend. If this one is el hijo of Norman Caruthers, our valuable chofer de camion, he is like hijo to Chucho Cruz." With his free hand he clasped Max's shoulder and executed a couple of kneads. Max concocted an ill smile and transferred the proposed bribe back into his pocket. The other cops lost interest and dispersed.

"The fight is over," Cruz said. "You are looking for a taxi. Come, I will drive."

There was no question of refusing, so they followed Cruz out of the building to his unmarked SUV, where Cruz herded them into the backseat. Cruz spun the vehicle around and raced toward town, which appeared from the ridge as a scattering of lights beside the void of the lake. Speeding down the winding road, Cruz glanced over his shoulder, showing his teeth. "You like the ladies, Norman? I bet this one likes the ladies." The rest of the trip occurred in exhilarating silence, Cruz cornering hard in spite of the SUV's high center of gravity, throwing his passengers from side to side.

At the bottom of the hill, they stopped at the red light outside of town. Cruz turned around, his right arm resting on the seat back. "Your ayudante is back, yes? Very good. Soon, we talk about business. You and me."

Caruthers didn't want to talk shop, especially not in front of Max. "Well, I thought we sort of took care of that," he ventured.

# A Candle for San Simón

Cruz clucked his tongue, as if agreeing. "Bad economies," he said. "Muchos problemas para todos. Even Chucho Cruz!" The light had turned green and a car behind honked its horn. Cruz ignored this, still twisted toward Caruthers, thinking. The car pulled around. Cruz emerged from his trance, brilliantly smiling. "I have the answer, my friend. To all the troubles. You will see. We talk later, okay? We all make money."

Caruthers smiled and nodded, though he wanted no further part in Cruz's negotiations. He was simply going to have to earn his own money, bribe Chucho out of any debt the gangster seemed to think he was owed, and that was that. He'd start tomorrow, by driving extra hours, doubling his time on the road. He could do it; he would do it. Tomorrow.

They roared down Santander and turned left into an alley. Cruz parked alongside a windowless building Caruthers had often passed over the years but had never so much as wondered about. A steel door took up the center of a one-story plaster wall, an easy structure to ignore except that it had been painted black, even the door and trim. Chucho Cruz knocked, three times quickly, a pause, three more quick knocks, another pause, and two slow knocks. A secret knock, Caruthers was amused to note.

The door opened a crack. Cruz mumbled, and the crack widened. Inside, wrapped in smoke and the scent of stale booze and mildew, a dozen men drank at cocktail tables or along a short bar. More sat around a stage supporting a nude woman shaped like a beer keg. The ceiling was so low she had to stoop as she rocked listlessly to the harsh trumpets and battlefield snare drum music.

Cruz took Caruthers's hand in both of his. "I'm going," he gestured with his head toward the shadows. "Come by some night. I invite you. Marta likes you very much, and she asks, 'when do we see the funny gringo?'" He regarded Max. "And you, be careful." He left, joining two other men at a table, all of whom disappeared behind a black curtain. When Cruz was out of sight, drunken weariness fell on Caruthers like a heavy, stinking blanket. To show Cruz respect, he asked the bar boy for a couple of beers. The kid placed two cans on the bar and popped the tops. Caruthers pushed some bills toward him, but he shook his head and backed away, scared of the money.

Caruthers sat with Max at a small round table by the door. A sour smell rose from the carpet. "So," Max whispered, slur evident in that single syllable, "who the hell was that?"

Caruthers leaned forward. "One serious asshole. What did he have on you?"

"Nothing."

"Nothing except inciting a riot."

Max exhaled, rubbed his face with both hands. "El Gringo strikes again," he muttered.

The crowd cheered. Max glanced toward the stage and frowned, but Caruthers was out of curiosity. He lifted the can, warm to the touch, and choked down a mouthful. It tasted like urine, and the night was done.

"There's something else," Max said, staring at his beer can. "The reason I'm here, and not with Karma, is that I fucked up big time." He told the story of their budding romance, the abandoned child, the night in a peasant shack, the denial at the orphanage, and Max's panicked flight. Caruthers' first impulse was to cheer the kid up, assure him that, taking the long view, this was not a big deal, and he was not a bad guy. The real villain is that mother, dumping her child on a stranger. True, bailing on his gal was a weasely move, but people have done worse.

"Let's get out of here," he said instead, the words thick in his mouth.

"I'm ready when you are," Max replied, eying his can with disgust. They left the bar, where a cab happened to be waiting just outside. Home was only a few blocks away, but Caruthers had an errand to run first. "Care for a ride?" he asked, climbing into the little yellow compact. Max shrugged and hopped into the other side.

"Cervesaria Monte," he told the driver. "A little detour," he said, and

# A Candle for San Simón

Max nodded, eyes closed. "I'll drop you off on the way back." The driver guided the car gingerly over every bump in the rough cobblestone road, and Caruthers felt so alone he wanted to cry. He hated himself, hated the liquor in his belly, the wrestling spectacle, the blown money, the new debt to Chucho Cruz, but he mainly hated that it all happened with his son along for the ride, a witness to and a participant in Caruthers' wasted night and wasted life.

They arrived at the all-night outlet. Drunks sprawled on the ground outside the take-out window like dead moths around a bulb. The driver put the cab in park and lit a cigarette, careful to exhale through the cracked window. Caruthers hobbled to the window. The grandfather who always worked the late shift hefted a case of Cabro onto the shelf and set a jumbo bottle of rum beside it. Caruthers paid. The transaction, as always, occurred in silence. Caruthers hefted his goods while the man retreated back to his seat and the black and white television on the table where he'd spend most of his dwindling hours on Earth. The saddest part of all was the eternal pity in his eyes; he felt sorry for Caruthers.

"¿A donde?" the cab driver asked, and Caruthers nudged Max to ask the name of his hotel.

"Well," Max said, waking, eyes on the new liquor. "How about a nightcap, and I'll walk home from your place?"

No, Caruthers meant to say, but "Yeah, why not?" came out. "Rinse the taste of Chucho's warm beer from our mouths."

In his apartment, they sat at the table behind rum over ice. Caruthers, dazed and out of sorts, regarded his drink with dread. No one ever visited his apartment, and he noted the smell of the place, the sharp, yeasty aroma of old alcoholic. Seems that he could have, at some point over the last decade, hung a couple of posters on the walls. Maybe he'd do it, after working that double shift he'd tasked himself with, tomorrow.

Tomorrow, he mused while Max faded into a bloodshot glaze, holding his glass, not drinking. The time was 5:20. Caruthers would be sick tomorrow, today actually. He hated that distinction between today and tomorrow, and how it always occurred to him at times like this. He was going to have to re-regulate his intake. Max kept nodding out toward his drink, catching himself, looking up surprised, smiling, breathing deeply and examining the beverage in his hand.

The kid was jumbling his program, Caruthers concluded. He'd been doing fine, for years, until the boy showed up, bringing with him all this bullshit. Caruthers stirred his drink with his finger, thinking it over until the silent grievance exploded into a revelation, the second over the course of this very night. How about the *kid's* program? Here he was, aided by his own pop, shirking crucial responsibilities, to his church, his decrepit peasants, and his girl. Who was jumbling whom? This sudden reversal of perspective filled him with goodwill and satisfaction, a feeling of wisdom. Something must be done, he decided. The instant called for radical measures, immediate action. A faint voice murmured through the cotton stuffed into his skull, telling him, No, wait on it; now was not the time to make permanent things happen, but a louder voice commanded him to move. Tomorrow it would be too late. He'd be too sober by then.

"Get the fuck out of my house," he growled, rousing himself. Max barely glanced over the rim of his glass, seeing nothing. Caruthers lurched across the table and grabbed the kid's shirt collar with both hands. Rum spilled and Caruthers' chair cracked against the floor. Max woke, staring at Caruthers' wrists under his chin. Caruthers clasped Max's throat, shook him, began to squeeze. Strangling him, belly on the table, Caruthers forgot why he was doing this. Max broke free, gulped air. The smell of spilled rum filled the room.

"What the hell?" Max asked, and cleared his throat. "What are you doing?"

"Out," Caruthers shouted. He turned his back. A crash rang out. Max had upset the table. Caruthers, furious, rushed him, and Max skipped to the side like a matador. Caruthers fell to his knees, hands against the

# A Candle for San Simón

breakfast counter

"Why are you doing this?" Max asked, retreating into the middle of the room, tears running from his eyes.

Caruthers climbed to his feet and made another run. "I'll kill you. I swear if I ever see you again I'll stab your heart out." Max dodged and Caruthers flopped onto his bed, rolled off it, and continued to attack. Broken glass crunched under his tennis shoes. Max ran out the door, and Caruthers followed to the landing. Halfway down the steps, Max stopped, turned. Caruthers leaned hard on the top rail, panting. "You go," he said between gasps. "Don't come back." He extended a finger toward the dark lake.

Max straightened his body, lifted his hat and shook his head, flinging the long hair back. "You're a really, really, profoundly sick man, Norman. I pity you. I truly do." He descended to the bottom of the stairs and started down the strip. Twenty feet away, he wheeled. "I hate you, you piece of trash," he shouted. "I'll kill you if I ever see you again."

And then he ran, full speed down Santander toward the lake. When he was out of sight, Caruthers returned to his room, where he sat on the bed long enough for his thumping heart to slow. He felt righteous and decent, satisfied, and only the slightest bit scared that he'd once again fucked it all up. In this state he collapsed on the covers, shut his eyes, and disappeared.

# Chapter Eighteen

For an insane second, Max thought to leave his room and catch the first Xela bus that came by. It was just after six in the morning, and his vision had narrowed to a spot the size of a human head. His memory of the night was already fleeing like a dream upon waking, fragments shattering into smaller fragments. Had his father really attacked him? Tried to strangle him? Max sat on the bed, clicked on the floor fan, and lay back on the mattress, where he drifted for several hours in and out of consciousness, never quite asleep, never quite awake. Burning light traced the plastic blinds. Occasionally, he sat up, throat so dry it felt like a plastic tube, and he would drink from the two-liter bottle of water he kept on his night stand. He woke shivering, his shirt drenched. He peeled it off, removed his socks and pants, flipped the wet pillow. His hands and feet were pruned. He drank water and fell back into the damp sheets.

The light dimmed, and Max considered food, but thought didn't lead to action. The room darkened, and he fell into deep, dreamless sleep. He woke the next morning, Monday, he calculated. The lucha was a Saturday night event. Sunday was gone, lost forever. He drank the last of the water. His head ached, his hands trembled, and he felt the contours of his stomach, burning faintly. Coffee seemed the logical first step back into the world, but the thought of it caused the acid in his belly to boil up into his chest. "Bad," he said out loud. "Bad, bad." He placed his bare feet on the carpet.

Showering would be a major undertaking; traveling to Xela, tracking down Karma, begging her forgiveness, accepting responsibility for the infant regardless of whether or not Karma forgave him…well, he'd never make it if kept looking that far ahead. Now, he needed to find his towel. He could do that.

Forty-five minutes later, he boarded a Xela bus and found a window seat over the rear passenger-side tire. Water bottle beside him, he opened his Bible to a random passage, Proverbs 31.17. "The eye that mocketh of his father, and despiseth to obey his mother, the ravens of the valley shall pick it out, and the young eagles shall eat it."

He closed the book. Eagles? he thought. It seemed a little much. At Solola, a large group of children in middle school uniforms climbed aboard. A couple of miles later, a police truck pulled alongside the bus, lights flashing. The chatter quieted and stopped. The ayudante looked nervous.

The driver pulled off the narrow, lonely road, overhung with tree limbs. The officer stepped out of his truck, wearing a beige uniform and tri-corn cap. He entered the bus, stood in the aisle before the passengers, and removed his hat. His round face was chubby, his mustache trimmed to a neat line. He fidgeted with the cap held over his belly. "Good afternoon ladies and gentlemen," he began, and then Max lost the thread of meaning. A name arose, Emilio Guzman, and everyone glanced around the bus, looking for Emilio. The officer kept talking, and the passengers turned to each other, smiling, the tension released. Many heads turned toward the back of the bus, where a skinny schoolboy stood at his bench, digging in his front pocket. He came out with a key ring, which he passed to a girl in front of him, and on down the aisle it went, to the officer's hand. He thanked Emilio, and everyone else for their time. He bowed slightly, and replaced his cap. Then he left with the keys, and the bus resumed its journey. Apparently, Emilio's folks were locked out of their place.

From the terminal, a queasy Max laden with his day pack and bottle of water walked an hour through the ugly, smoggy outskirts of Xela, all the way to Karma's school, where he found the front gate locked for siesta. With time to kill, he wandered to the park and settled on a bench in sight of a homeless man, dressed like a wizard in a winter coat whose ragged hem dragged along the ground as he ambled, muttering to himself. He fixed Max with hungry black eyes, and Max looked away.

Max arrived at the school just as Diego, the owner, opened the gate. Middle aged and blocky, he wore thick-rimmed, square glasses. "Welcome back," he said.

"Can I talk to you in the office?" Max asked.

"Of course." Diego led Max through the courtyard and into the building. "Sit," Diego said in Spanish, indicating the chair in front of his desk. "How can I help you?"

"Is Karma working today?" Max asked, in Spanish to show respect.

"No, not today. But if you care to sign up for another week's lessons, I can bring her back."

"No, no. It's not that," he said, reverting to English. "I need to talk to her. It's personal and very important."

Diego examined Max. The room was built of stone, like a castle chamber, with heavy tile flooring and walls of irregular hunks of rock embedded in mortar. "Certainly," Diego said. "I will call and tell her you'd like to talk."

"I want to see her in person, if possible," Max said, while Diego rummaged through a file cabinet.

"No problem. If she wants to see you, you two can work it out."

"Well, the thing is, I'm afraid she'll refuse to talk to me, from pride, but I really want to…I need to help her."

Diego lifted the telephone from the corner of the desk and set it before him. "You need, or she needs?"

"She has a baby, and I'm to blame."

"You work fast, my friend."

"It's not mine." Max briefly explained the situation. "Please," he concluded, "if you could give me her address, I'd never tell her where I got it. My motives are pure, I promise."

"I see." Diego lightly tapped his fingers over the phone buttons. "Go wait in the garden," he said. "I will talk to her and do my best to, how do you say, advocate you? If she agrees to see you, she agrees. If not?" He tilted his head and presented his open palms.

Outside, three pairs worked at tables, the teachers familiar. One of them, a slim, handsome man who always wore a suit, waved. Max waved back.

"Here is the address, amigo," Diego said, standing at Max's elbow. Max accepted the slip of paper.

"Thank you for your help. How did she sound?"

Diego patted Max's shoulder. "I will let you discover this on your own."

"That bad?"

"I didn't say bad. I said nothing. Go. She is home."

On the street, Max stared with longing at the swinging cowboy doors of a cantina on the corner before him. The Billy Joel song "Uptown Girl" played inside, God reminding Max that he was an idiot. He marched on, past single-story boxes of unpainted concrete that rose from weedy yards, down a once-cobbled street reduced to a rocky path. The road smoothed out after a few blocks, and the houses began to show minor signs of affluence, like painted walls, lawns, and fences.

He arrived at a white plaster cube with a second story addition over the left half, the original, lower roof of red tiles, the upper of corrugated tin. Beside the front door, a bronze plaque had been fixed to the wall: "Señor y Señora Muños, 29 Calle de Hannaphu." Max pressed the doorbell, and shortly a man answered, middle height and slim, with black hair wet-combed to his right. His features were fine, and only his small ears seemed to have been passed on to Karma. And perhaps his eyes, though they were hard to see through the black-framed glasses. "Good afternoon," Max said in Spanish. "Is Karma here?"

"Come in," the man said, opening the door, and then unlocking the security gate. "I am Antonio, Karma's father. You must be Max." His voice was calm and clear, like a public radio announcer's. Both Karma's parents were teachers, though Max forgot what subject or grade.

"A pleasure to meet you," Max said, entering a room with matching couches facing each other across a low table. Karma stood beside one of the couches, blowing steam from a white mug. She wore gray athletic tights and a white tee shirt. A man's voice came from upstairs, followed by a woman's, and then footsteps. Karma's father cleared his throat.

"I must return to work," he said. "Adios."

"Finished thinking?" Karma asked in English while Antonio exited through a sliding glass door in the back of the house. "Sit," she said, indicating the couch she faced.

"No," he admitted, leaning forward with elbows on knees, longing to lie flat, like a patient at therapy. "I didn't do much thinking at all. I spent the time drinking, actually. With my father. It didn't turn out so well." Karma sipped her fragrant coffee. "I'm sorry," he said, the words coming out flat, empty, totally insufficient. He had brought no gift, had given no thought to what he'd actually say.

"I'm surprised to see you," she said. "When things get difficult around here, men run to the States. It's always the solution. But for you, the States are always there, waiting. Why haven't you gone yet?"

"I still have business here."

She laughed, shaking her head. "Business. Is that what you call it? I can still see you in my mind, a grown man, running away from a girl and a baby..." She grew somber. "I was mad, but also I envied you. I would like to escape too, but I can't. This is my place, where I belong. I have nowhere else to go. No matter what you say, what you think, you're just a tourist here."

# A Candle for San Simón

Max had felt on the verge of weeping all day, a familiar effect of the worst hangovers, and now the tears fell, from pure shame. They embarrassed him, and the embarrassment added to the shame, and he cried, face crumpled, shoulders jerking.

"Don't..." she said, her voice gone soft, the voice she used for the baby. Max, blind, crawled from the couch, around the table toward Karma, and clutched her legs. "Come on," she said. "It's okay."

He kissed her knees, arms around her calves, sobbing, so aroused he thought he'd come from a few dry thrusts against her bare feet.

"Max, that's enough." She pushed him back, and he smiled, on his knees before her, wiping the tears and snot from his face. "Sit." She patted the cushion beside her.

He tucked his dick against his stomach as he took the seat, and sighed, head back, his whole body tender, electrified by desire and shame. "Sorry," he said, once the spasm had passed. "That was weird."

She shrugged.

"Did you find somewhere for, for him?" he asked, glancintg up at the ceiling where voices and footsteps sounded.

"Not yet. He's sleeping in my room. In the cradle I slept in when I was a baby. My sister was using it for her new one, but she's old enough for a bed now."

"Is he okay?"

"Yes. He's well. We're calling him 'Roddy.' My father says he looks like a Rodolpho. They'll probably change his name wherever they take him, but we have to call him something. We took him to the doctor. He's healthy, approximately four months old. We thought of inventing a birthday, but he'll be gone before he's one, so the orphanage can choose their own. We called another home in Guate, but it's the same there as here, too many babies, not enough people to care for them. The waiting list is the best option. He could get adopted by rich gringos. Who knows?"

Footsteps thumped from above, and a curly-headed man appeared at the back of the house. He glanced over at Max and Karma, and then exited through the sliding doors without a greeting. "My brother in law," Karma said. She seemed about to continue, but she let it go. "So you're here," she said instead. "Now what?"

"Can I?" he asked, moving toward her for a hug.

She sighed, shook her head softly, and opened her arms. Holding her, he kissed her neck, her ear, and finally, her mouth. She returned the kiss, and he slid his hand down her body, over her breasts, and, losing himself to the hunger, between her legs. She moaned quietly, and whispered in his ear. "Not now…"

He removed his hand and pulled away. "Sorry."

"Don't say sorry for that," she continued to whisper, caressing him through his jeans. "I want it too, but we have to wait."

"Yes," he said.

"Right now we need to talk about what comes next. What are we going to do?"

His passion waned, and he sat back as the shame returned, but fainter now. "I'm not sure, but I want, I need, to do what I can for the baby. I think I should take him back to Zunilito." He looked over at her, scared to take the next step, but not too scared. "I understand if you've had enough, of me and that place, but I want you with me." He couldn't read her face. "It won't be forever, and maybe after…" He looked away, shocked at what he'd been about to say, something about taking her with him back to the States after his mission, the ultimate gringo trump card.

"Okay," she said, staring evenly at him while the whining of a baby came from the back of the house. "You made one mistake, a pretty bad one, but I'll give you another chance." He turned away, squeezing back a new wave of tears. Before coming to Guatemala, he'd rarely cried since childhood, but he was making up for it today.

He breathed in deeply and exhaled in a long, calming release. He thought of the words in English, but then said them in Spanish: "I think I love you."

# II.

# Chapter Nineteen

Sundays, the residents of Zunilito crowded into the dead man's hut. On the occasion of Max's sixth week pastoring, rain hammered the roof and the sky was dark as night. Candles burned on the floor along the walls, and coals glimmered in the fire pit beside the cauldron that filled the room with wet heat and the smell of boiled meat, corn, and smoke.

"Good morning," Max said. "Can I ask you a favor? Please look this way and smile?" He raised the phone he'd brought from America, useless except as a camera. Plugging the phone into his laptop down in Pana or Xela, where he could find Wi-Fi, he'd posted pictures of the villagers, individually and in small groups, always outside working or hanging around, but Kent wanted shots of them in "church," praying, singing, listening, reading bibles… evidence that Max, and by extension everyone who sent money, was helping to improve their lives materially *and* spiritually—that, in short, the money was paying dividends, spreading Good News. Max clicked the button, freezing the room in white light and then plunging them back into dimness. "Thank you," he said.

Only Reina and Karma understood what it meant for their images to appear online, the amount of people and the kinds of people who would see them and the thoughts and feelings the pictures were designed to evoke—mainly pity. Max himself could not fully imagine the uses his posts might be put to in the vastness of the Internet. It was best the villagers remained ignorant, since knowing would only upset these private, simple folks.

The morning's talk centered on Philippians 2:13, Paul's letter from prison, randomly selected as always by Max's blind finger method. The letter endorsed hard work and humility, a message hardly relevant to Max's hard working, humble flock. Probably he should have chosen again, or given up the random choosing and actually read the Bible like a real minister, but he didn't know the Bible well enough to invent sermons from his head, and he didn't have the time or inclination to read it cover to cover. Besides, if the Bible really was the word of God—and of course it was—then every part should speak to every person. Today's challenge was to extract the nut from the shell.

He still had time to find the seam, the application of the chapter to his congregation. Everyone was eating, talking softly with one another. In the back row, Reina—lately become a typically sullen teenager—sat beside Karma, who was feeding the baby from a bottle. Max watched them unnoticed from his preacher corner, the good book stuffed with notes clasped in both hands before him. Karma had come to call the boy Rudy, a variation of the name her father had given him, but Max for no good reason referred to him as Beau, Beau the Baby, Baby Beau, just a nickname. Not that either name mattered much in the long run. Tomorrow, Monday, the first of November, they would finally meet with the head sister at Casa Luz Maria, who would finally settle the child's identity and place in the world, as an orphan.

While the parishioners ate, Max idly pondered his own future. Karma had begun to lose patience, with the mission, and, he feared, with him by extension. She hadn't said anything yet, but he could sense the dissatisfaction, boredom really, and he could hardly blame her. Their first month in Zunilito had tumbled by on a buzz of love, lust, and the plain weirdness of life in a primitive society. The sex took place in quasi secrecy, somehow both passionate and wholesome, natural in any event. As for sins of the flesh, he forgave himself. Jesus knew better than anyone that some sins were worse than others, and that touching and

# A Candle for San Simón

being touched by the one you love surely ranked low on His list, regardless of what some celibate priest might declare from his gilded pulpit. And if he and Karma eventually married, as he'd begun to hope and plan for, then all would be well that ended well. The prospect, of marriage, excited and scared him, as did the fact that he had no idea if Karma would agree to a proposal. She liked the words, "I love you," in English and in Spanish; she liked to say them and hear them, but she also had a habit of reminding him—just at that point of losing themselves in each other—that they hadn't been together long; that they didn't know one another, not yet, not really; that they might as well come from two separate planets in terms of their differing backgrounds; that shacking up in the mountains was one thing, real life was another. Sure, she was right, but who cared? Had love ever been about being right?

If anything, life in the village complicated the courtship. The cold and filth wore on them. Karma had begun to wonder out loud what they were doing, what they hoped to accomplish in this place, aside from pleasing Pastor Kent, whom Karma had come to mock. Max agreed that Sunday services weren't much, but the chimney project was going to save lives. His own brick oven and chimney even now funneled cook smoke up and out of the hut, a small, vital improvement. His goal was to install one in every hut, and in the process teach the others how to do it for themselves on future huts, improving the health of this village forever—or for however long the village lasted. He was now on the third chimney, and each time through got a little faster, a little smoother, the end product a little tighter.

While he worked on the huts, Karma taught English to the young ones (preparing them for life outside the village, and thus planting the seeds of the community's demise). Max had eight more months to give to Kent, a length of time that made him want to go back to bed and sleep until it was over. If they—he and Karma—survived it together, they'd do so day by day, not by looking toward the end. Their reward, endlessly played out in daydreams while Max trimmed bricks with a dull machete, would be clean cool sheets, hot showers, coffee, meat, and as much privacy as they wanted. No babies crying. No giggling children spying through the cracks in the wall. Tomorrow, after dropping Beau at his new home, they'd get a preview of the future, in the form of a hotel room. Max already had one in mind, half a block off the central park in Xela, three stars in his guidebook, expensive by local standards at twenty-five dollars a night. Large rooms, high ceilings, a central garden the size of a basketball court, lush with tropical trees and plants. They needed it, fuel to get them through the coming months, also something good to balance the way it was going to feel giving Beau away, whom they'd naturally grown to love. Besides, Max's posts had been a hit, and donations had been coming in strong. A modest travel budget was perfectly just. He could only spend so much on soup and bricks.

Across the room, the baby smiled from Karma's lap at Max, innocent of the coming treachery. Max had to look away. He'd decided not to mention the child to Kent, just as he'd kept Reina's age a secret, along with her recent moodiness and questionable motives. Kent didn't want complications; he wanted pictures and stories for Facebook, of success, saved souls, happy new Christians. Social media salvation. If Max did confide in Kent, he felt sure his pastor would talk him into adopting the child, the best Facebook story of all, for everyone except Max and Karma. Even Beau would probably be better off with the nuns. To send him to the orphanage was the right decision, though it felt pretty damn wrong.

The soup gone, everyone settled on the rugs and grew quiet. Max lifted his bible. "Today," he said in Spanish, nearly shouting to be heard over the rain drumming the roof, "we talk about Paul's letter to the Philippians. Paul writes the letter from prison. Why is he in prison? Only because he is Christian."

Max felt an unusual interest from the assemblage. He looked over the faces before him and settled on Reina, frowning deeply, agitated. She hadn't eaten, but nothing new there. Based on his own tortured eighth-grade year, Max figured she was mooning over a boy who didn't care about her at all. She surely didn't care about Paul's troubles in prison. The letter, Max explained as well as he could, was about how everyone should work for others and not just for themselves. It also cautioned not to complain or boast. "Jesus," he read from the notes Karma had helped him write, "could have gone around telling everyone that he was the son of God, but he didn't. He let them think he was just a carpenter."

Max considered mentioning that he too was a carpenter back in the States, but to compare himself to Jesus clearly cut against Paul's lesson of humility. The problem was that Max had nothing else to say. Out of notes, he looked around the room, like Pastor Kent would sometimes do to draw out the drama, only Max had no payoff, no more ammo, just another empty chamber. Back when he'd started giving these sermons, he'd encouraged questions, which led to painful silence broken only by his own sad pleading. Now everyone just waited until he was done, and then went home.

The exception to this indifference had been the first sermon, when Filomena, one of the unofficial leaders and a soothsayer in the village, had asked him who wrote the book, meaning the Bible. God, Max had answered, but then he'd felt compelled to explain further, that God had written it through many different people over time. Paul had written a lot of it. This recollection, standing there now without anything to say, inspired him to ramble. Who was this man in prison? he asked. What gave him the right to tell others how to be? Well, Paul used to be a disbeliever, a persecutor of Christians, just as he himself was later persecuted. He was an enemy of Christ who became Christ's biggest supporter. How? What happened to change his mind? It's hard to explain. He was walking along and the spirit of the Lord appeared before him, and he knew right then and there on that dusty road, without question or doubt, Jesus was Lord.

"Amen," he said.

"Amen," some of the others repeated.

Standing before them, Max relived the moment of his own revelation. It had come upon him, not on Sunday during the service but the next day at work. He'd been alone, a hundred feet back from the rest of the crew, redoing the sloppy work of a couple of smartass apprentices. The day had been sunny and cool, and he'd been chewing on resentment. The apprentices, two friends who'd gotten the job together, were mouthy, sarcastic, always dragging ass. One of them was the son of a state senator, and the other was his buddy, both slumming for summer money before starting college and the easy life. Probably, they'd use this time on the road crew for working man's cred the rest of their lives. Max, for his part, worked slowly, punishing the foreman for making him clean up the kids' mess. Bored and alone, he began replaying Kent's sermon of the day before. Then words came, not from his head but from the air, spoken in a deep voice that wasn't Kent's. Max had never been surer of anything, and he hadn't doubted since. God had picked that moment to speak directly to him, his lowly servant. *Forgive them, for they know not what they do.* A familiar line of course, but that day it made the hair stand up on his arms. Jesus Christ, a man in the midst of horrendous torture, said this to God, his father, the one who'd put him there on the cross. His own father! And now God, the father, both forgiver and forgiven, was delivering the same message to Max. Love your enemies, no matter who they are, no matter their crimes. He'd wept, helplessly, with joy and sorrow, joy from God's love and sorrow at how far Max was from Him and would always be.

Before he could form any of this into words, Filomena and her husband Baffi stood, and everyone else followed their lead. Max had paused too long. Oh well. It was probably for the best. Everyone ambled out, offering smiles and good days before braving the mud and rain back to their huts, while Max stood there nodding, feeling as always like a fraud. Soon everyone was gone except Karma, Beau, and Reina, who approached, biting her lip and looking to the side, waiting in the style of her people for Max to make the first move.

"Yes? Do you have a question about the service?"

"I need to go north," she mumbled. "I tried to wait, but I can't."

"North," Max repeated, looking down at her, his Bible awkward in his hands, big and chunky with nowhere to rest except the floor. "It's not paradise," he said. "America won't solve your problems. It'll create a lot of new ones. Plus, you have your people to think about."

"I'm scared," she said, and looked up at him, crying. Aside from small children, she was the second Mayan he'd seen cry. The first had been a woman weeping and hitting her thighs with her fists as she walked along a dirt road outside of Pana. Max had imagined the woman had lost a child. "Maria," Reina said, "a girl from my class—my friend. They took her on the way to school. They killed her father, her brother."

Max fidgeted with the Bible, the worn, soft cover, the dog-eared pages. He didn't know what to say, except that he was not qualified for this job. He was a carpenter, not a pastor. He could build chimneys, but that was all.

"They brought her to the prison, to give her to the men in there," Reina continued. "She was inside for three days before they let her out. She doesn't talk anymore. All the girls are afraid they'll be next."

Max squeezed the book until his fingers hurt, resisting the urge to fling it across the room. These people, he thought, these men he kept hearing about, were worse than animals. How could God have made them? How could God allow them to exist?

"They won't bother you," he said, lying to get through the moment. "I promise."

"How can you stop them?" Reina asked. "You don't understand. It's not just them. The boys in school want to join them, want to be them, and the girls want to be their girlfriends. They threaten the teachers, make them pay to get into the building in the morning. If you won't join them, they'll take you anyway, and if you do join them, their enemies will try to kill you. I can't go there anymore, but I can't stay here either. There's nothing for me to do."

"I…" Max said, "I'm sorry. No. I can't believe that. That can't be possible. That can't be happening at a public school."

"You want me to take you?" she asked, and he detected something new in her voice and on her face, a provocation, defiant and bitterly knowing. He wondered if she was a virgin, if she'd been raped already. She was so small, so skinny, he simply wouldn't accept it.

"Isn't there someone," he asked, "an authority?"

She was shaking her head, barely listening now.

"I'll do what I can," Max said. "I'll ask Pastor Kent. I'll recommend you. Maybe he can, I don't know, get you some kind of visa. There's got to be someone who can help. Don't they have amnesty programs for this kind of thing?"

"Are you asking me? How can I know? I'm just a girl. You're the gringo."

"Don't worry," he said. "I'll talk to someone."

"Yes," she said, and looked at the door. "Someone. I need to tell you, I will leave here if you can't help."

"Don't run away. It's not the answer. It'll just make everything worse."

"I won't run. I'll fight. Another friend from school, his father. Some others." She looked up at Max, that cold, challenging hardness in her eyes. "Something is going to happen, and if I'm still here, I will join them."

She walked out, plastic sandals sinking into the mud, her hair plastered to her head by the drops. The door swung closed. Max turned to Karma, still in the back of the room, bouncing Beau on her knee, pretending not to have heard the conversation, the way Guatemalans, accustomed to close quarters, got their privacy. "Teenagers," he said. "I hope she doesn't do anything stupid."

Karma glanced up. "I'll talk to her," she said. "Take him." She held Beau up, and Max scooped him burbling into his arms.

"What are you going to say?" he asked, while the child chewed on the shoulder of his shirt.

"I have no idea." She walked to the door. "First I want to know if she's telling the truth or making a story."

"Maybe you should ask Filomena," he said, and chuckled, hoping to lighten the mood. Filomena, the mystic, foresaw the future by scattering a bag-full of sacred knickknacks onto the floor and interpreting the results. Karma paused in the doorway, a cascade from the roof like a glass wall behind her.

"Maybe you should open up your little book and poke your finger in it."

# Chapter Twenty

The SUV was white, a Chevy Suburban with no plates, a vehicle he recognized from nightmares, though he'd always imagined it black. He sat in the aisle seat, Karma and Beau at the window. School children in uniform took up most of the other seats, relatively wealthy kids heading toward a private school somewhere up ahead. Max's vision grew sharp. A strap from his bag hung from the overhead rack, swaying. The bus driver's music, another narco ballad, barely covered the silence underneath; boxes of baby chicks filled the luggage racks, crying, cheep-cheep-cheep, and filling the bus with a barnyard smell. The air outside the windows was so clear, even under the gloomy sky and in the shadow of the forest, the trees practically twinkled.

Ahead, a thick tree had fallen across the road, and so the bus slowed, then stopped. No one moved until the ayudante climbed out of the open front door and up onto the roof, while behind them both front doors of the SUV opened like wings. Men emerged, dressed in bulky combat fatigues, complete with helmets and face masks, rifles slung diagonally across their chests. They came toward the bus, and the smaller of the two signaled with his gun for the driver to open the door. The driver hesitated, but then complied, and the two men opened fire. Max threw his arms over Karma and Beau, buried his face in Karma's hair, but not before witnessing blood flying about the front of the bus, mingling with shards of glass and plastic while the sounds of the shots exploding from the weapons and smashing into metal rang out, drowning the music, the cheeping chicks, and the screams that rose from the passengers.

The gunfire stopped. The chicks had gone silent or were too quiet to register over the cries of the humans or the ringing in Max's ears. The music continued as before, the tuba honking behind the boasts of men glorifying deeds like those just committed. Max opened his eyes, head to the side against Karma's hair. The killers scanned the passengers from the front of the bus, surrounded by blood and music. One of them pointed his gun at the ceiling and commenced to fire. He walked forward, spraying bullets as gardeners spray for weeds. Max again hid his face in Karma's hair, as if it would protect him, as if his soft arms and body would protect her and the baby. The firing stopped, followed by a mechanical clicking sound—a cartridge discarded and replaced—and then the job continued, closer to Max until the gunman brushed him with his elbow. They were after the ayudante, Max understood, just a kid with the wrong job.

The shots stopped, Max's ears rang with the echoes. "No, no, no," came a girl's cries, standing out from the general screams of terror. The larger of the gunmen had one of the school girls by her thick, long hair, and was dragging her into the aisle. She'd been chosen, Max knew, for her beauty. Max himself had noticed her, singled her out for the same reason the killer had. Her legs, bare between her skirt bottom and high socks, kicked as she slid up the aisle, grabbing at seat backs and writhing hopelessly.

White fire blazed through Max's veins, a feeling of power, the power of righteousness. He'd never felt such pure, immediate conviction, and he stood, and he shouted as loud as he could: "Stop," he said in English, his head nearly touching the riddled ceiling, breathing deeply the sulfur smell of spent bullets. "She's a child."

Everything did stop, except the music. The girl stared at him, as did the masked creature still clutching her hair. He let go of her, freeing his hand to take up the gun. Max would not cower, would not close his eyes.

If this was the end, so be it. The spirit had not left him. *Stay with me*, Max begged. The man raised the gun to his shoulder and took aim. His partner came into view then, passing Max to stand between him and the other. He raised a fist and executed some kind of signal, and then whirled on Max. The bigger man resumed dragging the girl down the aisle and off the bus.

The feeling of power, The Spirit, floated away as quickly as it had come, and he couldn't help cringing under the gaze of the monster before him, faceless behind the mask and orange-tinted goggles. Karma tugged at his pants to get him to sit, though now it was too late. He heard her whimper, and Beau cried thinly. "Come." The voice from behind the mask surprised him, the high pitch of a woman or a boy. Max didn't move. The gun barrel moved from him to Karma, and she let go of his pants to cower over Beau. The song stopped, and the chicks began again their sweet calls. Max stepped into the aisle, arms raised. Once begun, the rest was easy. He walked as if controlled by some other power, toward the mess at the front and the body full of leaking holes slumped to the side against the shattered window.

Down the steps as if floating over them like a ghost, he continued to the SUV, around its open passenger door to where the larger gunman kneeled between the legs of the girl, pulling on his belt. Her head was turned as far as possible to the side, and both arms clutched her open shirt to her chest. The gunman had removed his helmet and mask, revealing a shaved head. His rifle lay on the grass, and he unbuttoned his pants. Max stood by, no longer brave, just another mortal afraid to die, ready to do as he was told. The rapist wore a soul patch that met a sculpted chin beard, and a tattooed X marked each cheek. The gun barrel of Max's kidnapper moved from him to the rapist, and it lightly tapped his bald head. He turned, nostrils flared in surprise and anger, and the gun went off. A black hole appeared on the man's cheek, above an X, like a piece of mud had landed there, while the back of his head flew away in a puff of red mist. The expression of surprise on the man's face shifted to indignation, as he teetered and fell with a wet sound onto the screaming girl. Stars twinkled before Max's eyes. He clutched the hood of the vehicle so he wouldn't fall.

"Go," said the woman who'd just blown away her partner. "Around the front. Move!'

His vision cleared, and he followed her orders. From the driver's side door, he saw the bus, normal, peaceful even, viewed from behind. He raised his hand in salute, to say goodbye before sliding in behind the steering wheel. His door slammed shut, and the back door opened. In the rearview mirror appeared the black mask, the orange lens. "Go. Around the bus, and to the right of the fallen tree. There's a way through." She spoke English well, with an accent. The keys hung from the ignition. He turned them, put the vehicle in drive, and pulled forward. In the rearview mirror, he read the bus's marquee, XELA, each letter in a different color, red, blue, orange, green. The windshield was shattered and tinted red. Following orders, he maneuvered around the tree, and pulled back onto the road, which curved away into the forest. The SUV smelled new, like fresh plastic. He winced as the person in back moved, but she was only removing her helmet and mask. In the mirror, he saw the familiar face of a beautiful woman, with high cheek bones, thick lips, arresting tawny eyes, and a short, messy haircut. "Mad Max," she said, smiling. "I thought I might see you again, but not like this."

He nodded his head, gulping air.

"It's too bad that Hector back there was so excited to get to the bus, he went without me, and that crazy ass bus driver was packing. Shot Hector right through his mask. Lucky fucking shot. By the time I capped him, it was too late. You hear what I'm saying to you?"

Max continued to nod his head.

"Say, 'yes, I understand what happened back there at the bus.'"

Max cleared his throat of the phlegm that had gathered there, and then shook his head, to get it to function. "Yes, I understand."

"So tell me. What happened? What do you remember?"

Max's couldn't find any words.

"Come on, man. I know you're no genius. The way you stood up for that girl. Holy shit." She was laughing. "'Stop,'" she said, mocking the white man's accent, "'she's only a child!' Oh boy. I was thinking, who this guy think he is? Captain America?"

Max licked his dry lips. "What was the question?"

She shook her head, and he blinked at the road, vaguely aware of the harsh tingling in his hands. "What happened back there in the bus," she said. "What you're going to say if any of my men ask you about it. Come on, dude. Work with me."

"The bus driver. He shot your partner."

"Hey. There you go."

"And then you shot him. The driver."

"Muy bien," she said. "You're not so dumb after all. Not so smart, but not so dumb either. Behave and you might make it out. No promises though. You're most definitely in some deep shit. If you weren't such a handsome little gringo, and if Hector wasn't such a pain in my ass, you'd be seriously dead already."

Max drove in silence for a long stretch, out of the forest and down into a valley. Smoke rose from the chimney of a small farmhouse about a mile ahead. It felt strange to be driving again after so many months as a passenger or pedestrian, especially piloting this large, new vehicle. The gangsters had seen fit to place a pine-shaped air freshener on the rearview mirror. The time, digitally displayed on the dash, was 11:11. The date happened to be 11.1, which he knew because it was the date of their appointment with the head nun at Luz Maria. He concentrated on keeping the speed at forty.

When the clock blinked to 11:30, the woman, Vicki, told him to pull off onto a dirt road cutting through low scrubland. No car had passed in either direction. He'd feared cops, a roadblock, something that would prompt her to put the gun to his head or just blow him away. He now drove at thirty miles an hour, dragging a cloud of dust. "Stop by those trees," she said. He avoided looking in the mirror. He didn't want to see her, didn't want her to see him seeing her, didn't want to recognize or remember her, the combat boots and tight shorts, her mysterious connection to his dad, the taste of her painted onto his lips. All this knowledge scared him. He tried to come up with a reason why this shouldn't matter but couldn't find it. At least Karma and Beau were safe. At least the school girl was safe, if traumatized. Better to die for a reason than for none, if he had to die anyway. He stopped and put the SUV in park. "Turn off the engine," she said, and climbed out. She opened his door, and he took a long look at her eyes, so light they looked artificial. Perhaps they were contacts. She had him face the SUV, hands behind his back. She secured his wrists with a plastic zip tie. Next, she pulled a sack over his head that cinched around his neck. The fabric, which smelled new, drew into his face when he inhaled, and moved away when he exhaled.

"Come," she said, taking his arm and leading him toward the back of the SUV. "Down," she said, and pushed him softly so that he fell to his knees and almost toppled. "You believe in God?" she asked, and he nodded. "Time to pray." The fabric moved rapidly into his mouth and out, and he tried to contact God but wasn't able to find any words or thoughts. A sound came from very near his right ear, the unmistakable clatter of a pistol being loaded and cocked. The shot rang out before he could compose a single word, and he hunched down into himself, waiting for the pain and hot wet blood and for everything to end and the next thing to begin, but all that came through, all that happened, was laughter. "I'm sorry," she said, chuckling, "but that was pretty funny. Okay, up."

She ushered him into the cargo area in the back of the SUV and slammed the hatch. A door opened and closed, and the engine started.

They pulled back into the road. "You're in a dog cage," she told him. "So don't get any stupid ideas. We bought it at a Pet Smart. Isn't that some shit? I didn't even know they had them down here. You got Pet Smarts where you're from?"

"Yes," he said. "We have them." She didn't say anything else. A minute later, music came, more accordion, snare drum and wailing taunts, a cross between polka and gangster rap. A moment later, she clicked off the stereo.

"I'm sick of that shit," she muttered. "Got to get me some good music one of these days." After a pause, she asked, "What kind of music you listen to, güerito?"

A shock of fear ran through him, a sense that his answer would bring consequences.

"Hello?" she asked.

"I don't know," he said. "I don't listen to music much anymore. I used to like rock and metal, but I haven't bought any new music in years."

"I know what you mean. Getting old. Shit."

The ride lasted a long time, through changes in road texture, stops and turns, traffic noise and silence. "We're almost there," she said. "You better remember what happened back there, or you're a dead man. And I shouldn't have to tell you this, but I will anyways. Today is the first day we ever met. ¿Comprende, güero?"

"Comprendo," he said.

Several turns later, the car stopped. She got out and talked with various men, loudly, excitedly. Someone shouted curses, and the hatch opened. Max's captors dragged him out of the cage and goose-stepped him across gravel, one on each arm. Maybe a hundred steps later, they stopped, and one of them let go of an arm. A clicking and then squealing of rusty hinges. The hollow boom of metal on metal. He was led up a single step into an echoing room that smelled of rust. The hood came off, the door shut, a bolt slid into its slot, and a padlock clicked. The room, a steel storage unit like he knew from jobsites, was square, steel, eight-foot cubed. Small holes, put there by bullet or drill, let in fingers of light from around the top of the walls, too high for him to look through.

He walked the perimeter, clockwise, and after a long while, reversed direction. He wondered if he'd ever see Karma again, and he played in his mind, over the over, the moment he'd decided to stand up. Would they have killed the girl, or just raped her? he wondered, trying to account for his action, trying to decide whether he'd been brave or, as Vicki had said, stupid, whether he'd saved a life or was going to get himself killed over, over what? Chastity? Honor? Psychological trauma? He wanted out of there; he didn't want to die.

Pacing, images penetrated his mind's eye, the pictures and videos he'd browsed, giving in to a sick curiosity, on the Internet one night before coming to Guatemala, searching the subject of gang violence in Central America and Mexico. He tried to fight off the mental parade of brutality, but the grisly scenes redoubled their attacks, coming at him like wolves. A certain video took hold. Max attempted to dispel it by talking to Jesus, but the image was too strong, too vivid, unrelenting. The video had been recorded and posted by the torturers themselves, a way to brag and to threaten. It featured a man, bound arms and legs, being beaten to death by two masked men with aluminum baseball bats. They hit his body only, keeping him conscious through the long process of his slow and excruciating death. At one point the desperate captive violently began to jerk his torso at the hips and waist, the only movement afforded him. The effect was to flop across the floor like an enraged worm while his executioners watched, waiting for him to tire himself out so they could resume. Disgusted, Max had told himself that the victim was a ruthless criminal himself, but that didn't matter. No one deserved to suffer like that.

Even the men beating him? he now thought, pacing clockwise. Didn't they deserve to get what they were giving? An eye for an eye? If they'd ever had any humanity, a single molecule of decency, they'd traded it away at some point, and for what? A new truck? A sense of power? Women? A pocketful of cash? Did they believe in God? Surely not, since they'd know that hell awaited them, eternal torture that rendered their own cruelty mild. God, Max couldn't avoid thinking, all-loving, omnipotent, was the ultimate torturer, if you landed on His wrong side.

After the horror had its way with him, Max sat with his back against a wall, worn out. Mind blank, he filled it with a new picture, he sitting at a table across from Jesus, long haired and bearded like in the pictures, but wearing modern clothes, an old concert tee shirt too faded to read. They talked about music. Jesus didn't have a single favorite band, but he didn't like them all equally either. PJ Harvey was pretty great, he said, and Max asked Jesus if anyone had ever told him he looked just like Dave Grohl of the Foo Fighters. Everybody says that, Jesus responded, smiling gently, even shyly.

The conversation covered all the subjects that came to Max's mind— his history with women, the invisible wall between him and his mother, his father of course, Karma, Pastor Kent, young Reina, Beau the baby. Max rooted for the San Diego Chargers, no matter how bad they always were, no matter how frustrating football had become, games regularly decided by pass interference penalties that should or shouldn't have been called. He complained about the government bureaucracy that put him out of work, which led him in turn to come down here, where he'd likely be killed. He wasn't saying that he wished he hadn't come, or that he could predict the future. Only God knew. They were just talking. After a long while, they stood from the table, and Max lay on his side in the cell, hugging himself against the cooling steel, and they walked outside, to stroll side-by-side along a dirt trail edged in grass through sun-dappled woods he'd seen in story books. The woods grew denser and darker as they walked, and the path led Max to sleep.

# Chapter Twenty-One

Back and forth, they rode, endlessly and pointlessly. What a scene, Caruthers thought, these poor bastards and their tedious lives. He laughed out loud, drawing attention from the tourists sitting nearby. "We have a lot in common," he explained, waving toward the racers. The tourists pretended not to have heard.

He sat on the hillside with a view down upon the famous horserace of Todos Santos Cuchumatán. The occasion was the annual All Saints Festival, which Caruthers and most other highlands bus drivers forwent their usual routes to serve. Today was the final day of the festival, and since nobody was leaving until after the race, Caruthers figured to kill time by watching the show, letting Seba nap in the bus. The spectacle was a hoot, though depressing if he thought too much. To call it a race was to call lucha a sport. The racers to a man were drunk, and no one actually won anything. This was an elaborate drinking game, and Caruthers participated by following a single rider, and downing a gulp of beer in solidarity with him each time he reached one end of the track or the other, a course about half the length of a football field. The drinking and riding had been going on since morning and wouldn't stop until every last rider had dropped from his saddle onto the churned dirt below. The sky was clear, the mountain weather mild and cool. The travel warning having grown stale, a hoard of tourists had come for the party.

He killed his beer and climbed to his feet. He had to take a leak, for one thing, and the senselessness and debauchery of the race—so familiar—had grown dull. Maybe he'd find enough early exiters to fill the bus. Halfway between the race track and the village, he came to a wooden shack of a cantina, where he pushed through the swinging cowboy doors and entered the dim, fusty interior. Two old men sat at a table fashioned of raw lumber, and a young boy stood behind a sheet of plywood on saw horses. "¿Baño?" Caruthers asked the boy, who cut his eyes to the left, a barely perceptible motion in the thin wedges of light slicing across the room through gaps in the wall slats. Inside the bathroom, an invisible mist of urine burned his eyes, emanating from a wide concrete trough. Cockroaches squirmed about in his piss, apparently delighted, and Caruthers, who had seen worse, gagged. He finished, rinsed his hands and tried to shake them dry. He hadn't expected the Ritz, but soap and a towel would have been nice.

"Ron," he said to the boy. There was something about entering a bar and ordering a drink. What was it? Potential. Something might happen, starting from the moment the bartender poured the shot until the drinker walked out, and the longer he stayed, the greater the chance. The fact was, nothing much ever happened, and when something did, it was usually bad. But at least there was that chance, which was more than he could say for life outside the bar. "Copita," he clarified. The boy poured the alcohol into a mood-fucking plastic cup of the sort teenagers learned to drink from, and Caruthers threw it back, winced, and placed a coin on the bar. Outside, the scent of burning trash drifted by, along with a tinge of vomit in the general beer vapor, and yet, the air smelled pine fresh compared to that fetid pisser. Perhaps that explained the First World craving for the seedy. Without experiencing the dirty, nobody ever felt truly clean.

His bus stood with half a dozen others lined up along the highway, colorful as a graffiti contest. Inside, he found Seba—a fat, aloof cat— dozing on the wide bench in back. "Think I can pull us out of here?" he asked. Seba yawned. They were penned in pretty good.

# A Candle for San Simón

Seba sat up. "We going?" Caruthers tossed him the fortified thermos and started the engine. Once out on the main road, he'd wait to gather a few fares. Even without them, he didn't want to deal with the exodus traffic. The engine revved as he pumped the clutch, unable to jam it into gear. Finally he managed to slide into second gear, which offered just enough traction to bounce forward a few feet, up to the butt of the bus before him. "Not good," Seba informed him. They'd made it up the mountain in a cloud of burning clutch, the last hill the bus would climb without a trip to the shop. He fought the machine until sweat soaked the collar and pits of his shirt, but he made it out onto the road and pointing in the right direction.

The trip down was an exercise in braking and coasting, but in spite of the rattletrap state of his vehicle, Caruthers had a full load by the time they hit the level ground of the highland plateau. In Momostenango, a few fares hopped off and a few more entered, but they left him, every last one, the first chance they got after he had to kill the engine at a stoplight and start it, lurching, in first gear. Dispirited, he replaced the Pana sign with Fuera de Servicio, and limped home, the sweat that soaked his shirt never drying. By the time he rolled into the space behind La Mala, he and Seba knew tomorrow would be a day off. Unable to find the initiative to get up from his seat, he turned toward Seba, in the front passenger-side seat, arms resting on the horizontal bar that separated the bench from the steps. "What am I supposed to do now?" he asked.

Seba grinned, casting his eyes over La Mala, a lob to Cruz's offices.

"That's one option. Not a good one, but it's an option." The other was to give up the whole enterprise, sell the bus and route for whatever pittance he could get and catch a ride north, throw himself on the mercy of his native land, a zone notably short on mercy for the poor, but what did he expect? Likely he'd end up on the street, his humiliation absolute. Sitting in the broken bus with Seba, this option gathered a perverse appeal, the final degradation. Here I am, America, your problem now. "I don't know, Seba, but I'd look for another job if I were you." Caruthers counted out fifty percent of the day's earnings, reconsidered, and gave the whole of it to him, a sad little pension. "Wish I could have done better by you, my friend."

"No problem," Seba said in English, one of the few phrases in his repertoire. He stood, slipped the money into his pocket, and walked out. "Adios, Jefe," he said, back turned, one hand waving goodbye over his shoulder.

In La Mala, Red actually had a few customers beyond the regulars, two of the six tables occupied, as well as five seats at the bar, creating a general hum of conversation that covered Caruthers' entrance. Both ends of the bar were occupied, leaving a blank spot in the middle, where Caruthers sat.

"Norman," Red said, popping a Cabro and sliding it his way. He leaned toward Caruthers and spoke softly. "Don't get too comfortable." Caruthers put the bottle to his lips as Red fished something from his back pocket and set it before him, white paper covered in small blue squares, folded in two. Caruthers didn't want to open it. No, he wanted to stand and walk out the door, enter his bus, and drive away, and he likely would have done just that if the bus actually ran. "A young woman known to your boy came in here a hour or so ago, all in a huff." Red was leaning toward Caruthers but faced to the side, looking over toward the corner where the back door was. "Had this cute little baby in her arms like a ragdoll. She asked for you, and I told her you'd be in later. She wrote this out, practically breaking her pen. Hope you can read it. Didn't order a drink. Asked if I had an envelope and I said no. The craziest thing, she told me not to read what she wrote, told me if I read it, I'd be sorry. Trust me, she said, so serious she actually spooked me a little." Red smiled.

Caruthers tipped the beer back, chugged half, and replaced it on the napkin. "Little glass of rum, please," he said. When Red turned his back to fetch the booze, Caruthers opened the note.

"Ah, Max," he muttered, staring at the bottle in his hand. "You stepped in it this time, didn't you?"

Red served the drink, and then took a little tour from behind the bar to visit the tables. He did that sometimes, even though it wasn't expected of a bartender, one of the reasons Caruthers liked coming here, good service. He swallowed the drink and finished his beer, tasting nothing, not even the heat of the rum. He counted out some money and left it on the bar.

The decision had been made for him. He accepted that. With one yearning glance back at Mala's front door, Caruthers entered the tipica store. Up the steps to Cruz's offices. Inside, the Chief of Police was staring down at his secretary, who knelt before him. They both looked up at Caruthers, caught in the act. In the secretary's hand was an emergency-orange yoyo, its knotted string attached to Cruz's finger. She was helping untangle it.

Cruz grimaced, pulled the string from his finger, and tossed it to the secretary. "My good friend," he said, distancing himself from the yoyo. "I'm happy to see you." He wagged a heavy finger at Caruthers. "I almost come look for you."

"Well here I am," Caruthers said.

"This way, Norman my friend," Cruz said, signaling Caruthers to follow him down the stairs. "I feel like going on a drive. You feel like going on a drive?"

They exited through a back door, Caruthers not bothering to answer Cruz's question. Cruz climbed into his black-windowed sport utility vehicle, and Caruthers sat beside him. "Where are we going?" he asked.

Cruz waved impatiently, pulling into traffic. He drove carefully, with both hands on the wheel. At a stop sign he came to a complete stop, glanced up and down the empty cross street like an old lady. There were two Chucho Cruzes, Caruthers noted, one for the day, one for night. The sun hadn't yet set, but it was sinking fast, tinting the world yellow. They drove up the road that led to the lucho warehouse.

"My son's in big trouble," Caruthers said.

"I know. Chucho Cruz knows all." He laughed, accelerating up the mountain. "A pretty mestiza lady come to tell me. She is very nervous. These are very bad people, new people in my country." They drove for a few minutes, along the ridge, passing the warehouse and continuing on. Caruthers drank rum from his flask and eased back into the leather seat. Chucho Cruz was taking him out to the middle of nowhere, and there was nothing Caruthers could do about it. The realization came with a certain relief. All decisions had been removed. Now he merely had to endure whatever was going to happen.

They passed a cluster of large, concrete homes looking down on the lake. From this height, the lush pocket stood out from the surrounding rocky forestland. Cruz abruptly pulled off the road and rushed toward a wall of dense, bushy trees. "Shit," Caruthers said, and the grassy earth under the tires dipped before impact. Without slowing they pushed through the feathery leaves and emerged onto a field of yellow grass. Twin tire lines marked the way. Cruz was laughing.

"Oh, I scare you so bad!"

"You did," Caruthers agreed, clutching the dash. They parked at the edge of a pit, about fifty yards square.

Cruz killed the engine and smiled. "Come. You will enjoy."

Caruthers followed Cruz to the edge of what turned out to be a very old, neglected amphitheater of some sort, with terraced steps leading to a square field covered in weeds. They climbed down to the field, about the size of a volleyball court.

"I like this place," Cruz said, and inhaled the loamy air.

"Ruins?" Caruthers asked, examining a stone block on the bottom ring of seats, decorated by faint markings.

"A ball court." Cruz stood in the center of the field and spoke as if addressing an audience. "You have heard, yes? The players, sometimes the king himself, kick the ball. To them, the ball is the sun."

Caruthers knew all about the ancient game, part of the ubiquitous tourist script. "Whoever lets the sun hit the ground loses the game," he said.

"Exactamente," Cruz said. "Then what?"

"They'd sacrifice him. Rip his heart out so the blood could fuel the sun's journey, or however those savage bastards justified their cruelty."

"Savage?" Cruz asked. "Maybe. In Tikal, they say, they bring the loser to the top of the very high temple, tie him in a ball, and goodbye. Down the steps. Bump, bump, bump." Grinning, Cruz pantomimed the final shove. "¿Muy funny, no?" Caruthers shrugged, in no mood to find the humor in torture and execution. "Of course, not so funny if you are sacrifice. I understand this. I don't make fun." Cruz frowned. "Sacrifice," he said in a softer voice, then looked to a sky full of pink clouds on a field of steel blue.

Caruthers had become terribly depressed. He sat on the lichen-veined stone. It was cold and hard. "Chucho, please," he said, addressing the dirt. "What do you want from me? My bus just died. I've got no money. My son's in the hands of the bad guys." He raised his eyes. "I need help, man."

"Norman. My friend." Chucho approached. "I know. I see trouble on you like, how do you say? All over." He contemplated the terraced stone.

Caruthers imagined feathered and painted onlookers filling the seats. The vision did not improve his mood. He dug the flask from his coat pocket and drank deeply.

"The winner," Cruz said. "This is why I bring you today. What happens to the winner?"

Caruthers wiped mist from his eyes. "I don't know," he admitted. "Land? Slaves? Cocaine?"

"I don't know, too," Cruz said, and laughed. "Nobody talks of the winner, but I think of him." He took Caruthers's flask. "There is more than to cry for the loser, my friend. There is to drink for the victor." He belted one down. Shadow covered all but the far edge of the court. Caruthers leaned back against the next step up and rested his head on a pad of moss. "I have another chore for you," Chucho said. Caruthers turned his head so that the moss cooled his cheek. Chucho stood with both hands tucked into his back pockets. He wore a revolver on his hip. The black, textured grip appeared utilitarian, a mere handle on a mere tool.

"What?" Caruthers asked. "Where?"

"A pick-up and delivery," Chucho told him. "Salvador to Xela, like last time."

"Again?" Caruthers asked, and sat up. "More girls?"

Cruz shook his head, frowning. "No, no. But another good plan, a better plan, and not so far this time. My people at the border. A gringo in the bus." He tossed the flask to Caruthers. "Some pasajeros for disguise," Chucho continued. "You drive there. They put some stuffs on the roof. You know, packages, boxes, baskets. You come back, and some other peoples take the stuffs. Simple."

"Who's it for?"

"Who cares?" Cruz laughed.

"The same gangsters as last time, right?"

Cruz stared at Caruthers, turned his back and walked toward the strip of light. "Who won ball? We don't know. Do we care? No. The sun hits the ground for all. True? The players, they play." Cruz turned, evidently pleased by his speech. Caruthers considered telling him that he'd been following this philosophical stance his whole life. But he let it go. He'd come to play ball.

"So you're telling me you can free my son?"

Cruz, smiling, returned across the shadow-covered court. He reached out and tousled the cringing man's hair.

# Chapter Twenty-Two

Max woke shivering and achy. His wrists hurt especially, and his shoulders felt as if they'd been injected with ice. He struggled to a sitting position. Light still came through the holes, but from a different angle as before. The cell smelled of blood. He hadn't noticed it before, but now he could hardly breathe through his nose without retching. He was thirsty, and he ran his tongue over his dry lips. With some effort, he slid the bound hands under his butt and brought them behind his bended knees. The position afforded some relief to his shoulders, though not much. He loosened the laces of his work boots. All was silent inside and out. The boots came off, one after the other, and he wiggled his toes, stretching the muscles in his feet. Some part of him, at least, felt good. Likewise, his cell was warming. He pulled off his socks.

By squatting and exhaling, then rolling onto his back, he was nearly able to fit his heels into the space under his wrist ties. He tried the right one only, and it shot through without trouble, leaving his hands caught between his legs. His left leg, less flexible than the right, proved more difficult. He strained, the tie cutting into his wrists. Sweat broke out over his body, dripping down his spine. The cell had gone from too cold to too hot. He tried again and toppled to his side, where he lay panting, reconsidering the whole venture. That's when the bolt at the door squealed and clanged, and the door swung open with a nerve-grinding whine.

Two men, mouths covered in bandanas and eyes hidden behind

sunglasses under brims of baseball caps, stood in a square of white light. They didn't move, taking in the scene: Max on his side, arms and legs tangled, boots and socks scattered about. The one wearing square, black glasses and a New York Yankees cap chuckled; the other, in mirrored aviators and a camo-print hat, didn't. They came at him. He shrank back as the one in aviators drew a machete from his belt, and the other grabbed his legs, spread them while rolling him to his back. Before he could shriek or fight back, he was on his feet, hands free, being marched out of the unit into blinding light, half dragged over the dirt and gravel and weeds of a compound of some sort. He hobbled on hurting bare feet alongside a metal structure, a warehouse or industrial garage. To the left rose an old stone wall, a dozen feet high and topped with new razor wire mingled with rusty old barbed wire. A vague background noise of traffic and city activity murmured from no particular direction. The sun beamed from overhead, and Max's shadow lay at his feet. Past the garage, a two-story structure appeared, constructed of plaster with a red tile roof, a good seventy feet long. Closed wooden double doors fronted the house, in the shadow of a balcony, on which Vicki stood watching his transport. She'd changed from her special forces gear into jeans and a white sleeveless undershirt.

The guards dragged Max around the side of the building, down a stairway that descended into the ground, and through a new steel door. They continued along a dark hall, around a corner, and through a second door. The man on his right flicked a switch, revealing a concrete, commercial-sized shower facility. The smell was the same as in every other locker room Max had known: soap, mildew, and human funk.

"Strip," one of the men said in Spanish, indicating the row of four showers against the wall.

"¿Baño?" Max asked.

They allowed him to relieve himself in one of the stalls, and when he emerged, the man with black glasses tossed him a plastic bag, in which he found soap, shampoo, and a plastic razor. The water was cold, and the men watched as Max showered. After he'd shaved at the sink, at his captors' insistence, he was tossed a towel and a comb with wide teeth on one side and narrow on the other.

Watching himself and the two men behind him in the rusty mirror, he pulled the comb through his long, wet hair, experiencing a sense of unreality, of playing out a dream. For some reason, he recalled one of Karma's lessons. The word the ancient Maya often used for human sacrifice was "suckling," a euphemism and play on words. This, Karma had explained, was one of the ways the gods tricked their victims into agreeing to sacrifice themselves, for *suckling* in their language meant both to nurture and to drain of fluids. Max had been darkly fascinated by these ancient people, who often kidnapped passersby from other villages, bound them to stone altars, sliced open their chests, and yanked out the still-beating hearts. Max had been unable to reconcile these stories with the mild villagers all around him, until now, facing himself in the mirror. The villagers of Zunilito had not descended from priests and lords, the torturers, thieves, slavers, and murderers of the ancient Mayan empire. His people, the firewood collectors, the weavers and vendors, the diggers and stackers, the poor, were the children of the persecuted, the sacrificed. The progenies of the ancient nobility now ran the gangs, organized death squads, brutalized and bribed their way into government seats and corporate boardrooms. From whom did Max emerge? The mighty or the humble? The mighty, until his father broke the line, plunging himself and his sons into the peasantry.

One of the men handed him a stack of white fabric, pants and a blousy shirt of the same white cotton, snowy white, the kind of thing Jesus Christ might have worn over his last days. Max slipped them on, wondering where he'd lost his hat.

The guards led him up two flights of stairs, and through a creaky wooden-floored hall to a heavy door painted white. One of them knocked. "Pase," came the familiar voice. One man swung the door open, and the other pushed Max into a large, oblong bedroom with a high ceiling. The door closed behind him. Vicki sat with her back to an old fashioned desk supporting a mirror with a thick frame carved with flowers. She stood, hands on her hips and her expression serious. Between them, the queen-sized bed, covered in a neat white spread, projected from the wall to his right, across the narrow width of the room from French doors, one of them open to the balcony he'd seen over the entranceway. Filmy white curtains swayed, lit by the bright day outside, though the room remained dark and cool. He imagined running, through the open door and leaping off the balcony, a fall that would probably break a leg. "The hero has come," Vicki said, "dressed in white." She took a newspaper from the desk and approached, her beauty disorienting, mixing fear and desire. Flat sandals slapped the floor faintly as she walked. Her toenails were painted red, and her jeans rode low on her hips, exposing a thin strip of skin between her belly button and the top button of her pants. Dark tufts of hair grew from under her arms. Yesterday she'd shot at least two men, one innocent and one not, killing them forever, without hesitation or remorse. She handed Max the newspaper.

"Stand there." She pointed to a blank space of whitewashed plaster beside the bed. "Hold the paper under your chin. Like county jail. You been to jail?"

"Yes," he said, his voice small.

"What for?" she asked, drawing a phone from her back pocket.

"Assault."

"Don't smile," she said, and snapped a picture. "Now, take off the shirt."

He placed the newspaper on the nightstand, and then pulled the shirt over his head. She looked him over, focused the camera on the dragon covering his right breast. She instructed him to turn to his side, so she could capture the cross on his shoulder, the old, faded cartoon coyote below it on his bicep. Then there was the gothic lettering across the top of his back, spelling out "Let There Be Light." The ace of spades on his other shoulder over an evil joker. The homemade cross scribbled on the meat of his left thumb, and the rosary bracelet around his right wrist.

"Now the pants."

He looked down at his bare chest, his belly, for the first time since high school, rippled with muscle, a result of the Zunilito diet. "I'm not wearing anything under," he said, and she laughed.

"Off," she said, and he slipped them down, stepped out of them, and threw them onto the bed over the shirt. He stood straight, gazing past her at the curtains, hands covering his groin. "Arms at your sides," she said. He uncovered himself, stealing a glance at his genitals. Fear had shrunken his dick to its smallest state. Why this should matter at a time like this, he couldn't know, but of all the emotions coursing through him, fear, confusion, dread…embarrassment felt most urgent.

"Turn to your side," she said, and moved in to photograph the dolphin on his ankle, his second worst tattoo. Number one on that list came next. She instructed him to turn all the way around, so she could snap a picture of the red lipstick print on his left cheek. Kiss my ass, had been the message his nineteen-year-old self had wanted to relay to the world. He hadn't even been drunk. "Now," she said, setting the phone on the newspaper, "come with me."

She led him to the desk. "Stand very still," she said, sitting in the chair. She removed something bright and silvery from one of the drawers. A tiny, high sound escaped Max's lips when he recognized it as a straight razor. "Don't you think about moving or I'll call my men in to hold you down, and everything you're afraid might happen, will. Understand?" She dipped the razor into a silver ice bucket full of water, and then she placed the cold blade against his skin, just under the belly button. Off came the strip of hair, down to the mass around his shrunken penis. He looked away, as he used to do at the lab before they pushed the needle in. The curtains had stopped moving. "I am going to ask you some questions, and you need to tell the truth, the whole truth, and nothing but the truth. Do you understand?"

"Yes."

Shaving him, she asked about his mother, his father. Where they lived, what they did for money. Were his grandparents alive? Did he know anyone in Guatemala? Where was he staying? Was he married? Children? A girlfriend back home? Had he slept with the Spanish teacher? What was her name again?

"Spread your legs," she said, and began to scrape away the hair from the base of his testicles and up. He answered every question, holding nothing back. As she worked, he felt the skin of his scrotum writhe, expanding and contracting like a creature separate from him. Over her shoulder he saw his own red pocket knife, folded on her desk. He imagined taking it up, stabbing her and running off, his dick and balls a bloody mass on the floor by this time. She slid the blade over his denuded genitals in short scraping strokes. Again, he closed his eyes.

"Pretty good," she said, and set the razor down. "Here." She placed a plastic bottle of lotion on the desk in front of him. He pressed the dispenser and rubbed the stuff into his tingling skin. He looked like a child, and reflexively he pulled on his dick a little, to bring it out from hiding. "This way," she said, and walked to the foot of the bed, her back to the window, indicating that he stand directly before her. He did as told, standing with the backs of his legs against the blanket tucked into the mattress. Breeze from the French doors played across his body.

She lifted her shirt, up along her belly and over her head, showing the silky hair under her arms and uncovering teacup-sized breasts. The rustling of clothing released a smell from her body, sweet, like walking into a place that made candy. She stepped out of her sandals and unzipped the jeans, showing black hair to match her armpits. Nude

# A Candle for San Simón

herself, she stepped forward so that her nipples touched his ribs, enveloping him further in the smell of sugar, now tinged by something else, a bright scent like expensive vinegar. "I'm taken," he said, amazed at the stupidity even as the words came out.

"So am I," she whispered. "This is for him, not you. My man's a sick little fucker, but I guess I am too." She placed her hands on his face. They were cold, dry, and smooth, without texture. She brushed them over his forehead and through his damp hair, down to the back of his neck. Her belly touched his dick, and she kissed him. He returned the kiss, eyes closed while he fell slowly backward onto the bed.

She straddled his head, the phone clicking pictures as he did her bidding, not from fear but because he was lost in her, her smell and feel and taste, the idea and material fact of her. She moved over him, doing what she wanted and commanding him to do what she wanted, all while documenting the progress click after click. He lay on his back, rolled over, sat up, bent down…complied without pause. He felt free, free from decisions, free from himself, free from thought except this one: that freedom and bondage circled around and met on the far side.

# Chapter Twenty-Three

Vicki attached the final jpeg to the email address Angel maintained only for their special talks. Outside the window, José Luis, the dead man's younger brother, crossed the grounds from the workshop to the living quarters. He knew she'd killed his brother, but not why. At least one *Prensa* article, citing an anonymous source, said that the gang member was shot by his partner, not by the bus driver, as she had claimed. José Luis hadn't said anything to her, hadn't challenged her version of the story, yet, but he'd talked it over with others in the crew. She reduced the email screen without sending, and then she opened the security cam application. On the screen, José Luis entered through the front door. Spock and Gabo on the couch in the common room took turns on Grand Theft Auto. Ernie and Chuy shot pool behind the couch. She turned up the volume until the sounds from the video game came through, along with the crack of a pool ball. Fat Eric lay on his back on the other couch. Ruben, Jorge, and…who was that? Zipper? eating sandwiches in the mess hall, while doña Antonia and her daughter Liza did the dishes in the kitchen. Running a crew was harder, more complicated, than Vicki had anticipated, especially one that had tripled in size in just a few weeks. Rico never had to deal with this shit, like managing a hotel. His boys all had their own places, but in the end one of them killed him. It took a lot of effort to keep shit tight, but she liked the work of putting everything where it belonged. She'd always liked details.

The shower was empty, and a figure slept in room two, Pablo, who'd gone out the night before. She gave them the day off today, a reward for the hard work these last weeks. They'd been busy getting rid of or hiring the local amateurs, which meant conversations, payoffs, snatchings, interrogations, and two executions, which Vicki recorded on video and posted online, to get the word out in case anybody remained uneducated on the matter of the new kids in town. Door-to-door, they'd introduced themselves to local businesses, explaining politely that the slight rise in fees represented a higher-value, a more advanced operation and ultimately better security. It didn't take much persuasion. Just last week they finished the third phase by reaching deals with local leaders, starting with Chucho Cruz and going outward. They weren't strong enough yet to make the big move, the reason for the whole operation, to establish an alternate, overland supply line from Columbia into Mexico. That would mean dealing with both FARC down south and the narcos up north, as well as establishing a safe port in Guatemala and the infrastructure to move the goods by land. But before any of that, she had to seriously arm her men. No point in going big if you can't defend your gold.

The gringo had fallen into her hand by accident. She'd merely been teaching a lesson to a rebellious bus line, a hard strike to serve as example to all others. On the surface, the kidnapping had been a dumb, impulsive act to take him, almost as risky as executing Hector. The gringo's move, shaming them for taking the girl, had required a response. In normal circumstances, she'd have blown him away right there, but she didn't, for a few reasons. For one, his connection through his father to Cruz might prove valuable, a little extra leverage for the upcoming deal, something to give or withhold.

Maybe she should thank Hector for grabbing the girl and fucking everything up. With chaos comes opportunity, and with opportunity, risk. Hector, a pain in the ass from the start, deserved what he got, but the boys wouldn't see it that way. They'd forgive and forget, if she could hold out until the big delivery. Money, power, weapons…these trumped the life of a maggot like Hector.

She returned the screen to the unsent email, with its thirteen attachments. A risky move, as all her moves were with Angel. He'd gotten off on her taunting him about taking lovers, but how would he react when talk turned to action? She could end up in a dozen trash cans around the city—but you don't do the crime if you can't do the time. The truth was, Angel was Vicki's little pet worm, and she couldn't afford to let him forget it.

The last time they'd met in person, she'd driven across the border to the old apartment in the desert. After playtime and the gradual reversion into their professional roles, he gave her the money for the weapons, a pretty big investment even for him. Angel himself had negotiated the details once Vicki put him into contact with Cruz. Her job was to exchange the cash for the goods. She didn't even know how much the locked, portable safe held, but she had an inventory sheet for the guns. Angel had left her with a warning. It wasn't necessary, and she told him so. She knew what to expect if he caught her stealing. A typical employee was bound, beaten, interrogated, and finally got to watch both hands get sawed off by the same chainsaw that would—before he could bleed out through the wrists—remove his head. She'd have it much worse.

"I'm yours, and you're mine, forever," she'd said.

She considered adding a note to the email, to prepare him for the pictures, but instead, while a blast of energy coursed through her, she clicked "send" without explanation, without even a subject line. The message paused, stuck "sending." In the security cam window, nothing had changed except a new pool game. She counted eleven men, which meant five were out, probably still in the city sleeping off hangovers, pawing whores, maybe still drinking, still smoking, still sniffing. Edgar and Francisco weren't around. She'd seen them jacking each other off in the showers a few days before, while the others were in the shop. She held onto this secret affair in case she ever needed to blackmail the happy couple. You never knew what might be useful.

She closed the cam to give all the tablet's power to the email. The message was "still working." She hoped it wouldn't fail, or only send a few but not the rest, or strand her not knowing one way or another. She needed the packet to arrive on Angel's screen as one big, unfolding shock, sudden, like the build to an orgasm. She paced the room, and then pulled on her boots. She'd assemble the men tomorrow morning to tell them about the shipment—some welcome good news. Morale had been low, as the promises she'd made about bonuses hadn't yet happened—this on top of the usual grumbling about having to work for a woman. She slung the leather jacket over one shoulder and checked the message once more. Delivered. She stared at the screen. Sometimes Angel replied to her demands, insults, and pictures immediately, like he'd been waiting for her at his computer, dick in hand. Other times he took up to several hours to write back. No response came as she watched, so she killed the page and turned off the machine. Needing out of that place, she pulled on the jacket.

She slid the phone into her back pocket, and her pistol into the holster sewn into her jacket. Angel had given her the gun, a black 9 mm he called "sexy," and he also outfitted the crew with a small, start-up arsenal, with two AK47s, various rifles, shot guns, and two boxes of used body armor. In addition, crew members were expected to carry their own personal pieces. The gun bulged from her jacket, easy to notice for anyone paying attention, so she replaced it in the desk drawer next to the gringo's cute little knife. Camouflage was a better defense than packing, at least today, out on streets where nobody knew her.

She locked the door behind her and walked downstairs. She wished to slip out like a ghost, but she showed herself in the rec room because she couldn't start hiding from her men, not this early. Everyone shut up when she walked in, and the air turned brittle like it could break. For years, she watched Rico work his boys, joking with them, praising them,

shouting them down, threatening and once executing a motherfucker—
this last for the benefit of the living; the dead man had no more lessons
to learn. He'd build them up but not so high they started feeling big, and
he'd knock them down but mostly not all the way down. He never let
them feel like fools or like equals, always kept them somewhere in
between. At first she thought she could imitate him, but because she had
a pussy and tits instead of a dick and balls, she had to play it different, a
game whose rules she had to make up every day. "Rest tonight," she said,
touching the phone through her pocket to check a phantom vibration.
"Tomorrow's a big day. I won't say what it is until we're all here together,
but you'll like what's coming. I promise." Cute Ernie, the youngest in the
crew, who liked to shave crazy designs into the buzzed sides of his hair,
gave her a smile. "It'll be like Christmas," she said. "Enjoy the rest of
your day off."

She left on this good note, out the front door. Instead of driving, she
aimed for the narrow gate at the back corner of the compound, near the
containers they used as cells that lay scattered about, where poor Max sat
in storage. She almost felt like knocking on his door, saying hi, but
instead she pulled out the phone, checked that the vibration alert was on.
It was. The silence meant nothing yet, but if it lasted a whole lot longer,
she might have trouble.

Aside from the rolling electronic front gate, there were two other ways
in and out, one known to all, the other a secret from everyone—even
Angel—except her and the contractor who built it. Now, she approached
the simple iron door in the wall, locked by a thick deadbolt. The other
exit was some real spy shit she invented, a trap door covered in plywood
disguised by glued-on gravel, that led to a ladder going straight down into
an old aqueduct made to catch the mountain runoff. During the rainy
season, the pipe nearly filled, but in the dry season the river turned to a
green trickle slithering down the center of the tunnel, ending in a dump
outside the city.

# A Candle for San Simón

She locked the gate and took the dirt alley behind the compound, high wood slat fence on one side marking the edge of the saw mill next door, her own fortified stone wall on the other. This alley joined a larger dirt road that wound around trees, over a rocky hill, and then descended into Xela. The city center spread below, hundreds of boxes outlined by vein-like streets, the whole thing organized but random, like clusters of cells she'd seen on the Discovery Channel, like life, a pattern too crazy to figure out even though you see it before your eyes. Brown air hung above. She walked down into it, step by step losing the view from above and then finally entering the pattern, becoming part of it, a cell moving through a vein.

She entered an open-air market, a smaller version of the city itself, like every part is a version of the whole thing, always repeating. She found too much to see, too many things to buy for her to focus, but it didn't matter. She was just killing time, killing time before time killed her. Someone once said that to her. Who? Rico. He'd been funny that way with words. Time finally did kill him. A man killed him really, but it had only been a matter of time. The crazy life is not a long life, but nobody lives forever anyway. If Rico'd heard her say that, he'd have repeated it himself, taking the credit like he always did. She didn't used to mind.

She entered a hot passage of cooked food stalls, whose smells all finally gave way to corn: roasted corn, boiled corn, corn blended into a drink, smashed into a paste and cooked on a plate of iron over a small wood fire kept hot by a woman fanning it with a flattened cereal box. Next came the heavy, sweet smell of fruit and colors so bright she had to squint. Orange mangos the shape of cashews and round ones, green tinged with red; papayas like American footballs; pineapples; heavy bunches of bananas hanging from hooks, green and yellow marbled with black. A boy with a red stain over half his face pressed orange halves in a silver juicer with a long handle. She bought a plastic cup full, drank it down at once, feeling its energy filling her belly and moving out to her limbs. At the end of the fruit lane lay hills of rotten stuff so rank she breathed through her mouth, cans and bags and simply piles on the ground, covered in black flies.

Raw meat took over like a new neighborhood, pale yellow to purple, bones sticking out of hunks of muscle, carcasses on hooks, all in an invisible cloud of blood. A dozen eyes bulged from a table covered in skinned beef heads, almost funny their looks of surprise, yellow fat and strands of silvery sinew standing out from the dark flesh. Rico once showed her a video of men skinned alive this way, tied down tight and their faces ripped off to reveal the same expression as the cow heads before her, like underneath the skin we're all just animals. She passed mounds of slimy or dried fish and tiny shrimp all salty and funky, and finally entered the land of vegetables, with their mild colors and clean smells, a good part of town. A little girl in traditional dress, five years old but with the serious face of a tiny woman, nicked a sliver of green flesh from a halved avocado with the tip of her machete and held it out for Vicki to sample. She ignored the girl and cut into a passageway barely wide enough for one person to pass, which dead ended in a dozen overflowing trash cans.

She passed through a tunnel of electronics, buttons and switches all silver and black, but with a few pearl-white or ruby-red plates of plastic. This hard, shiny material gave way to the softer, older, women's zone of fabrics, with its subtle, honest smell and quietude. A teenaged girl staring at her phone watched over tights painted like jeans, hats, belts, boots, sneakers, shorts, and women's underthings. In the next stalls lay stacks of tee shirts, men's business shirts in boxes, dresses and skirts hanging from lines, sexy clothes and exercise gear, all cheap, all made in China and flown across oceans to this land famous for its textiles.

Alone, she lingered at a tipica stand, surrounded by huipil blouses, skirts, sashes, and an assortment of tourist junk, like reggae-colored berets, purses, baseball and sun hats made from the traditional weave. An

# A Candle for San Simón

old woman appeared, gray-hair parted in the center and hanging down on either side in thick braids, dressed in a red huipil, purple skirt, and light blue apron, looking the same as all of them. On her dirty feet she wore ballerina slippers. A small woman, under five feet tall, she stepped aside and invited Vicki to enter a dark cave of clothing. Vicki complied, though she'd originally planned to move on.

The place was deeper, more intricate than she'd thought from outside. "Would you like to try something on?" the woman asked, surprising Vicki with her clear voice, her ladina accent, like how sometimes a black person will sound white when he talks. "A pretty girl like you would make a beautiful Indian." She smiled, slyly or simply it was hard to tell, rubbing between two fingers the edge of a golden shawl hanging from the ceiling frame. Vicki, playing tourist, considered the goods before her, wondering if she would ever experience a circumstance to wear this stuff, pretty as it all was. "Everything in this shop, except for a few things up front, is authentic," the saleswoman said, "woven and sewn by women from villages all over Guatemala."

"What do you think when you see white people wearing your clothes?" Vicki asked, only to extend her time in this quiet, cool place.

The woman smiled, showing long, yellow teeth. "I feel very happy, if the clothes are from my shop! Did you know the designs came from the Spanish? When they arrived here, they made these clothes to cover our nakedness, an affront to God. They would have forced us to wear them, but they didn't have to because we liked them. They were gifts, along with the knowledge of the one true God." She let go of the cloth to cross herself in the Catholic way. Vicki, a product of a Salvadoran orphanage, repeated the gesture without thinking. "The Spanish invaders taught our women to weave the clothes. Each group had its very own colors and patterns. Why?" She chuckled silently, her shoulders moving up and down. "So the Spanish could tell us apart! Without clothes, we all looked the same."

"And you still wear them now, all these years later."

"Of course! They're beautiful. We are proud of our skill. Gringos and ladinos like you buy them. Sometimes to wear, and sometimes…" she laughed out loud, "to hang on their walls! A gringa from the north told me this." She continued laughing, shaking her head in amazement.

Vicki smiled herself, enjoying the sense of camaraderie between her and the old woman. "Show me what they wear in the smallest, farthest-away, least-known village of all. Do you have anything like that?"

The woman nodded her head, as if to herself, and led Vicki by her jacket cuff deeper into the shop, to a messier area, a maze of folded and stacked cloth rising like model skyscrapers from tables. "Here," the old woman said, "from high in the mountains, far past Chichicastenango. Perfect for you. The people there are taller than the rest of us, whiter. Like you."

Vicki examined the textiles. They looked much like the others, and she had the feeling the woman was hustling her. Probably all the stuff came from a single factory somewhere, but if she was telling the truth, that the people who'd made these clothes were taller, whiter than the rest, that could only mean more fucking than usual among the conquered and the conquerors. More rape. More wiping out of the men, knocking up the women. This was Vicki's story, the story of her people, the rapists' blood in her veins making her better, prettier, more valuable than the old Indian before her, who now held draped over one arm a slate-blue skirt with vertical white stripes, a rust-colored huipil embroidered with brown flowers, a lighter blue belt, and a red cloth ring to be worn on the head like a fallen halo. She held the items one by one against Vicki's body. "Go ahead," she said, nodding and smiling.

Vicki looked around to find them still quite alone in the shop. "We wear our clothes without underthings," the woman said, "but you don't have to." Vicki stripped, hanging her clothes on a painted wooden chair. The woman wrapped the long skirt high around Vicki's waist, coming to just under her breasts. The blouse hung loose over her chest and shoulders, and the belt pulled it tight around her middle, above her belly button. "Sit down," the woman said, indicating another wooden chair. She ran her fingers through Vicki's hair, combing it while massaging the scalp. "When your hair grows longer, this will keep it in place," she said, and set the circle of fabric on her head, angled back.

Vicki stood before a full-length mirror, staring at a stranger. The bottom half of her body appeared long in the skirt, but mainly she looked like a taller version of the kind of woman she saw every day but never noticed. "If you were one of us, all the men would ask you to marry them," the woman laughed. "And the girls would hate you and want to be your best friend, all at the same time."

A foreign sound entered the space, a series of grunts, three sets of two, her phone vibrating in her pants, of course. Vicki forced herself to ignore it. "Go ahead," the woman said, turning her attention to a stack of folded swaths. With a downward brushing motion, Vicki smoothed the new clothes, which felt heavy on her body, like armor. She walked calmly to the chair, withdrew the phone. "The young girls tuck their phones into the belt," the woman said, going through the swaths without looking up. Vicki brightened the screen. One email message. No subject line. She opened it. No message, just an attachment. She clicked on it and waited as the image filled the screen: Angel's short, thick cock, pushing the material of the panties Vicki had left him as a gift, a wet spot visible at the head. Over the image, he'd learned to impose script words: "Awaiting your Instructions, my Love." She blacked the screen and reflexively slipped the phone into the belt, like the young girls did.

"Your boyfriend?" the old woman asked, smiling, maybe lewdly, maybe sweetly.

"Why do you ask?"

"You were so happy when you looked at the phone, I thought, this must be love."

Vicki turned from the woman, busied herself with her street clothes. "I'll take these," she said. "And two other outfits just like it, but in different colors if possible. You choose. Package them, and I'll pick them up later." Vicki pulled her jeans on. "Make that three more."

"You'll need a shawl," the old woman said. She held out a golden length of material, striped and complicated like most of the tipica cloth, folded over one arm. "You wear it this way." She hung it like a banner over her left shoulder, so that it covered half her body down to the thigh. "Or you can wrap it over your head and around your shoulders if it's cold, or, when the time comes, you can make it into a little hammock for your baby."

Vicki tied her boots, paid the woman, and left the shop. Outside, the sun had set. She was hungry, and tomorrow would be a busy day.

# Chapter Twenty-Four

The phone vibrated, two faint hums announcing a text message. Or was that part of the dream already sliding from memory? Karma blinked up into the familiar darkness of the bedroom at her parents' house, Baby Rudy breathing evenly in the cradle against the far wall. A series of explosions like gun fire cracked from the street outside, and she sat up, fully awake and heart fluttering. It was only a packet of firecrackers thrown into a neighbor's yard, the traditional birthday prank, marking the time after midnight but before dawn. On the dresser, the phone lay hidden in a clutter of clothes, two handbags, a leather belt, and a folder full of papers from Luz Maria.

She'd missed the appointment, and so Luz Maria had dropped Rudy from the waiting list. When Karma finally was able to call, they would only put him back at the end, refusing to consider the reason for the absence. She'd been tempted to simply leave him at the front door some dark morning like everyone else did, but once again she'd be punished for her conscience, for doing the right thing. She sat up, feet on the floor. The baby shifted and moaned but didn't wake. Occasionally he screamed in his sleep, apparently caught in nightmares, but what a child that age could dream about was a mystery to Karma. Hooded men with guns? Blood spraying a shattered windshield? The screams and whimpers of the adults who cared for him? Yes. Too nervous to get back to sleep, she flipped open the phone, revealing two new text messages, both from a single blocked number.

Attachment notices filled the screen of the first text, headed by a brief note in Spanish: "I like to share. Enjoy." Normally she'd delete without pause such a random message, especially one with attachments, but tonight was not normal. Her tongue thick and foreign, like a strip of leather stuck in her mouth, she opened the first attachment. The picture loaded slowly, from the top down. She saw damp shaggy brown hair, pale eyes…Max's face. Karma looked in panic around the room, at the crib, her bed, the barred window covered by a red curtain. She pulled open the door of her wardrobe, shoved her hand through the hanging clothes to be sure no one hid behind them. Of course, this was crazy. The gangsters hadn't broken into her home during the night. The invasion had come invisible through the air, into the little box she held in her hand. She breathed, resisting the impulse to check under her bed, listening hard for strange noises.

In the picture, Max held a newspaper under his chin. She thought about waking her parents, but what could a couple of teachers do? She opened the next attachment. It was a tattoo from Max's arm. The following attachments showed other tattoos, most of which she'd seen, one she hadn't over the course of their hurried love making. Attachment nine confused her as it loaded. She saw bare skin, but at first couldn't make out what part of the body it was. Then she recognized it as a close up of an erect penis. There was something strange about it, and soon she saw that all the hair had been removed, as if for an operation. Sitting down on the bed, she opened the next attachment. A full body picture of Max, on his back, face turned to the side on a pillow, legs together and that same bare erection pointing toward his belly button. She opened the last five attachments quickly, sensing as each loaded that this would be the red one, the documentation of mutilation and murder. She saw a hand, thin, hairless, gripping the penis. Then from the opposite direction, from Max's perspective, the hand guiding him into a vagina surrounded by black hair. Picture fourteen featured that same vagina, but now over

# A Candle for San Simón

Max's face, his eyes squinting, as if trying to see into bright light, the lean thighs taut on either side of his head. The final picture was another close up of Max's genitals, now curving half hard up and over like a question mark, glistening.

The phone trembled, and Karma dropped it to the floor. Barefoot in a night shirt, she lifted the phone gingerly, as she might a dead mouse. Though the room was cool, a sheen of sweat covered her body. The pictures, depraved and frightening, had stirred her, and not just the pornography but what lay behind it, the captivity, the disloyalty that wasn't disloyalty; and especially the faceless woman making all this happen, for reasons Karma couldn't begin to fathom. She imagined herself in Max's place, captured, shorn, straddled, fucked, photographed. She opened the phone, hands trembling. "You can have him if you want him. Central park. Your city. Now." She snapped shut the phone and set it on the dresser, frozen by urgency. Rudy whined, smacking his lips. She should wake her father, but he'd want to call the police, and the photographs would eventually come to light, shared among the officers, and eventually finding their way into the tabloids and across the internet. The police could not be trusted in any case, except to blackmail her, to contact their underworld bosses with the information. Whoever sent the texts knew Karma's name, her phone number, certainly her address, and probably a lot more.

She dressed and, before leaving, stood at the edge of the crib. A pale night light low on the wall threw the baby and his blanket into dark relief. If she found Max dead in the park, she'd leave and let someone else discover the corpse, answer the questions. If he was alive and hurt, she'd take him to the hospital if possible. If alive and well, she'd take him home. That was enough to go on, and Rudy would be safe for the time being. If he cried and woke the house, they could call her. She slid the phone into her jacket's inside pocket and slipped out to the back yard where she kept her scooter.

Far enough from her house to avoid waking anyone, she started the bike and set off. Ten minutes later, she pulled onto the one-way loop around the park. Art deco streetlamps lit the walkways that wound through the lush garden-like grounds, soft-yellow, shaded and silent. Puttering along, she came upon a body on a bench. Her ears rang and she breathed in sharply, and then an arm rose from the figure, scratched a head of greasy black hair and dropped back to the bench, just a bum sleeping under a ratty blanket.

She continued around the park, the puttering of her scooter the only sound. She'd almost completed the circle when, twenty yards ahead on the perimeter walking path a large person, bearded and long haired, dressed in a coat that reached the ground, stared down at something at his feet. Karma recognized him as the eccentric beggar who lived in the park. She pulled over, still sweating in the chill of the morning. The lump on the ground, a body in white shirt and pants. Though missing its head, the thing somehow squirmed on the sidewalk, even managing to roll onto its side. Karma gasped, and the park-dweller retreated into the shadows. Familiar green triangles marked the bottoms of the boot soles, bound together but moving, and as her horror grew, Karma noted the black hood, blending into the dark sidewalk and hiding Max's covered head. He was alive, apparently intact, but bound at hands and feet.

"Hello?" he said, quietly. "Is somebody there?"

"Max?" Karma said, approaching warily.

"Is that you?" Max asked.

"Yes," she said, and kneeled beside him. She touched his shoulder, and they both startled. "It's okay," she said, stroking his back while he panted. "It's over."

He let out a long, shuddering breath. "My god," he groaned. "I thought I'd never see you again." She helped him sit up, and then fumbled with the hood, managing to untie the drawstring. There he was, his beard a few days thicker, his eyes wet and red, nose running, but otherwise the face she knew—the face between the thighs in the picture still in the phone in her pocket.

Plastic tie bands secured his hands and feet, too tough to break without a blade. "In my pocket," Max said, twisting to the side to present his hip. "I couldn't reach it."

She shoved her hand in and found the red folding knife, left there, she assumed, by Max's captor and lover. She cut him free, hands and then feet. He rubbed his wrists, and then shook his arms as if trying to fling his hands to the ground.

"Hurry," she said, helping him to his feet, "before they come back." She led him to the scooter. He climbed on behind her, and she rode away, into the dark part of the city where she lived. Max locked his arms around her waist, squeezing her, chin on her shoulder, body heaving gently from deep breaths. "Thank you," he murmured into her ear, his breath a warm spot in the cool wind pushing her hair back. As she navigated dark side streets, he slipped a hand under her jacket and caressed her belly. That part of her, especially when leaning forward, embarrassed her, its three rolls of fat, but Max had often told her how much he loved it, the soft flesh. In the primitive setting of Zunilito, Max had been a gentle but timid lover, and she could not reconcile the man she knew with the subject of the pornographic pictures.

She flipped through the pictures in her mind's eye, aware of the hum of the scooter's seat between her legs, Max's big hand resting passively along the waistband of her tights. She pictured this hand slipping down, cupping, rubbing, entering her. Up ahead, a man stumbled along the sidewalk, so drunk he'd never make it home. She pictured Max's face between her legs, imagined his tongue, his lips. Rolling into the alley behind her parents' house, she revved the scooter in neutral while tilting her hips forward on the vibrating seat cushion. Outside the gate, she killed the engine, leaned the scooter on its kickstand, stepped off and clutched Max, straddling his thigh and kissing him deeply. "Let's go," she whispered. "Quick, before everyone wakes up."

# Chapter Twenty-Five

Caruthers inspected the bus, parked as always behind Red's place. It looked the same as before, except for the cabinet installed over the driver's side window, its metal door secured with a padlock. The clutch was practically new, good for the rest of his life, the same amount of time he'd be indentured to Chucho Cruz. But he'd saved Max, a good deed that more than balanced out the dirty deliveries in his future. Cruz informed Caruthers of the good news, and soon after the kid's girlfriend called La Mala to confirm. Max himself hadn't deigned to get on the phone, but that was okay, understandable. He didn't know who'd rescued him, and Caruthers preferred it that way. Finally, he got to do something good and get no credit for it. He left the bus, a brief chore in mind before retiring to La Mala for the rest of the day.

Walking across the spongy grass lot, Caruthers felt light, hopeful. Working part-time for Cruz carried risk and reward, like every endeavor in life. Either way, he was going to have enough gas to get around the last lap, and that's all he wanted. On Santander, he entered a cluttered stationary shop for school kids, where he bought a pad of paper, a pen, and a stack of envelopes. Walking home, he passed Frank. "Going to the bar, Norman?"

"I'll meet you later," Caruthers replied. And then, several steps away, he added, "I'll buy you a drink if you're around."

In his apartment, buzzing and pacing, he popped a can, drank, and placed the pad of paper on his table, admired it for a few seconds. He sat and removed the cap from the pen. He drank from his beer. The can sweated a pool onto the table, so he got up for a towel. He didn't want to smudge the ink.

To hell with it, he thought, and upended the beer, gulped until it was empty. His eyes watered and a belch burned through his throat. He picked up the pen and wrote, "Dear Son," and then stood so quickly he knocked the chair to the floor. He was too restless to sit, and his beer can was empty, so he retrieved another and paced in front of the window, drinking and looking out on the town, slowly coming back to life. Tourists, Mayan men and women in traje, all scurrying around like ants. The street wasn't exactly crowded, but Caruthers counted twenty bodies coming or going before he turned from the window to continue pacing, a meteor storm of words shooting through his mind, accompanied by a flickering slide show of pictures. I remember the day you were born, he thought, and then he remembered just that, the hospital room with its sharp antiseptic smell. He recalled laughing the first time he looked into Max's scornful, blue-black eyes, saw the shock of black hair on the wrinkly little creature. So serious! He and Pam had been high on a chemical sort of love back then, an instinct to protect this helpless thing they'd made. When had it worn off, the love, the impulse to protect? He couldn't pinpoint the day, but it had happened. He'd plain lost interest somewhere along the line.

The words and walking kept going for some time, until finally it all slowed to a few phrases, small steps, an image or two flaring up and burning. Then silence and a deep pulsing through his body. The world outside his window had not changed, but everything was different somehow. Slower. A dog skulking down the lane, slower. A woman fanning herself with a newspaper outside the travel agency, slower. Caruthers breathed deeply, set the beer down, stretched his fingers and sat. He read the two words he'd written, "Dear Son." He took up the pen and rested the point on the next line down. "Sorry," he wrote, and added

# A Candle for San Simón

a period. He breathed in, breathed out. "I'm sorry," he wrote again, "for all the shit I've put you through," and then he kept going for a long time.

Massaging his aching, dented finger, Caruthers left his room, marched up to the police station and past the secretary without a word. She stood behind him at the door to Cruz's office, saying something Caruthers didn't catch. Cruz shooed her away. So far, he'd given Caruthers a hundred U.S. cash, plus the new clutch and his son's freedom. Eight hundred more would be paid upon delivery of the weapons, a bonus, Cruz had called it. Caruthers asked for six hundred up front, and Cruz could keep the other two. "That's a hell of an interest rate," Caruthers said.

Cruz scowled from his desk, tapping a pen into his open palm as if it were a tiny nightstick. "Interesting," he said, puzzling it out, glancing up at Caruthers, who hadn't taken a seat. "You are interesting today. Different. What is going on in Norman's mind?"

"I've got debts that won't wait, Chucho, and I haven't had anything to lose in years. The difference is that I just now noticed it."

Cruz threw an offer his way and Caruthers countered. They settled on four hundred and fifty U.S. dollars. Caruthers extended his hand and Cruz shook it. "I'm waiting for the cash," Caruthers said. There was a pause and Caruthers thought he'd blown it, until Cruz laughed. He left the office for a minute and returned with the bills.

"You are not thinking something stupid, Norman?"

"I've got white hair and a turquoise bus," Caruthers reminded him. "How far would I get? And for what? A couple hundred bucks?"

Cruz stared at him for a long moment. "Today, I believe you," he said. "Why? Because you are right! Nowhere to run, my friend. You know this." He slapped the money into Caruthers' hand. "Good luck," he said as Caruthers left.

Now, seeing to more pleasant affairs, Caruthers crossed to Mala. Frank was the only customer. He spun on his stool. "You said you'd buy me a drink," he reminded Caruthers.

"Hoping you'd stop in," Red said. "What's the status on that thing we were talking about?" In a moment of weakness, Caruthers had confided his troubles to Red the other night, alone in the bar.

"Solved. All but a little job I've got to run to pay the piper. I'm here to celebrate. Do you mind setting me and my associate up with beverages?"

"Good news," Red said, serving the beer. "We can all use good news these days."

Caruthers drank, the coldest beer of the day. It tasted like hope. Frank threw a plastic arm over Caruthers' shoulders.

"So tell me," Red said, "did your boy split the country? I know I sure would."

"Nope. The crazy son of a bitch is going back to the boonies to finish his religious thing there. Said he wasn't heading home until he finished the job."

"That'a boy. Wonder where he gets the stupidity."

"Change of subject," Caruthers said, "while it's not too busy and we're both more or less in our right minds." He dug Chucho's money from his pocket and set it on the bar. "This," he said, peeling the hundred from the top and placing it in front of Red, "is for whatever my friend and I drink tonight. And this," he laid another hundred on top of that one, "is for you."

Red pulled a stool from under the bar and sat facing Caruthers. He opened himself a beer. Caruthers hadn't looked into Red's eyes in years, maybe ever. They were yellow-green, a touch diabolical. "Now tell me what this is all about. An inheritance?"

"Fuckshit," Frank said. "Why you asking questions. Take the money."

"That's awfully generous," Red said. "What's the catch?"

"No catch," Caruthers said.

Red stared at him. He hadn't touched the money. "You planning on taking off?" he asked.

# A Candle for San Simón

"The thought has occurred to me. Heard nice things about Nicaragua. You know they have freshwater sharks in that lake down there?"

"That a selling point?"

Caruthers finished his beer, and tucked the remaining $250 into his front pocket. "What do I care? I don't swim."

"The top one for the tab. Okay. You guys'll drink it eventually, but what about the other hundred?"

"A tip, of course" Caruthers told him. "You've been a hell of a bartender." He stood, taken by a sudden instinct. "Hold my spot and keep a cold one ready. I'll be back in ten minutes."

"We'll be waiting for you, buddy," Frank said. He wiped his wet eyes with his rubber-covered hooks.

"I'll hurry."

Caruthers stepped outside and stood still in the sunshine. Cruz was looking down from his office. Caruthers waved, and then started back toward his place. He wanted to stash the remaining money before the real drinking began. The binge, unlike most of the others throughout his life, was planned. The idea was to be at his sharpest for the delivery, and the mornings he woke up most clear-headed were the days following his worst hangovers, hangover days when he'd be too sick for more than basic maintenance drinking.

In the bathroom, he pulled out the medicine cabinet and exchanged the stack of quetzales there for the greenbacks. He nearly left off the screws when he replaced the cabinet, but he reminded himself that now was not the time to cut corners, so he twisted the four screws back into place, returned the screwdriver to the tool drawer in the kitchen, popped a beer for the road, and headed back to Red's.

Along the way he passed two teenaged Indian girls, pretty as could be in flower-embroidered blouses, each balancing an enormous basket heaped with miniature bananas on her head. Caruthers killed his beer and tossed the can to the gutter with the rest of the trash. Usually he did the gringo thing and held on to his waste until he came across a legitimate receptacle, but tonight, the sky yellow as the sun set behind the volcanoes, he didn't feel like holding on to anything, saving anything for later.

Jimmy Buffet played inside. Not Caruthers' favorite, but not so bad really, a fellow drunk at least. The rat man sat at the bar next to Frank, and the hippie gal who sold bread and mysticism had even come, accompanied by the tall Australian with watery blue eyes, fair weather drinkers Caruthers hadn't seen in La Mala Senda for months. Red placed a beer at Caruthers' spot. "I saved your seat," Frank said, and smiled his big baby smile.

"Round of rums on me," the rat man said, and Caruthers saluted him. Everyone raised their glasses and knocked them back. It was early, and they had all night. Suddenly the place was crowded, roaring all around. Someone bumped into his back, and Caruthers turned to Billy, with two pipsqueak friends and a couple of local girls huddled together whispering to each other. Rap music was playing, and the happiness of a moment before, an hour ago, several hours ago whatever, turned to anxiety and dread. Caruthers attributed the change to Billy and his hoodlums. He swiveled around to the bar counter and settled in to wait them out.

He raised two fingers, the signal for a rum and a beer, but Red was swamped by customers three deep shouting drink orders. Caruthers sat there battling himself. Red was busy. That's how it went at the bar, first come first serve. On the other hand, Caruthers had tipped the motherfucker a hundred dollars a few minutes ago. Had he already forgotten? Caruthers looked to the right, at the hippie girl and her Australian, and to the left at Frank and his new best buddy the rat man. Everybody was ignoring him. Fuck them, he thought, tapping his empty rocks glass on the bar. Even the ice was gone. He considered standing up and shouting. Red. Here I am. But he sat stewing instead, hardly noticing the fresh rum on rocks and beer with vapor still rising from its newly

# A Candle for San Simón

twisted cap sitting before him. He looked up, but Red was working the right side of the bar, where a faceless cluster clamored behind the hippie and her positive vibes.

The rap music ended, but before Caruthers could appreciate the relative quiet, heavy metal took its place, a drum smashing, guitar twiddling invasion of noise performed by sweating boy-men with scowling pimply faces. God, he hated it. What the fuck had come of the world? The rum disappeared and another appeared in its place. The beer was warm, neglected, so Caruthers chugged it down before he forgot. Red set another in front of him and Caruthers couldn't find the right way to say no, he didn't want another beer just then. Words had gone, from his mouth at least, but they bounced around in his skull so fast he couldn't catch up to them.

The place had cleared out some. Frank and the rat man were gone, and Billy's two hoodlums had taken their stools, while Billy sat on Caruthers' other side, laying a line of bullshit on the two girls at the short leg of the bar. The three were singing along with the current music, drug runner polka rap. As sometimes happened when he got especially drunk, Caruthers understood Spanish as clear as if he'd been born to it.

In one-two-three, one-two-three waltz time, the singer crooned: "I'll pull out my piece, I'll cut off your head, I'll wipe out your family…" Caruthers looked for the physical source of the music and found it on the television. The band—dressed like sloppy mariachis—strutted around on stage before a shrieking audience, one guy rocking an accordion and the singer holding a bazooka over his right shoulder and the microphone in his left hand. The stupidity was too much, too-too much. Something had to be done about this. He bided his time, waiting for the song to end, the music program to fade to commercials. Billy had scooted over close to the girl beside him, practically in her lap. She wore no expression, and her friend sulked at the far end of the bar, but that was the way these kids always looked, blank or sad or angry.

"Hey Guillermo," Caruthers shouted into Billy's face, exaggerating the gringo *r*. "Nice music you're singing to. Real smart stuff. Real sophisticated."

"Hello old man!" Billy said, smiling broadly, acting as if he'd not noticed Caruthers until now. "Why are you still awake? This is the time for the young peoples. Not old mans like you." He laughed, enlisting the additional laughter of his crew.

"I'm here to tell you something important. You listening? Someday somebody's going to call you out on your punk ass shit. And you know what will happen then? They'll knock you straight off, right out of this world. And you know why? Not because you're a crook, which you are, but because you're a little asshole, and the thing about little assholes is they grow up to be big assholes. I say this to help. Because I care."

Billy stared at him, fierce and puzzled. Caruthers strained for more words, to make himself understood.

"Pretty soon the girls will be gone. They're already bored. Look at her." The girl beside Billy had been roped back into conversation with her neglected friend. Whatever spell Billy had cast had been broken by Caruthers' intrusion. "That baby mustache and soul patch around your mouth looks like ass hair." Caruthers laughed. It did look like ass hair, even more so now that Billy had puckered his wet red lips in anger.

Then Billy laughed, a change in demeanor so sudden it surprised Caruthers, even from the distant, foggy place where he floated. "Hey Red," Billy called out lightly, "you be careful with this one. He's a little intoxicated." Billy then turned to the girls and spoke in Spanish. He signed his boys on the other side of Caruthers, pointing toward the exit and yawning theatrically. "You be careful," he said, hand on Caruthers' shoulder. "This is a very dangerous country. But you already know that, right?" Laughing again, he led his entourage out of the bar. Caruthers felt bad for chasing them off. Hadn't he started with good intentions? What had they been? Oh, yes, the gangster mariachi music they liked so much.

# A Candle for San Simón

He wanted to give them a lesson in taste, was all. Don't look up to these monster clowns on television, singing about killing like it's a joke, worshiping bling and pickup trucks. Even the richest of the drug lords lived scared and died young. That's what he'd wanted to say, but he'd botched it.

Red was washing glasses, the bar about empty. Caruthers would buy the kid a drink next time he saw him, if he ever saw him again. "See ya, Red," he mumbled, but Red was dunking glasses. Caruthers slid off his stool, one hand on the bar to steady himself. He took small steps around the tables, a couple occupied, the rest empty. He'd stop in for one or two tomorrow.

The air outside was cool, fresh. Caruthers started up the empty street, shaking some of the fog from his head. A single floodlight over Chucho's office lit the area. Caruthers left this halo of light and walked through darkness toward home. His feet knew every cobble, even half blind. Ahead he locked on the diagonal stairway leading to his door. At the bottom step, he rested a bit, clutched the handrail, and then he heaved himself up, all the way to the landing. He fumbled with the key and finally fit it into the lock when a shadow rose beside him and he fell to the side, his head bright and ringing with pain that reached deeply into him through the numbness. He ducked against blows raining down on his arm and side and back. An orange glow behind his eyes, he fell, tumbling, slow enough to think that this might be it, the end of him. It wasn't so bad, he thought, resting on the ground, eyes closed, the hurt crawling over him and settling on the side of his head and in his left leg. Dully, he heard crashing and stomping high above, followed by footsteps drawing nearer and the electric heat of bodies leaping over him and disappearing like bats into the night. He was alone, still alive. That seemed like a good start. He opened his eyes to a sideways view of his bottom step over the dirty cobbles of the road. Something had to be done about this, but later, he thought, closing his eyes and slipping away.

# Chapter Twenty-Six

He opened his eyes, and the dog that had licked his face stepped back, a brindle cur with a web of scars over its muzzle. Dawn had broken, tinting the low clouds pink from his own building's overhang to the jagged horizon to the east. No one was about, and a sense of urgency, alarm even, settled in, while the pain that had been there all along pulsed for attention, pain from two sources and with two different styles. The pain on his ear was shallow and sharp, lemon squeezed onto a cut. Flat on his back, he reached up and touched it, felt the ridges of drying blood along the broken cartilage. A deeper, sickening pain had taken over the area of his left ankle, booming like old time railroad workers swinging sledge hammers. He sniffed, blinked his cloudy eyes and compiled the facts of the moment: he was on the ground, outside, injured; in approximately twenty-four hours a grave responsibility awaited, a duty requiring the use of all his senses and limbs. "Get," he said to the dog, his voice an incoherent croak. The dog, watching from five feet away, ignored the command. Caruthers sat up, and the dog backed away a couple of steps.

Hoping for relief, he untied his left sneaker, releasing a new, more fluid variety of pain into the foot. After the hurting, the next concern was thirst, for water first and then for something more medicinal. He needed a doctor. He needed off of the street. He arranged those needs into a workable order. The ringing in his head was loud, like the whine of a giant mosquito. He breathed in deeply, grabbed the bottom post of his stairway, and pulled himself up on his healthy right leg. He didn't attempt to put pressure on the other, not yet.

He swiveled toward the empty street. Billy. That's who rolled him. Well, shit, he thought, and fell into a fit of coughing, the present version of laughter. He gently set the left foot on the step, moved it up and down on the hinge of his ankle without too much pain. He slowly put some weight on it, breathed in deeply, and hopped his right leg up to that same step. Pain like a molten poker shoved into the marrow of his ankle bone exploded and slowly subsided as the right leg took over. Sweat dripped from his nose onto the next step. He crawled up the stairs on hands and knees. At the top, he hopped on one foot into his apartment, torn apart quickly and, to Caruthers' mind, amateurishly. The key was still in the door. He removed it, caught one last glimpse of the dog, its front paws on his bottom step, and locked the door behind him. The kids had taken the beer and liquor, emptied his drawers onto the floor. In the bathroom he found the medicine cabinet open. He found the bottle of ibuprofen on the floor, shook out eight pills, and clutched them in his fist, thankful they hadn't gotten his money or papers. He hopped to the kitchen, washed down the pills with a gallon jug of water from the fridge.

Belly full of water, he regarded the trash on the floor. Mostly cans, stuck in a tangy glue of beer residue, a white paper bag among them that had once contained a roasted chicken and now held bones and gristle. This is what archeologists would learn about him centuries hence. Oh, what a fuckup he was. The thought threatened to knock him across the room and down into bed never to rise. He'd done it to himself, yet again. Memories of the previous night floated like goblins in the dark of his brain. He didn't want them to come out into the light, but he couldn't avoid glimpses, bits of talk. Not now, he thought. He simply didn't have time to wallow. The steps listed on the ground out front now had to be followed. There'd be time later to slop about in the filth that was him. The notepad lay unmolested on the table, beside it, the pen. He dropped into a chair and wrote numbers down the left side, one to seven, with plenty of room between each. "Undress," he wrote beside number one. 2: "Remove shoe from fucked up foot." He drew lines and arrows, signifying a swap in order between two and one. 3: "Shower." 4: "Catch tuk tuk to Dr. Jimenez." 5: "Don't let Cruz see you." The last wasn't a thing to do, but it belonged on the list. Briefly, masochistically, he entertained the notion of coming clean to Chucho, informing the gangster that his new gun runner was already broken and out of commission. So sorry. He'd just have to tell his new criminal buddies to reschedule.

Caruthers shivered. He'd likely blow Caruthers away immediately, the best of the many unpleasant potential reactions. 6: "Drive to Salvador tomorrow." Failure, as he was always hearing the latest generation of gringo backpacker say, was not an option. Oh, how wrong they were. Failing was not everything, it was the only thing.

He slid the chair to the side so he could get at his foot. He untied the right shoe, pulled it off and unpeeled the damp sock. Then he loosened the other and removed the suture-like strings. He breathed in and out a few times, rocking slowly as if to gather momentum. Sweat trickled down the groove of his spine. He pulled the shoe off. He didn't yell out loud, but inside he lifted his soul's snout and howled like a wolf. The purity of the pain just made sense, burned all the shit away, leaving nothing but ashes. He felt better. On the sheet of paper, he crossed out item two, scribbling until the page tore.

The tuk tuks would start patrolling around eight. That gave him an hour. While the coffee brewed, he removed the medicine cabinet. Ignoring the cash, his papers, and passport, he trucked the pint of rum he kept there for emergencies into the kitchen and emptied it into the thermos recovered from the detritus on the floor. The day began to feel manageable. He poured a finger into a cup and threw it back. This provided enough warmth the get him undressed and into the shower. Another shot waited as a reward for cleaning and clothing himself.

# A Candle for San Simón

The foot, like the freed genie, would not again be confined. He considered a sock, or a flip flop, but finally he elected to tote the pale, bloated, purpling hunk of meat naked out into the world. He clutched the Stanley and hopped out the door. Five minutes later, the first tuk tuk buzzed by and toted him down Fifth Street to Dr. Jimenez's. The only medical facility in town, it was known simply as the clinic.

A family of Mayans—mother, father, child, toddler, infant—bunched at the far side of the waiting room, taking up a quarter the space an American family would have commandeered. As always, the children were quiet and calm, eyeing Caruthers with open curiosity. He hopped to the sliding widow where Jimenez's assistant, a Mayan girl, asked for Caruthers' name and the nature of his ailment. The urge for a smartass response did not lead to a smartass response. Instead he pointed down at his foot and said "sprained," in English, an expression of wishful thinking meant to influence the eventual diagnosis. He hopped back to a plastic chair across the long, narrow room, as far from the family as possible. The old American conviction arose as he settled in to wait: his trouble was more important than theirs. But wasn't it true, at least today? He saw no evidence of illness or injury among them. Probably a routine visit, offered pro-bono by the good doctor. Charity patients should have to wait for those who pay, Caruthers thought, smiling at what an asshole he truly was.

A few minutes later—the Stanley a quarter drank—a young woman with an Indian face but dressed in leggings and a large sweater over her pregnant belly walked out quickly, head down as though ashamed. Weren't we all ashamed to be seen at the doctor's, an admission that things weren't okay, that we needed help? He doubted she was sixteen. As the family ventured as one through the open portal to the magic land of health, Caruthers recalled that abortion was illegal in this country, that contraception was discouraged and difficult to find, even condoms. A strange place, Guatemala, the freest of free markets on the one hand, a land of tyranny on the other. A sort of op-ed ran through his mind. Want to open a business? Put a sign up and go at it. Few paid taxes. Virtually all deals took place under the table. Laws were suggestions, and the government—separate from the military—was too weak to enforce them anyway. Security and education were mainly private. The wealthy lived in fortresses, sent their kids to school under armed escort. These kids were valuable commodities on the open market; the sentimentality of their rich parents paid bundles. And the gangs were the ultimate players in this game without rules. The strong survived long enough to reproduce, the most anyone in that life could hope for. Pure Darwinism. A fat, pampered American conservative's wet dream. Then you had the Catholic Church, the big check to all this freedom, this free for all, whose peculiar rules were all over these girls' bodies—not the boys', just the girls'. How many generations had passed since Cortez sailed up with his guns and horses and more powerful god? How many conversions had he accomplished under torture?

The Mayans themselves hadn't been saints—not the ruling class at least, not the priests and kings. They were into human sacrifice, sometimes quick deaths but more frequently slow and excruciating, or at least horrifically gruesome. But they hadn't tortured, never thought to use pain and terror to gain information or conversions. They hurt people for the fun of it, to appease the gods, the embodiments of their own sadism. Christians brought torture, hurting for profit and not just amusement. Progress! And by God the present batch of leaders would make Cortez proud.

Caruthers hoped he'd die quickly and with a minimum of pain when the time came, be it sooner or later. He didn't mind the thought of not existing. He found it even comforting, especially at a time like this. The actual dying, however, filled him with dread.

The assistant summoned him, cutting off this line of reflection. He passed through the door and into a small, windowless room with an examination table like those in the States, minus the covering of paper. The doctor, a bald, light-skinned ladino with extremely thick-lensed glasses, stood waiting for him. His white coat bore a trail of brown stains down the front, large as a penny at the top, getting smaller as they descended, like the little wakes of a skipped stone. Caruthers had been in this room before, with its white, bare walls and tile floor, on three separate instances in fact: for an infected boil on his back, which had grown from the size of a marble to that of a baseball overnight and hurt like a stiletto in his kidney; for a hand broken by punching a stone wall while dead drunk; and for a case of diarrhea that had nearly killed him.

The doctor, now as then, went about his job in tranquil silence, occasionally broken by soft humming. "It's mainly the leg," Caruthers said, as Jimenez began wiping the area around his smarting ear. The doctor paid no attention, and with the gentlest of motions, cleaned his broken flap. It stung, a little, but not much. After ten patient minutes of cleaning, Jimenez ripped open a bandage and secured it over Caruthers' ear, a big surrender flag attached to his head. What the doctor didn't do was inquire about Caruthers' habits. He took his blood pressure but didn't share the results. Didn't ask about smoking, drinking, even as the smell of rum filled the closed chamber. No concern about cholesterol. Caruthers scooted back on the table to present the injured leg to Jimenez. "I drive for a living," he said, "and I've got an important job tomorrow." He was looking at the ceiling, crumbling drop tiles around two florescent lamps with their plastic covers removed. Probably discarded after the first time the bulbs were changed.

"Can you move it like this?" Jimenez asked in confident English, mimicking with his hand and wrist the motion of a foot depressing a gas pedal. Caruthers was happy to comply, to show that the foot still worked. It hurt some, but he could move it fine. If he passed the tests and avoided saying anything stupid, he'd be given permission to drive his bus tomorrow, and the permission would lead to the ability. "This way?" the doctor asked, making a side-to-side movement. Caruthers, more painfully this time, again accomplished the task.

The doctor had Caruthers hop down the hall to the x-ray room—the apex of the clinic's technology as far as Caruthers knew. He took the opportunity to down a few sips of the coffee, and then set the thermos on the floor in the corner of the room. He lay on the table, posing this way and that as the doctor snapped pictures. Caruthers wore no lead apron, and why should he? The potency of his sperm mattered about as much as the temperature on Venus. Zap the whole damn thing off for all he cared. He'd done his damage.

Jimenez left the room, and Caruthers retrieved his beverage from the floor. Other, more subtle pains, his right wrist, the hinge of his jaw, both elbows, appeared under the cover of the pulsing ankle and squealing ear. His foot had continued to swell, all the way to his toes, which poked from the end of the ballooning flesh like nipples on an udder. He imagined five little piggies feasting there. No, six, the runt going hungry on the table. Oh, it was a bleak world. The whimsy of his thoughts signaled that the rum was taking effect. He removed the lid to take a long drink. The doctor was good enough not to notice the strong smell when he returned with the pictures.

They showed, he explained, a spiral fracture in a small bone in his ankle. After the swelling went down, Caruthers could go to Xela or Guate for surgery, or Jimenez could do his best to set it and apply a cast—though the last option held the greatest risk for decreased mobility. Caruthers stared at the four images of his bones, fuzzy white things closer to clouds than the rigid stuff that kept his body from crumpling to the floor. "You need to understand, Doc, I have to drive tomorrow. Decreased mobility is not a concern at this point in time. Decreased aliveness is my present worry."

The doctor blinked like a reptile. "You can't put pressure on this leg. If driving requires depressing a clutch, for example, you won't be able to do it."

"Please, Doc. Can't you do something to get me through one day?
Afterwards you can amputate the damn thing for all I care."

"Do what? Your leg is broken. Six, eight weeks minimum before you
can walk without a cast. More if you keep drinking the way you do."

"A brace, or something like that. Some pills to numb the pain."

The doctor cracked a thin-lipped smile, an expression of indulgence.
"Take the day off, sir. Even God rests one day a week. Would you like
me to write you a note?"

"Great," Caruthers said. "Perfect. A note. Please don't kill Mr.
Caruthers. He's got a hurt foot."

"I can't help you, except to write a prescription for pain. Keep your
foot elevated. Put it on ice." Jimenez produced an ace bandage. "Relax,"
he said, and began to wrap the ankle. "If you are still with us in two days,
come back and I'll check the swelling." Caruthers watched the doctor's
face as he worked, searching for a sign of humor. He was rewarded with a
flicker of a smile as the doctor fastened the bandage with its little metal
set of fangs.

Will you care, he wondered, if I disappear? Light freckles accented by
a few darker moles covered Jimenez's head. He wore a wedding band. An
unattractive little man with a pretty good job in a poor country on a
beautiful lake, he was making the most of it, unlike Caruthers, who'd
taken the opposite tack.

"Wait here," Jimenez said, and left the room. Caruthers studied his
smoky bones again. They were like everyone else's, as far as he could tell.
The sadness and self-pity ebbed. For a second there he thought he was
going to cry—at nine thirty in the morning and barely drunk. Jimenez
returned with wooden crutches, used. Fine cracks covered the rubber
handles and padding on the tops.

"They charge hundreds of dollars for these things in the States,"
Caruthers said. "Probably thousands by now."

"I know. It's all we talk about, we poor doctors of the world, the healthcare problems in the U.S. It makes us feel better."

Caruthers tried them out, and the doctor helped him adjust the handles. "I can charge you five hundred if you like," Jimenez said.

"You're a regular cut up," Caruthers responded, slinging himself forward and back. The problem, he saw, was the Stanley. The Stanley was always the problem.

"Cut up? I'm not much of a surgeon, if that's what you mean."

"Comedian. You're funny. I never knew."

The doctor was pleased. He stooped to pick up the thermos from the corner. "Sometimes. I try to make people happy." Caruthers accepted the Stanley. He was able to hold it by the handle with his fingers while maintaining his thumb on the crutch. "Would you like me to attach it to your body?" Jimenez asked. "I have some tubing somewhere around here."

Caruthers practiced a step.

"An intravenous drip would be even more efficient," the suddenly hilarious doctor added. "How much would that cost in the United States?"

"Keep your day job, Doc, and thanks for the help." Caruthers crutched out the door before being subjected to more of the doctor's wit. At the front desk, he paid with a U.S. fifty dollar bill, and the girl returned about twenty bucks worth of quetzales. She informed him in Spanish that he could sell the crutches back when he no longer needed them. Jimenez held the door open for him, and he exited into the waiting room, where an old woman hefted herself up from her chair with the help of a homemade walking stick. Others filled the rest of the room, but Caruthers avoided looking at them. The sick and injured depressed him.

Outside, an SUV drove toward him from Santander Street, and Caruthers held his breath. An old vehicle, rusty around the wheels, it served as a reminder he needed off the streets before Chucho or one of his spies happened by. But where? What would he do? His torn up apartment didn't appeal to him. Red would open in fifteen minutes, but no. Too close to Chucho's roost, and too many flapping lips there. He eased himself from the non-accessibly narrow sidewalk down to the street and started away from Santander, aiming for a little ranchero dive he'd popped into a few times over the last years, just around the corner where Rancho Street dissolved into a dirt road beside the river they used as a dump, a place to camp out for a few minutes and plan his next move.

On Rancho he slung himself along the dirt road toward the bar, a shed really. He pushed through the swinging door. The place had room only for a five-foot long bar counter and two tables. A man slept on the floor against the wall to the right of the door, the lone customer. Caruthers ordered a beer, and the bartender, a young man wearing a Lakers jersey, flicked a switch behind the bar to fill the room with Billy Joel bragging about his rich girlfriend. The boy Billy and his fellow muggers sometimes hung out here, Caruthers remembered, and a thought occurred to him. He could probably end Billy's life, if Cruz waited long enough to hear Caruthers' story before plugging him. He leaned the crutches against the wall under a poster of a bikini girl tipping a Cabro toward her wide open mouth, and eased into a twisted wooden chair.

Where was his notebook, his list? Well, the only list that mattered had one item: Find someone to drive the bus. The obvious answer was Seba, except Seba had never even driven a car, much less a 67-seat passenger vehicle with a split axle transmission. No way, not even if he was willing to try, which he wouldn't be. Seba valued this deficiency. Once you learn to drive, he'd told Caruthers, you need a car, and once you have a car, you need to put gas in it, buy it new tires, clean it, bribe cops, get a license that allowed the government to keep track of you. Seba was right, Caruthers thought as the kid bartender set a beer on the table, driving eventually led to running guns for vicious criminals. How about Red? Nope. Wouldn't do it, and Caruthers wasn't going to embarrass himself by asking.

He could run. Just hop a bus and get as far away as possible. With $300 and some change to his name, he might make it as far as Mexico City, a nice place to be broke, gimpy, and hiding from gangsters. The better solution would be to off himself. Why not? He'd considered it before, plenty of times. He'd gone over various methods in his mind, which is where the desire to be gone tended to break down. A bullet? Too messy. He didn't want his final act to involve spurting blood. Drowning? Where? He didn't own a boat and couldn't imagine flopping into the water from the shore. Hanging. Ugg. It would hurt too much, and imagine the person finding him. Pills? He'd screw it up, survive and have to start over except this time with brain damage. No, he'd always settled the matter by reasoning he'd be dead before he knew it anyway. He'd made it nearly to the finish line. Might as well limp across.

The counter argument was that suicide would be less horrible than torture. But he no longer owned a gun, forgot to ask for the pain pill prescription, and his ceiling didn't have anything to tie a rope to. He'd have to buy a hook at the store, and a drill to install it, plus a length of rope. What a pain in the ass that would be. The real solution, which had been hovering around his mind from the moment he'd felt his leg break but only now, half through his beer and well into the day's second song, "The Piano Man," was he able to recognize it. His son, Max, could drive the bus.

No, no, no, no way, Caruthers told himself. He ordered another beer, and by the end of that one and onto side B of Billy Joel's Greatest Hits he'd managed to turn "no" into "maybe." The third beer ushered the danger to Max from grave, to moderate, to minimal. Billy Joel, meanwhile, stepped aside for Bob Seeger. The noon hour approached, when the second of three daily busses headed to the hinterlands down south where Max hunkered with his steaming peasants.

Outside, he propelled himself along the dirt road east toward the

A Candle for San Simón

highway, the back way through town to avoid an unfortunate run-in. He didn't have much time for self-justification, but he used what time he had. The kid could always say no, and really, if he hadn't gotten himself kidnapped to start with, Caruthers wouldn't be in this mess. In the end, it would all equal out, and they'd be fine. It was just a simple drive, there and back. They were only a delivery service, after all. *Uptown girl,* Billy Joel sang in Caruthers' head, *she's been livin' in her white bread world.* He let the song stay there as he navigated the ruts and stones in the road, while the dog that had woken him hours before watched from the shadows under a porch. "What are you looking at?" Caruthers mumbled.

# Chapter Twenty-Seven

Karma was sitting in the dirt beside Reina when the dogs began to bark. She cradled a tin cup of elote in both hands, warm in the sun watching Boo the baby sift dirt through his fingers, endlessly fascinated by the stuff. She'd been telling Reina about Max's experience in captivity, minus the sex. Reina's knowledge of the gang was either extensive or incorrect. Mara X they were called, founded by imprisoned Salvadoran immigrants in Los Angeles, California, and new to the Guatemalan highlands. Ruthless murderers, they'd made short work of the local thugs, introducing the next level of organized crime to what had been a backwater. The only hope against them, Reina thought, was a militia of outraged citizens forming in Xela. Karma agreed in principle. The answer to bad government was popular uprising, and in the absence of government, wasn't this criminal enterprise acting in that role?

The object of the dogs' attention appeared on the path outside the village, an old white-haired man hobbling on crutches, a green thermos swinging from one hand. A pall, a black cloud covering the sun, attended Max's father's arrival. He waved with his free hand at Karma, leaning forward on his crutches. "Hola," he called. "Getting up that hill on these things is a bitch."

"You hurt yourself," she observed.

"It's nothing," he said, unscrewing the lid on his thermos while glancing around and behind him. "Glad to see you guys back in the saddle. Max come through the ordeal okay?"

# A Candle for San Simón

"You can ask him yourself," she said, pointing toward the center of the village, where Max ambled along one of the paths that had appeared with the growth of the grass. He'd changed since the brief captivity. She could see it even in his walk, the way he knocked the dust from his hands against his thighs. Since returning, he'd devoted himself to the chimneys full time. The day before, Sunday, he'd served soup as before but offered no sermon, or any explanation for the absence. "Eat," he'd said. "Enjoy." At the same time, he exuded more force and confidence than before. She didn't know she welcomed the change. She'd felt tender toward his weaknesses, his confused anguish and uncertainty. She didn't know what to do with the new version.

A stew of feelings attended his approach, chief among them shame, tinged with a reckless excitement. They'd made love often, as much as three times a day since arriving here, a passion initiated by her but having taken on its own life. The new intimacy always took place in silence, the silence of certain dinner tables, where the focus was on the hunger, the satisfaction of relieving it.

The people of the village had shown signs of pious disapproval, or perhaps Karma had merely imagined this silent reproach. She didn't care much either way. She wasn't one of them, didn't want to be one of them, and was free to leave whenever she liked. Meanwhile, an unspoken pact formed between her and Max. They'd discussed nothing about his internment. She'd not deleted the photographs. They burned in the phone in her pocket even as she sat talking to Max's father.

"There he is," Caruthers said. "The man of the hour. How's it feel to be free?"

Max assessed the situation, looking from Karma, to Reina, to Boo, and finally to his father. "I was only there three days. People spend years locked up like that."

"All the more reason to be thankful, especially with Thanksgiving coming."

"I'm thankful," Max said, looking at Karma. "I might be the luckiest guy around."

"Luck, yeah, you might call it that. How about God's will? You're into that kind of thing, aren't you?"

"Let me guess," Max said, gesturing toward Caruthers' bandaged ear and leg, "you got drunk and fell down the stairs."

"Close. I had assistance. To be specific, I got rolled by a pack of juvenile delinquents. They trashed my place, even raided the fridge. Could have been worse though."

"Why are you here?"

Reina stood and gathered Boo. "We're going to see the pigs. He likes to watch them eat," she explained to Caruthers. A group of children marched by in line, guided by nine-year-old Maria, who barked at her underlings from beside their ranks, a military game she always tried to initiate.

"Can't I drop by to see if my son's okay after his brush with dangerous kidnappers?"

"Please. I have a lot of work to do. Get to the point."

"Fair enough and well said. None of us has a lot of time these days." He shifted on the crutches, fiddled with his thermos but didn't open it. "You mind if we talk in private?" He directed this at both Max and Karma. She was about to excuse herself when Max protested.

"Anything you need to say to me you can say to her."

"You sure she wants to know? I've got some, well, potentially hazardous information."

"I want to know," she said.

"Well, okay, in that case." Caruthers took a long drink. The elote in Karma's hand had gone cold. "It's nothing really. I have a little errand to run tomorrow. I need to take the bus over to Salvador and back. A one-day trip is all. Start in the morning, back before dark. Unfortunately, the doc says I can't drive, not for a couple of months. Rotten timing."

# A Candle for San Simón

Max stared at his father like he couldn't quite place him. "Are you kidding me? You want me to do your job for you? Does it look like I'm on vacation here? I've got four more chimneys to build, and every day these people live without one increases their risk of cancer, emphysema, who knows what else? We're talking about little kids."

"I wouldn't ask if it wasn't important."

"Important. I see. And my work is, what?"

"It's a matter of life and death, son. I'm not talking about emphysema someday in the future. Immediate death. Mine."

"You're nuts."

"True, but that doesn't change the facts."

Max paused to let Filomena and Baffi walk by. Karma wondered what these diviners would advise in this situation, what the rolled bones would predict. On their way to talk to Reina, they took in the gringo summit and kept going, as if out for a stroll. The village "daykeepers" always consulted the young Reina, educated in the mysteries of the outside world. Karma didn't believe in their magic, but she recognized their basic good sense and the wisdom that came from experience. The bones were just a gimmick, a symbol of authority, like a judge's gavel and robe or a cop's badge. Karma admired the structure of it, though the system would break down if the village ever grew too large for everyone to personally know everyone else. That's when charlatans and thieves got hold of the bones.

"Let's pretend you're really in trouble," Max said. "Out of all your friends at the bar, you come to lean on me, who you barely know."

"What can I say? You're right. The people I associate with don't give a rat's ass about me, and I don't blame you if you feel the same. I'm here for one reason. You're my last chance."

"No," Max said. "Sorry, but no. I can't, and I won't save you."

"I didn't want to bring this up, but I'm going to. That's how desperate I am. The reason—"

A dog fight broke out nearby, and everyone whirled around to watch. The conflict ended as quickly as it had started, with the smaller dog scuttling off low to the ground, the bigger dog standing his territory proudly while three others of his species crouched in witness. "What was I saying?" Caruthers asked. "Oh, I got into this mess by saving your ass, Max. That's the truth. I made a deal with the devil to spring you from the gangsters, and now I owe the devil a day's work. You'd never have had to know any of this, except that I can't do it by myself anymore, and I need your help."

"No," Max repeated, looking to Karma as if for clarification. "Can this be true?"

"I don't know," she said, the picture of Max's dick sliding into the hairy vagina appeared in her mind, and she cleared her throat. "I just got a text message telling me where to find you in the park. That's all."

"Believe me or not, son. I'm sorry to put you in this position. I really am. I'm sorry about a lot of things, pretty much everything. You turned out to be a good man without my help, or in spite of me. I'm proud of you. If you can't do it, that's okay. I'll figure something out. Oh, and before I forget." He pulled some folded papers from a pocket in his coat and separated out three envelopes. "Here. One's for you, the others are for Danny and your mother, whenever you see them. Read yours when you feel like it. Nothing important, just some thoughts I had."

Max made a sound like an animal, half groan, half growl, his hands covering his face as if keeping it from falling off.

"What's the job?" Karma asked.

"How's that?"

"What are you delivering? Where? What's the plan?"

"Oh, that. The less you know the better. For your own safety."

"The people who kidnapped Max know my name and where I live. They know who my parents are. I was there when they took him, when they shot the driver."

236

"I hardly know anything, and I promised not to tell. That's part of the whole deal."

"If Max is going to help you, he needs to know what he's getting into."

"Excuse me?" Max asked. "Am I going to help him now?"

"Max, please. We need all the information we can get before anyone makes a decision." The sun had sunk behind the trees, whose shadows covered the village. Karma stood, accepted the envelopes flopping in Caruthers' hand. "You're smuggling, right? Drugs? People? Weapons? It's got to be one of them."

Caruthers shook the thermos to test the level. After some internal calculations played over his fleshy red face, he opened the lid and drank. "Guns," he said. "We set out tomorrow at eight. Drive to a certain backwoods border crossing and just into El Salvador, where we'll meet the contact. I'm not sure what happens there, except I'm not supposed to leave the bus. Everything will be taken care of, except driving. On the way back, we're supposed to take on fares as a front, up to the final stop in Xela, where we'll drop off the load. After that, we're done. There's not a lot to worry about. The cops are in on it. That's one of the only things I know for sure. It's basically a business deal. Sales. And we're FedEx."

"We?" Max asked.

"Hypothetically."

"Max," Karma said, placing the envelopes in his hand. "Let's take a walk. Do you mind waiting here, Mr. Caruthers?"

"Please," he said, "call me Norman. Norm. I'll keep your spot warm." He hobbled over to Reina's hut and eased himself to the ground.

Max was already walking, into the center of the village and toward the corn field. Karma jogged up to him. Soon they waded into the chest-high stalks of green corn. A peal of giggles rang out ten meters in front of them, and the stalks there rippled as the kids ran off, perhaps waiting for Karma and Max to have sex.

He stopped in the middle of the field. Gnats flew about their faces. Over the past few minutes, he'd lost the recent focus and conviction, and he stood confused and scared, a little boy who's run away from home and can't remember why. His eyes, so large and sad, always made her feel a little like crying. It was a large part of the attraction. "Where are we going?" Max asked. She took one of his hands in both of hers. His other still held the envelopes.

"This way, away from these bugs." She led him toward the back end of the field, to the evergreen forest outside the village. The kids broke free of the corn and disappeared among the trees. "I think you should do it," she said, and Max stopped at the base of a tall pine.

"Really?"

"It's dangerous. I know that. And after everything you just went through..." She dared to look him in the eyes. "Such a terrible experience." He held her gaze, his expression placid, blank. "I'm thinking about how you'll feel if, if he's telling the truth, and they do something to him."

Max nodded his head. "I'm surprised. I thought you'd try to talk me out of it. I was thinking we could send him back to the States, but, well, I don't personally have the money, and what would I tell Kent? Can I really expect the church to bail out my deadbeat father?"

She looked at the hand in hers, traced the calluses with her fingertips, calluses grown rougher since the chimneys. "Will the embassy help?" she asked, knowing the answer.

"What would they do? Give him some forms to fill out. No. He wouldn't go anyway. And even if they do send him back, what's he going to do? He'll be broke, with nobody to call."

Karma imagined Caruthers walking out of a giant, gleaming

airport, his thermos in hand. She'd never flown, never gone farther
from home than Guate. She'd seen the U.S. in pictures, in movies,
but she couldn't imagine it really, except for tall buildings, wide
streets, beautiful people in fine clothes. An absence of dirt, except
for dark soil in pots and flower beds. Nothing but new cars on the
roads, and no busses anywhere.

"You're right," Max said. "This is my duty. I see that now. My
feelings about him don't matter, and it doesn't matter if he deserves
it or not. None of us did anything to deserve this life anyway. I've
been wondering why I'm here. To build chimneys? No, it's simpler
and more direct than that. I came to save the father I've hated for as
long as I can remember." He closed his eyes and nodded his head.
Karma kept to herself the observation that Max's arrival had directly
led to his father's predicament. "Yes," he said, "I think I
understand."

Karma experienced a surge of misgiving, an urge to withdraw
support for the venture, but what could she say at this point? She'd
helped dislodge the stone from the cliff, and now it would tumble
down the hillside. Maybe Max was right, about his higher purpose.
Who could know why things happened the way they did?

"Let's go back," she said. "You'll need a change of clothes."

They held hands like sweethearts, through the village and back to
their hut. Inside, she slung her briefcase over her shoulder as Max
surveyed his things.

"Should I bring my passport?" he asked, sliding the envelopes
into the small pocket of his backpack.

She thought about his question. "Yes," she said. "It could help.
I'll go tell your father your decision. Meet us at Reina's."

Caruthers stood as she approached, the way one stands at the
appearance of a judge. "Max has agreed to drive your bus," she said,
"but only if you tell me everything. Where you're going, the

timetable. The whole trip there and back." She removed a pad of paper from her briefcase.

"You sure you want to know all that? Seems kind of unnecessary, even dangerous. And writing it down, well, that's evidence, isn't it?"

"I want to track Max along the route. We'll stay in phone contact."

"You're not thinking something stupid, are you? Like calling the police?"

"Which police? The ones who ride mopeds and can't afford their own bullets, or the ones employed by the gang you're working for?"

"Okay. Just making sure you understand the situation. You start messing around, even with the best intentions, you're likely to get your boyfriend killed."

"I only want to know where he is. He'll call when it's over, and I'll come meet you."

"If those are your terms, I guess I have to accept them. You ready? We leave at Pana at eight, like I said." He removed a piece of paper from the coat pocket and dictated names of streets, meeting times and locations. "It's all approximate. You can't predict traffic, closed roads and such. Also, the other people involved. Maybe they show up, maybe they don't. Lot can happen."

Max came down the central footpath carrying Boo, Reina beside them. The name "Rudy" had fallen away for some reason, and Max's "Beau" had slid into Boo. Karma fit the notebook into her case. Max kissed the child on his fat cheek and passed him to Reina. He embraced Karma, squeezing. He kissed her on the mouth, the stubble of his beard and mustache scratching her face. A familiar stirring of blood, a blooming, moved within her, and she had to smile at the folly of the body, craving sex at a time like this. Max released her and turned to his father.

"I guess we're going to do this thing."

# A Candle for San Simón

"I'm grateful, son. You'll never know."

"Are you staying here?" Max asked Karma.

"I'll take Boo to my parents' house, wait for you to call."

Max nodded his head, looked around at the gathered dogs, sitting or standing in a group, watching. The defeated dog, his place re-established, had rejoined the club. Baffi and Filomena also watched, from the front of their hut. The kids assembled behind the dogs made up the rest of the audience. "I hate to leave Anton's chimney unfinished," Max said.

"You'll be back in two, three days tops," Caruthers responded. "He'll survive."

An amorphous grief entered Karma, watching Max and his father walk down the path, shrinking and then disappearing down the hill. She shook off the useless feeling and took Boo from Reina. "I need to talk to you," she said to the girl, the first of many urgent duties.

# Chapter Twenty-Eight

They met at the bus an hour early, to give Max some practice time behind the wheel and to avoid an unannounced send-off by Chucho Cruz. Caruthers sat at Seba's usual spot, first row of the passenger side, which provided the best view of the guest driver. Max bounced on the seat, testing its spring while examining the instrument panel. He wiggled the stick shift, and started the engine. The sky was bright even though the sun hadn't risen over the eastern mountains.

Caruthers reminded Max of the concept of the manual transmission with dual axle speeds. You go through the gears like a normal car, and then raise the red button and start again in first. Max, familiar with construction yards, had heard of this kind of thing. He put it in gear and pulled forward, cranking the wheel to get in line for the narrow alleyway exit. "It's not as big as it feels," Caruthers said. "You think it'll never fit, but it does." Max guided the bus carefully to the edge of Santander, stopped with a jerk as he tested the brakes, and then lurched into the empty street.

Slowly they crawled toward the highway at the top of the strip, where the challenge for Max would begin. Already busy with bus traffic, the winding road switch-backed up the ridge, swinging along the edge of sack-shriveling plunges. Max paused at the intersection, ground the gear into first, and apologized. Caruthers said no problem. He'd get the feel for it. Confidently, Max entered traffic, looking good at the helm in the green Hawaiian shirt with orange

# A Candle for San Simón

blossoms that Caruthers had pestered him into wearing. Caruthers felt proud of his handsome, competent son, in spite of the little bun on top of his head like Buddha's second cousin. What had happened to the cowboy hat? Caruthers wondered.

He relaxed as Max settled into a rhythm with the bus. As they ate the miles, Caruthers took some petty satisfaction in the disappointment of the waiting passengers as the bus sped by, flying the day's flag: Fuera de Servicio. That's all he wanted in life, Caruthers understood, to be out of service but still running, to cruise along without passengers, not heading anywhere special, just moving. Leaving the lake area, the drive got easier, straighter, more level, with lighter traffic. Semi-arid scrubland gave way to dense forest. The sun rose behind, but Caruthers didn't look back. He'd seen enough orange sky in his life. Underrated were the soft greens through which they drove, the opposite side of sunrise. Besides, his neck ached.

An hour later, as they approached the left turn onto the 9 toward Salvador, Caruthers located the worry that had haunted him all morning, that sense of forgetting something. He'd intended to use a little of his buyout of Chucho on a new pistol for the trip. Oh well. What was he going to do with it anyway? Kill the bad guys and save the day? Soon enough they'd have an arsenal on the roof, just out of reach.

Max drove well, relaxed now they'd left traffic. The clutch did its job crisply, and the engine still sounded strong, an old bus, having come down from America for a second life. Caruthers felt pretty good about things, verging on the sentimental. He'd never compared himself to the bus before. In any event, something was definitely going to happen today, and for all he knew it could be good.

"Feel like a beer?" Max asked, pointing at a spray-paint-on-particleboard sign advertising a store a kilometer ahead. Caruthers recalled long drives down desert roads with a cooler full of cans and ice, the bright days of ditching college.

"You serious or messing with me."

"Serious, more or less. I'm thinking, why not?"

"Sure," Caruthers said, and Max put it in neutral and drifted to the small dirt parking lot. He left the bus idling and returned with a cardboard box lined with plastic and filled with cans and ice. Caruthers thought he'd wait for Max to make the first move for the beer. They'd descended from the plains without quite noticing the change, onto a basin covered in limp grass and pools of standing water, giving off a swampy smell. Gulls and ducks flew about among lesser birds.

"Good thinking," Caruthers said, giving in and cracking a beer, while the full Stanley nestled on the bench against the wall. "Will you have one?"

"Not just yet, but soon. I'm starting to figure out that I want to drink, but not so much."

Caruthers laughed. "The key to life, kid."

Dunes supplanted the marsh as the sun climbed three-quarters up the pale sky. "This reminds me of a trip I took into Mexico," Max said. "The only time I've been. I was young, a couple years out of high school. I saw a sign for a spring break trip to Mazatlán while doing some contract work at a junior college. Walking through campus, I could see I was the same age as the students all around, and I kept thinking that I could be one of them, should be, instead of laying carpet with the old burnout I worked for. I tore off the little registration card at the bottom of the poster." He laughed. "I did it while the boss—I don't even remember his name—was eating lunch, and I looked around to be sure nobody would see me, like I was stealing something. The trip was for students, but how would they know?" Max tapped the steering wheel and looked back at

# A Candle for San Simón

Caruthers. "I'll take that beer now, if you don't mind."

Caruthers popped one for him and opened a second for himself.

Max placed the can in the cup holder, and Caruthers felt a stab of jealousy. A bus approached from the opposite direction, its ayudante sitting on the roof with his feet dangling over the windshield. "I paid the deposit, and after that, I was stuck. I wasn't exactly fired when I told my boss I was going to take a week off, but I wasn't given the days off either. Construction's like that. You work when they need you, you stay home when they don't. I knew if he liked whoever he hired while I was gone better than me, I'd be out of a job, not that I cared. Nobody owed anything to anybody was both our attitudes toward life. Anyway, the trip turned out to be a little bit of a scam once I added it all up, a Greyhound ticket from Santa Ana to Calexico, a Mexican charter bus with a keg of beer in the back and some hotel rooms in Mazatlán, where we slept four to a room. I didn't bother to do the actual math, but I knew I could have gone on my own a lot cheaper and not have to share a room. But I guess I was paying for the company, to be a part of something, even though I wasn't really in the group.

"On the Mexican bus, I sat next to a girl, tall with a pretty face and nice black hair. I wanted to hide that I wasn't a student, and so I hardly talked, but she liked me right off anyway, without asking questions about my life. The deal was, her hips were a little too wide to make it with the top college boys, and she saw that I wasn't one of them, that I wasn't so picky."

"Fuck those jackasses," Caruthers opined. "I remember them well."

Max nodded in the affirmative. "We drank beer after beer, and I felt, for the first time I could remember, that everything was just like it should be, the bus, the girl, everybody yelling and laughing, the desert with its shacks and junked cars. Late at night, completely drunk and sleepy, she asked me to tell her a story, and she curled up on her side to sleep in the seat, her face against my shoulder, my hand on her leg. I don't remember what I told her, some story about wizards and elves. I read those kinds of books back then, one after another, so it was easy to make something up. She fell asleep, and later I did too, leaning against each other. I woke up the next day, my back killing me, my head aching. The worst hangover I'd ever had. I thought I was going to throw up in the nasty toilet in the back of the bus."

"I take it you'll drink more moderately today."

"You got that right," Max said, his eyes behind aviator sunglasses.

"You, uh, how do the kids say it, hook up with this gal?"

"No. It was one of those things that happened on the bus, and the next day we both felt too sick to think about anything except surviving the drive. Then came all the confusion of moving into our rooms and we just sort of lost track of each other. Over the week, I'd see her at the bars at night while the other kids danced on the counter, and we'd both be sitting there, apart from one another and also the others, but we never really talked again. We'd just look away, kind of embarrassed. Getting together would have been like admitting nobody else wanted us. Something like that."

They crested a dune, and the Pacific Ocean spread before them, creamy caps and diamonds of light all the way to the horizon. It had been years since Caruthers had seen it. White and black birds circled over a spot beyond the breaking waves. One of them dived. They came to the outskirts of a port city and turned onto a narrow, poorly paved road dusted with sand and hugging the coast. Several miles later a town appeared, one of those fabled undiscovered fishing villages. A gaggle of kids in shorts stood on the side of the road outside of town, hailing a ride. Max honked the horn twice and shrugged an apology as he sped by. One of the boys threw him the

Candle for San Simón

finger. The village—a handful of sand-blasted buildings along an brief avenue, the usual central square fronting the usual church with the usual dead fountain in the middle—passed in an instant. A tattered flag on a pole, its insignia bleached away to nothing, snapped in the wind. "Ever been to Costa Rica?" Caruthers asked, feeling good and free but also a little sad, the purpose of the trip loitering on the border of thought, a leash around their necks. "What do you say we ditch the whole thing and head south, see how far we get?"

Max sipped his beer. "Sounds good to me." He smiled over at his father, reminding Caruthers how infrequently he'd smiled as a boy, and how good his occasional smiles made Caruthers feel, then and now. Caruthers wanted to give him something, some advice maybe, some love. He didn't know how, but he thought he might figure it out in the next hours. They still had a lot of driving to do before the day was over.

Ten miles later, the road T-ed into highway 7, where they turned away from the ocean. Caruthers glanced over his shoulder for one more look. They climbed up, onto the southern tail of the Sierra Madre range. Cruz, with Caruthers at the secretary's computer, had planned the route and timing, avoiding certain highways and certain territories, the circuitous way a drunk driver meanders home after a long session at the bar, hoping to dodge the cops. By now, Chucho's cohort should already have bribed away the guards at a mountain crossing called Cerro Brujo, a rough bit of road that kept most drivers away, according to Cruz.

They rose into cooler, thinner air. Pines and occasional hardwoods made shadows in the sunlight falling straight down. A rusted sedan passed in the other direction, the first vehicle they'd seen in hours. At a junction surrounded by what looked like a ghost town, they turned onto a smaller road, rising sharply toward mountain peaks. The going was slow, and once around a sharp bend Max lost track of the gears, kept grinding and looking around until he had to stop the bus in the middle of the curve and start over in first. "It's okay," Caruthers assured him. "I used to have to do that about a dozen times a day before I got the hang of it."

"Glad nobody was coming the other way," Max said, cranking the starter.

"That's what recommends this road," Caruthers said. "It's unattractiveness to everyone else. Kind of like your girl with the wide hips."

Fifteen minutes later, the sign appeared ahead. "Cazadoras," it read, "gasolina y cuchillos," a landmark Caruthers had been expecting, the last stop before the border. The road dissolved as it rose, until the pavement turned to chunks in the dirt, obstacles. Caruthers watched with as much energy and more stress than if he were driving himself, willing Max to move this way or that, to no effect. Max hit the potholes he hit, avoided the ones he avoided, all amounting to a randomness that sapped one's will to do anything. They entered clouds. Gray moss hung from branches in the forest around them, and the world took on a cold fecundity. Caruthers finished his flat beer and opened the Stanley. Their shirts, covered in flowers and Tiki gods respectively, looked dumb in this climate, and Caruthers hugged himself for warmth. Several minutes later, they passed the tree line, and the land opened onto low table rocks and brush dotted with red berries.

The border crossing appeared in a field of grass. A chain link gate topped with razor wire blocked the road and butted to a shed, outside of which stood a small pickup. Max stopped and a man wearing a collarless coat jogged out, his brow so low his hairline practically touched his eyebrows. Face down, he opened the gate. Max ground first gear, tried again and eased forward. The gate closed behind them.

"Easy enough," Caruthers said out loud, his voice startling him. They still had to descend the mountain, where Cruz's partner in trade would, in some way Caruthers wasn't privy to, facilitate the exchange. Five minutes and half a mile later, the mirror winked. A polished black SUV followed a hundred yards back, unmarked, even its windshield tinted black. "What should I do?" Max asked.

"Keep driving," Caruthers said. "Act naturally. This part is going to happen to us. Our job is to not freak out. No gunning the engine. No running away. No screams, no sudden movements. Let's just be cool."

The road dropped abruptly. Caruthers swore he could see the ocean, miles across the brown desert to the wavering edge of world. Just beyond the jutting peak of the mountain's shadow, a city glittered in the sun, a handful of coins dropped in the sand. This side of the mountain was steep, rocky, all the soil eaten away over the centuries, stripping the bones bare. The road had been carved into the face, long switchbacks all the way down like a suture. Warlock Mountain.

Max kept it in low gear down the first leg of the suture, a gentle grade. The SUV followed fifty feet behind. They approached a terrific precipice where a deep canyon cut into the mountain. The bus hugged the edge for a span of road turning hard in the other direction. A wink of light caught Caruthers's eye, down at the base of the mountain. He looked closer at a greenish area at the foot of the mountain, making out a large truck painted military green. Two jeeps flanked it. Figures wandered around. The wink returned, perhaps a reflection off the lens of a binocular, a phenomenon Caruthers knew from movies. All was well, he told himself. This was how it was supposed to be, the trailing SUV, probably Chucho's representative there to check the goods, the retail station down below manned by the selling party. Unless it wasn't okay, the SUV a rival gang, Salvadorian army waiting below. They'd find out soon enough.

The road cut back again, this time toward the canyon. Once there, Caruthers stared down the striated rocky wall on the far side. Trapped mist pooled at the bottom. Probably there was a stream down there, a waterfall surrounded by ferns. One level up, the SUV passed in the opposite direction. Caruthers felt like waving hello. Instead he capped the Stanley. With too much time to think and nothing to do, he imagined getting caught, that the people fore and aft were the bad guys, or rather, the good guys. In this vision, he and Max were brought to trial, used as propaganda, political leverage on an international scale. They'd make *USA Today*, gun-running gringos. Perhaps they'd share a cell. Plenty of time to get to know one another then.

The road straightened out at the bottom of the mountain, and they coasted the final straight stretch toward what was clearly a checkpoint. A man in uniform stood in the road, signaling Max to pull to the side, into a tent set up for the occasion. Caruthers sat still, staring forward. He wished he'd brought sun glasses. Max killed the engine. Another soldier entered the bus, said nothing, stood over Max, reached up and opened the padlocked storage cabinet over the driver's side window. From in it, he removed and spirited away a metal box. The money. If Caruthers had known, would he have been tempted? Maybe. Costa Rica might not have been a joke with enough cash, not that Max would have considered running, leaving his girlfriend behind to take the heat.

Men climbed onto the roof, and a clatter of boots and boxes hammered into the cabin. The load would be hidden under peasant baskets, Chucho had explained, tarps, cardboard boxes...the typical freight topping Guatemalan buses. The dangers, Caruthers understood, came not from casual scrutiny of passing cops, but from double agents, captured insiders, anyone who knew the plan and could gain by ratting them out. But the odds were on his side, Caruthers told himself.

A half hour later, a soldier stood in front of the bus and motioned for Max to back out. He did so, carefully, executed a three -point turn, and began to climb back up the mountain. Rolling through the border checkpoint up top, the air in the bus sizzled with a heatless electricity. Out of the cloud forest, past Cazadoras. The money delivered. The freight secured. Caruthers popped a beer and let out a long sigh.

Flouting Chucho's assigned route, they skipped the dogleg down to the coastal road, kept straight on CA 9. They passed a tanker, a slow bus, a jalopy, and then a pickup going the opposite direction. A troop transport passed them, two soldiers on the open tailgate, legs dangling, betraying only vague interest in the gringo bus, out of service but loaded with cargo. It would have made sense if they'd placed a Xela sign on the marquee for the trip home, took on passengers, as Chucho had planned it, but Caruthers couldn't do the ayudante thing even when healthy, and neither of them needed the extra complication. The military truck grew smaller along the straight road, disappeared behind a hill, and was gone for good. The long grass on either side of the road lay on its side, to the right, like combed hair.

They intersected the 11, the way to Panajachel, keeping on the 9 toward Xela, a virgin strip of road for Caruthers. Every few miles a village appeared on one side or another. The road adopted a new number, according to a government sign. A few minutes before three p.m., they began to ascend the highland plateau. The grass turned to brush, the brush to trees. The road bent to accommodate the broken, rising land, land like scar tissue. Along tight curves and steep climbs, dodging potholes the size of kiddie pools, they made slow time. No problem, though. It wasn't even four yet.

Caruthers finished his beer. The cardboard box had disintegrated into a wet trail of sludge flowing down the aisle toward the back door. He crumpled the can and threw it into the back of the bus. Fuck it, was the attitude. He felt shaky and raw, his foot throbbing. They hadn't eaten, a foolish omission. He should have brought a couple of sandwiches. Maybe they'd stop up the hill once they entered more developed territory, grab some Pollo Feliz from a drive thru even. A bus appeared behind them, about a hundred feet back. Green. Rainbow striped Bluebird symbols visible on either side of the destination marquee. The route printed too small to read from Caruthers' seat.

"Hey, watch it," Max shouted, braking hard. Caruthers, facing backward, braced himself against the rail, coming upright with feet on the floor. Another bus had pulled from a dirt road, nearly invisible in the woods that had grown around them over the past several minutes, and stood, apparently stalled diagonally across the highway. The driver looked over his shoulder as Max tapped the horn in annoyance, idling a few feet away. The trailing bus pulled up to them, nearly touching the bumper.

"What the hell?" Caruthers asked, and two men came around from the far side of the stalled bus, the one in front waving his hand in a more or less friendly manner. He was short compared to the other, and thick, the usual Mayan fireplug to his companion's quixotic dimensions. The short one wore a lumberjack shirt, the other a beige zip-up jacket. They came to the door, signaling to be let in.

Max looked from them to Caruthers and back into the bus. Caruthers rose his aching foot onto the bench. Something was in his hands. The Stanley, about a third full. Max opened the door. The men entered, the shorter one all the way up to Max and the tall one stopping on the steps, his head level with Caruthers'. He was not a young man, but he wore a teenager's dewy mustache. "Do you mind?" the short one said to Max in confident English. He made a slight shoveling motion with one hand, shooing Max off the driver's seat. "We must get off this road as quickly as possible," he explained. "It will be easier if my friend drives. Please forgive me."

The politeness seemed to win Max over. He stood, crossed the aisle to sit beside Caruthers, who scooted over to make room. The tall man supplanted Max behind the wheel, while his partner stood behind him, facing Max and Caruthers. He had a round, jowly face, clean shaven, somewhere around thirty years old. He smiled and his eyes turned to cheery crescents.

The bus blocking the way backed into the dirt road, and the tall man, a professional driver clearly, followed it into the woods. The bus behind them brought up the rear. A hundred yards in, they came to an expanse of tree stumps. The leading bus stopped, backed up for a quick exit. Caruthers' own bus backed in beside it, and the third did the same. The engines shut off, two buses with long snouts on either side of Caruthers' snub-nosed bull dog. A number of men came from the buses and began to climb onto the roof.

"Is this it?" Max asked. "Are you the people?"

"We have no name," the stocky one said, "no organization or creed, other than self-defense." Sounds of rummaging came from above. The spokesman introduced himself as Marcos, owner and operator of a taxi cab in Xela. Like everyone's, his business had been suffering lately, as the violence scared off visitors, the gangsters extorted more and more from honest businessmen. Others in the group, he explained, had lost more, suffered worse. Daughters and wives snatched, raped. Barbaric murders. It dawned slowly on Caruthers that they were being hijacked, that someone had informed. High-caliber shots rang out overhead, ending the thoughts and forcing him down, hands over head. "Don't worry," Marcos shouted. "Just for practice." A thunderous explosion shook the bus, and Marcos' eyes went wide. "What was that?" he asked, smiling. Chatter and laughter came from the men on the roof.

"We don't know," Max said. "Nobody ever told us what's up there."

Of course, Caruthers thought, putting it all together. Max's goddamned girlfriend had alerted these vigilantes to the plan. That's why the bitch had been so curious about everything. He watched his son carefully for signs of falseness, to see if Max was also in on it, but he saw only distress, worry, confusion.

"Now," Marcos said, "I will offer you two options. Are you listening?"

Caruthers nodded his head, letting go of the suspicion, the blaming. Here they were. That was all that mattered now.

"First you must know that we are not like them. We will not hurt you. Option one is this: you stay here with one of our associates. We will, I am afraid, have to take the bus. I hope you understand. When the thing is over, you are free to go. Simple."

"That's a good option," Caruthers said. "I'd like that option." He played the potential aftermath in his mind. Chucho couldn't really blame him for getting hijacked—but of course he might anyway.

"Or you can help us," Marcos continued, and Caruthers thought, no, no thank you. Forget it, bub. "In a few minutes, we will surprise the criminals. To do this most effectively, we ask you to continue as before. Enter their headquarters as planned. Once inside, we will jump out from hiding, disarm them. Twenty of us. Ten on the roof, ten in the bus, all well-armed." He smiled, his eyes disappearing. "They will have no chance, trust me."

"Love to help, gentleman," Caruthers said, "but my strong

preference is to stay out of the way."

"I'll drive," Max said. "I'll help you."

Caruthers laughed, a squeaky, hysterical sound. "Wait a minute here. Son, with all due respect, you don't know what you're talking about. Marcos, you seem like a good man. Could you explain to my naïve child here how this thing will go down?"

"We hope it will be peaceful. But your father is correct. This is a dangerous mission for which you have volunteered. It will take much bravery. Yes."

"Much stupidity. Much insanity. We're talking bloodshed, Son. Bullets like rain. Rivers of blood."

"I'm going." Max kept his back to his father, but Caruthers could picture his expression, the crease between his eyes.

"You are welcome, sir. We thank you. All the good citizens of Guatemala thank you."

Caruthers recalled, so vividly the moment was as real as when it happened, Max at three, defiant for no good reason. He didn't want to change out of his pajamas, thought he could halt the day from happening, getting dressed, eating breakfast, brushing teeth, going to daycare. Pam was working then, managing the front of the store while Caruthers took care of the back warehouse and mail order catalog. The scene with Max was typical. He'd lock onto some idea, some vision of how he wanted things to happen, and it seemed, in the moment, that he'd rather die than give it up. Stubborn was the word for it. Everyone used to say so, mostly with affection, and Caruthers saw it now, understood what they meant in a way he'd been unable to at the time. Oh, how angry Caruthers would get, savagely tearing off an equally furious Max's pajamas, using all his grown-up strength to force the clothes onto his son's writhing little body, finally locking him into the car seat, where he'd thrash and flail until wearing himself out. How wretched Caruthers would feel afterward, talking to himself out loud in the warehouse, pleading his case, explaining to an imagined child that he'd had no choice. You have to get up. You have to go to daycare, school, work. Why can't you understand that? And yet, all these years later, it was he, Norman Caruthers, who'd run out on the whole societal pact, unable to stand the very system of order he'd enforced so brutally against his own son. Today, to close the circle, here sat Max, set in that same stubbornness for the opposite reason as before. He intended to go to work, at any cost, no longer a child but a man, too large for Caruthers to subdue.

Caruthers opened up, the layers unfolding, exposing the soft, tender middle. It was all right. He looked out the windshield, saw the stumps of trees stretching over a hill and disappearing behind the slope. Untouched forest grew on the next ridge a half mile over. The men had stopped firing the weapons. Caruthers reached over and rested his arm over Max's shoulder. "If you're going, I'm going," he said. He felt more than saw Max's nod, a whole-body motion of the affirmative.

"Excellent, my good friends," Marcos said, and stood. "We have little time. Hold on."

Caruthers sat back and watched it happen, the movement sharpened by a purpose. Marcos left the bus, shouting orders. Men, perhaps women among them, climbed onto the roof. Others, now helmeted and covered in armor, entered the bus, machine guns at their waists. Marcos himself strapped a vest on, tossed one each to Caruthers and Max. "Put these under your shirts. When…things start," he said, "drop to the floor. We will keep you safe. Stay calm. You are protected."

Max, thick as a linebacker in his armor, started the engine, pulled onto the highway. Someone threw the soggy cardboard out the window, along with two vagrant cans of beer rolling about. Nobody spoke. They sat on the floor, out of sight from the road. Marcos told Caruthers to let them know when they were nearing the place. He ordered all windows open.

Forest turned to small farms, plots of harvested corn, a few cows, pigs, chickens, horses and burros, a little building here and there, constructed of poured concrete or loose wood slats, rusty tin roofs. Billboards featuring the same old politicians, noses painted red though the election was over. Other buses joined them on the road. Small urban clusters centered on gas stations, featuring Pollo Feliz franchises with their happy cartoon chicken on plastic signs. Caruthers, shivering, his face thick and stiff as if covered in a heavy clay mask, had lost his appetite. He took the paper with Chucho's instructions from his back pocket. They were in the city now, the sprawl outside of Xela characterized by slums, the smell of burnt trash.

They exited the highway onto a cobbled road between high fences protecting various commercial interests, such as junk yards. They turned left and left again, onto a narrow dirt road. "Go a hundred yards," Caruthers said, voice tight in his throat, "and honk the horn four times. Not too long, not too short. Four regular honks."

The militia inside the bus hunkered into the spaces between the benches, each under a window, guns ready. Max pressed the horn. One, two, three, four. A man appeared in the road ahead of them, signaled to his right like a traffic cop. Max followed the directions through an open gate made from thick sheets of metal on rollers, between ten-foot stone walls topped by brambles of wire. The tires crunched on the gravel drive as they rolled slowly into an industrial-looking space. The man who'd signaled them in, masked and wearing a black ball cap, guided Max to a parking space on the left, between an old two-story stone building and a metal-sided warehouse. A figure in a helmet and armor stood on the tile roof of the stone building, machine gun with a long curving clip resting on his right shoulder.

Gunfire thundered overhead, first one trill and then a full symphony of noise. The figure on the roof flew back, disappearing, and the man directing the bus fell, twitching in a storm of bullets. Max threw himself to the floor and lay curled around the seat, arms over his head. The bus still moved forward in the granny gear, toward the downed man as bullets smashed through the shell of the bus. Caruthers broke the paralysis of shock and dropped to the floor, face against the grooved rubber pad in the aisle, still damp from the makeshift ice chest. Something hot and wet hit his neck, and he waited for pain and death to follow. Neither came. Had the Stanley spilled? No, it was still in his hand, upright. He touched his neck, and the hand came back bloody. More of the liquid landed on him, and he glanced around and up, where blood dripped from a hole in the ceiling, while still the shots cracked all around. A great explosion rocked the bus, seeming for a moment to silence all other sounds. The men inside fired out the windows without pause. Bullets shredded the bus. Grunts and shouts sounded, intimate behind the din like backstage whispers. Sulfur and iron lay thick in the air. The bus lifted slightly, the front tire rolling over a dead man. Caruthers looked at Max, hugging himself like an infant on the floor a foot away, the top of his shaggy head toward Caruthers, the bun unraveling. "Max," he yelled, but his voice couldn't penetrate the gunfire. "Son!" He crawled forward, slid onto his side to get face-to-face with Max, each upside down to the other, curled like a yin and yang sign. Max's eyes were closed, his teeth bared. Caruthers brushed away the hair from his pale forehead. Max opened his eyes, bright with fear and pain.

"I'm hit," he whispered into a sudden pause in the shooting.

# A Candle for San Simón

Someone from the back leapt over Caruthers and Max, opened the door with the lever, and ran out, machine gun stuttering. Another followed him. Still the bus rolled forward.

"Where?" Caruthers whispered, stroking Max's head. Max closed his eyes, and Caruthers threw an arm around Max's curved back but felt only the stiff vest while also pressing Max's chest through the Kevlar with his other hand, holding him as closely, as tightly as possible, feeling the rapid breathing of an animal in distress. "You're okay, Son. You're okay." Caruthers wormed his right hand down the neck hole of the vest and stroked Max's back, just as he'd done when Max was a baby in his father's arms, crying over some little thing until finally slipping into sleep, just like now—except today's tears fell from Caruthers' eyes, not Max's. The thing Caruthers had most feared in the early years after Max was born—his young son's body, obsessively checked during sleep, no longer expanding and contracting—was happening, had happened. "Wake up," he shouted, shaking his son gently, and then with increasing force. The bus jolted to a stop, sending Max and Caruthers into the shifter. The engine sputtered and died. "Come on," Caruthers said, now on his knees looking down at Max's face. "Open your eyes." A warm puddle surrounded them, and Caruthers saw the smear of it where they'd slid across the floor. "Help," he cried, joining other pleas: moans, whimpers, someone screaming outside.

Tears had been falling, but now Caruthers cried with his entire body, his face nestled against Max's neck. "Help," he managed to burble between ragged jags of weeping, clawing at Max's vest.

"I'm sorry," someone said from far away and above. Caruthers would not open his eyes, would not let go of his son. Sirens grew louder, closer. "He was very brave. We couldn't have defeated them without him." The sirens halted, cut off, and Caruthers knew that around him the wounded were being treated, the dead carted away.

He saw the scene in the dark space beyond his eyelids. Two men spoke Spanish nearby, talking about him and Max, a father still living, a dead son, a delicate situation. Caruthers recalled a morning from his own youth, when he'd endeavored to stay home from school by refusing to get up, refusing to acknowledge that he'd woken, by lying there as if dead. His mother shook him, shouted, stripped the blankets off, and still he'd lain, eyes clamped shut, body limp and unmoving except a slight shiver from cold. Finally he'd had to accept that the ploy couldn't last, and he'd opened his bleary eyes, sat up yawning in the gray light of morning, his mother shaking her head in amused irritation. So it would happen today, eventually. They'd force him to let go of Max, to stand aside and watch them cart his boy away, covered in a sheet, into the back of an ambulance and away forever, but for now he was going to lie still, pretending to sleep, his son dozing in his arms.

# Chapter Twenty-Nine

Caruthers swallowed his morning pills with water. Dr. Jimenez had stated the name and purpose of each of the five tablets, but Caruthers hadn't listened at the time and didn't care now. He knew the morning ones kept him alert and empty; the nighttime pills put him to sleep. That's what Chucho had paid for and that's what Chucho got, a driver awake during the day and asleep at night. Caruthers prepared the Stanley, out of habit these days. The pills did something to him so that the rum had little effect. Sometimes Caruthers forgot to drink the stuff, a personal improvement, he supposed.

He set out down the stairs, no longer sure if his ankle was still tender after the surgery or if he only imagined the pain. Not that any of it mattered, reality and perception and whatever differences there might be between them. Caruthers no longer needed to worry about anything, not rent, not gas, not vehicle maintenance, not permits and passport visas. Chucho took care of all that now. He also told Caruthers where to drive on any given day. Caruthers should have given up years ago, his bus, his route, the freedom he'd never needed or used. All this time he'd valued these hassles for no good reason, only to discover at the end of the line his mistake. Never too late to learn, they said, and they were wrong as usual.

He still parked behind La Mala Senda, though he seldom drank there anymore. The evening pills knocked him out so quickly he had to be home when he took them, and after a day's driving, he was eager for the oblivion they delivered. Besides, now that the tourists had returned, especially in the height of summer, the bar had become too loud and crowded for Caruthers' tastes. Good for Red though. Caruthers wished him well. He wished everyone well, even the assholes of the world. The pills did that to him too, filled him with well-wishing that might be real or might be fake but was there in him nonetheless. He walked down the drive into the weedy lot, home now to the new bus, bought at auction in Iowa a few months back and gussied up by Chucho's body man. Barely 70,000 miles when the school district deemed it too old. "Santa Cruz" was written along the sides in a red, white, and blue motif. Chucho liked to imagine a whole fleet of these busses someday, but now it was only Caruthers, his handlers, and the Xela line. Edgar and Benny, the new assistants, sat on either side of the aisle in front, waiting for him. Edgar collected money, as Seba once had, except that now, at the end of the day, Edgar tossed Caruthers a few bills and kept the rest, instead of the other way around. Caruthers didn't mind. He had little use for money. Benny's function was to carry a gun.

Caruthers entered, waving good morning as he sat. He placed the Stanley in its holder and turned the key. The engine woke quickly, without requiring extra gas. "Normal," Edgar told him, meaning today they'd simply run the route until quitting time. Other days they drove south to the port at San Jose, or north into Chiapas. Chucho recently told Caruthers during a dinner meeting at a new Texas-style barbeque joint in Pana, he'd eventually add another destination, a poppy farm and production facility now in the works. Mexico's version of the war on drugs was creating all sorts of new opportunities, the Chief of Police and future Mayor of Panajachel had said, pointing for emphasis with a half-gnawed rib bone. One of Caruthers' new duties was to listen to Cruz hold forth whenever the urge took the boss. Chucho's English had been getting better.

He'd been angry at first with the outcome of the bloody delivery. Caruthers never knew exactly how much money Cruz had lost in the ambush, but the amount was significant. Luckily, plenty of good fortune followed the setback. The vigilantes—who now called themselves the Citizen's Safety Brigade, if Chucho's translation could be trusted—proved amenable. They simply wanted a modest cut of the action and for the violence to stop, or at least slow down some, or at least move out of their neighborhoods. Meanwhile, Cruz's prestige in legitimate circles grew fast when, a couple of months after the raid, he collaborated with the government of El Salvador to nab one of Mara X's top dogs, an arrest that made the news all over the continent, if only for a few days. Cruz was running unopposed for mayor.

Caruthers put the automatic transmission in drive and maneuvered onto Santander, turned left toward the highway, and passed what would soon be the new indigenous culture center, three storefronts covered by scaffolding. An artist from Antigua had been commissioned to turn the entire façade into a mural. Chucho stipulated that the brave gringo missionary who'd given his life in the fight against vicious criminals be fit in somewhere. Max's old girlfriend, Delilah, as Caruthers now thought of her, had supplied a recent photograph of Max laboring for the unwashed peasants. Caruthers looked forward to the completed mural, to seeing his son every day up there among Guatemala's heroes, though he understood the gesture, ultimately, as a sacrifice to the great god of tourism, Chucho pandering to outside money. As painful as it was, Caruthers enjoyed visiting Max's grave across the lake, in the little cemetery outside of San Pedro, a pretty spot: peaceful, crumbling, overlooking the lake. Max would have liked it, and Caruthers told him just that, among other things. Sitting with his back against a tree trunk, he spent long hours on days off talking to Max, telling him everything, listening to Max's replies. Otherwise, Caruthers clung to small pleasures, a glimpse of the ocean, fields of poppies in bloom, the smell of rain in the air, his evening pills, the ferry trip across the lake to visit his son.

\* \* \*

Carmela closed the textbook, smiled at Doug, and folded her hands on the table, signifying that the day, the week, the course was over. "It's been a pleasure," she said in English. "You are a very good student, and I know you will go on to be a fluent Spanish speaker, if you continue to practice." Doug—tall, skinny, pale-skinned with hair so blond it was nearly white—had returned to the classroom after several months administering vaccinations out in the campo. Little round glasses added no particular character to his narrow, long face. She found him pleasant, easy to teach. Soon he'd return to Canada to practice medicine and make money.

"Thank you," he said, fumbling with his pencil in those long, nervous fingers. "I was wondering. Now that the course is officially over, if I can take you to dinner. To celebrate."

Carmela, still smiling, widened her eyes, a flicker meant to express surprise, a certain pleasure but not too much pleasure. About half of her male students asked her out at some point during the studies, usually after the final class. She hadn't generally put much effort into sparing their feelings. Americans mostly, their self-love tended to match their muscles, swollen from weight lifting and unconditional praise. But Doug was different, a man who didn't appreciate his own worth—or did he? Sometimes she couldn't judge the difference between the way people seemed and the way they were. "You didn't have to wait until the course was over to ask me out."

# A Candle for San Simón

"Wanted to keep everything proper, you know."

"You didn't want it to affect your grade?" She grinned.

"Well, you know. Our professional relationship."

"I see. I should tell you first that I have a son."

"Oh, I'm sorry. I never heard anything about a, a husband or partner or anything."

"Almost. I almost have a son. The adoption isn't complete, not yet, but it is happening. Beau is his name, and he just turned one." She looked around the courtyard, full of students and teachers. The gringos had returned, and with them her job. She hoped for more, better pay eventually, but for now, she was glad to be back. "We don't know his exact birthday, so we invented one. July 14th. I closed my eyes and pointed my finger onto a calendar in the month the doctor estimated he was born. Isn't that funny?"

"That's, very interesting," Doug said. "I'd still like to take you out, if you're up for it."

"Yes," she said, even as she saw him shrinking, back into his protective shell of foreignness. After Max's death, she'd decided to adopt Beau, to name him officially, Beau Caruthers Muñoz. Along with the guilt of sending Max to his death came anger, at him. Why'd he volunteer to drive? They'd promised to let him go. Even the drunk father admitted that it was Max's decision. She'd only wanted to put the guns into the community's hands, not turn her boyfriend into a martyr.

After the raid, she'd stayed in Zunilito for a few days, doing what she thought Max would have wanted, though he didn't want anything anymore. She'd helped Reina write the message—on Facebook—to Max's church, which turned the church Facebook page into a tribute to their "fallen warrior," who was now "with God." She'd stuck around through the discussion of what to do with his remains. For a while, it seemed that the church pastor might pay for Max to be shipped back, and even that Reina might get an emergency visa to accompany the body, but finally he was buried near his father. His mother had changed her name when she'd remarried, and nobody knew the new one. The last Carmela had heard, the pastor was trying to find Max's brother, who'd moved abroad somewhere for business.

"Yes? You don't seem so sure," Doug said, stooping to look into her face.

"I was just thinking about my schedule," she said. "I'm busy Friday and Saturday nights."

"Big dates?" Doug asked, smiling to show he was kidding. She saw, or imagined, two things in that smile: confidence that he had no rival of his stature, and fear that he did, a lurking possessiveness she didn't like—or maybe she just found him dull and was looking for excuses.

"The truth is," she said, "I'm on patrol this weekend." She waited for him to process the words, strange as they must have sounded in his ears, so unlike everything else she'd ever said to him. "I belong to an organization that keeps the city safe from criminals."

He shook his head, scowling and grinning at the same time. "So you drive around looking for crimes?"

"Something like that. We check in on businesses that were targeted by a gang that formerly operated here, until we, my organization, hunted them down and killed them. Now we make sure they don't return." The expression of alarm and confusion on Doug's face made Carmela happy. She didn't mention the role that collecting donations played in the patrols, how at first the businesses placed money in their hands without being asked, donations that soon turned into fees. "They're like roaches, these criminals. You spray and spray, but they come back. You can never give up, never stop spraying."

## A Candle for San Simón

Doug sat back, smiling, his former confidence resumed. "You're kidding me, aren't you?"

The students and teachers were either gone or clustered at the gate, filing out. Diego sat hunched over his desk in the office. Carmela unzipped the front pocket of her briefcase, on the ground beside her chair. She brought to her lap the pistol they'd found in the gang house, where she now lived with others in the group, a woman's gun, Marcos had said, lightweight but plenty strong enough to kill. "Look under the table," she told Doug. He paused, and then bent down, one hand on the edge of the table to peek under. She held the pistol between her legs, aimed down at the floor for safety.

"My God," he whispered, still under the table. "Is that real?"

"Oh yes," she said, sliding the weapon back into its pocket, "it's real all right."

\* \* \*

On Sunday, Itzel walked along the black-sand beach, enjoying the cool early morning before the sun rose higher and sent everyone running into the shade of church. After mass, she'd return to her rented shack, stand in front of the floor fan and strip off the clothes that identified her, if anyone ever got the cojones to ask, as a Kekchi Mayan, from a far-away village nobody ever heard of. She knew her story well—the places, times, events, and names—even if she never needed to tell it. For now, the clothes kept her apart from everyone else in the village, apart and invisible, even with her crazy pale eyes, short hair, and thin ladina body.

A gang of vultures stood on the sand nearby, facing the ocean with their backs to her, wings spread to catch the breeze, watching the waves that slapped and sucked at the shore. She took the sandy walkway up into the town square, like she did every morning. A fountain stood in the center, round and ringed by four mermaids facing inward, cupping their naked breasts to spray water onto the fat cherub in the center, except those stone chichis were as dry as the rest of the fountain. She'd seen gangster mausoleums bigger than the church that faced the square, but she never missed mass, always sitting in the back and leaving right after the farewell blessing like the bashful religious Indian she was. She stood at the counter of the town café, one of four businesses on the square, and ordered her usual coffee and sweet roll from Angelo, the owner.

Movement from beyond the church drew her gaze to a raggedy, dirty man scratching his beard with both hands while he shuffled off the highway toward town. Sitting at the table under the café's awning, she watched him approach, wondering how a guy on foot got so far from everything else. She swore a bus hadn't passed since the night before. He locked eyes with her until she had to look away, wondering why these weirdos always picked her.

He stopped at her table, staring down with crazed, hungry eyes, shaded by the bill of a ball cap so filthy she couldn't read the logo. She thought about saying something, but this guy didn't look like he even spoke human. Plus, Itzel was shy, and spoke little Spanish. She glanced over at Angelo like she might need help, and he shrugged, a little fat man sad about the world.

Vicki never cared for bums, and never gave them change or smokes or booze or whatever they wanted. Get a fuckin' job homey, she always thought. Learn to steal at least. Something, anything was better than begging. Show some self-respect. But Itzel—soft, weepy, gullible, religious, and a little simple—was different. Looking at the man's glazed eyes, she felt him, and set her roll and cup of coffee before him on the table.

Looking away from her, he picked up the roll like it was his all along, like he was some kind of king, so used to everyone serving him he didn't even notice. Roll in one hand and coffee in the other, he went toward the fountain, while one of those vultures from the beach came swooping down and landed between two of the mermaids. Ignoring the nasty bird with its face like a rash, he stepped into the fountain and sat with his back against the cherub's pedestal. Angelo came over and placed a fresh roll and coffee in front of her, shaking his head toward the bum. "Thank you," she said. "I feel bad for him."

"It's okay," he said, sitting across from her and waving toward the man in the fountain. "Every time I see a man like this, I ask myself: what if this is Jesus, come back in disguise?" He shrugged, smiling at his own foolishness. He looked more closely at her, taking in the fine features and yellow eyes, nothing like any Indian he'd ever seen. Instead of asking the question in his head, he turned back to the man in the fountain, who smiled like an idiot up at the sky, a toothless baby, the roll about to fall from his hand.

Itzel wished to answer the questions Angelo couldn't ask, to get the story out there before other stories, truer stories could creep in, but she, a Kekchi far from home, shamed and exiled, would never talk to a stranger without first being asked. They, the entire village, including Itzel, would have to wait, for the belly to grow out under the high Mayan belt. Ah, they would say. Now we understand. The poor thing. And later, they'd learn more of the story they themselves would invent, when the baby arrived, pale skinned with eyes the color of the sea and hair as black as a vulture's feathers, child of a tourist passing through, a charming gringo poor, simple Itzel hadn't been able to resist—an old, sad story of betrayal, shame, an angry father and guilty gringo dollars that explained how Itzel could afford to live among them without working. The questions answered, they'd pity and accept her as one of their own. They would love the pink, foreign baby, not just her child but a child of the village, born by chance out on the edge of the world but like a bastard prince, destined for the best schools, travel, money…glory.

The vulture jumped down from the edge of the fountain, breaking Itzel's dream. It hopped toward the bum, who was too busy smiling up at the sky to notice, and snatched the roll from his hand. The church bells began to ring, summoning the village and startling the bird, which rose from the shadow of a mermaid, dropped the sweet roll, opened its wings, and flew away.

## ABOUT THE AUTHOR

Kelly Daniels grew up on the road, living for stints with his parents in a Hawaiian commune, a lonesome desert cabin, and in an old delivery van outfitted with bunks. As an adult, he set off on his own, traveling extensively through Europe, Mexico and Central America, picking up jobs along the way, jobs such as production manager of a furniture factory (Guatemala), newspaper reporter (Mexico), and bartender (all over).

He is the author of the memoir *Cloudbreak, California*, and his short stories and essays have appeared widely in literary reviews. A regular contributor to the *Sun* magazine, he lives with his wife and son in Le Claire, Iowa. He is an associate professor of creative writing at Augustana College.

CPSIA information can be obtained
at www.ICGtesting.com
Printed in the USA
JSHW050957210920
8028JS00003B/13